P9-DNR-423

DISCARDED

DARK LAKE

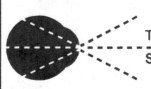

This Large Print Book carries the
Seal of Approval of N.A.V.H.

DARK LAKE

CLARE REVELL

THORNDIKE PRESS
A part of Gale, a Cengage Company

Farmington Hills, Mich • San Francisco • New York • Waterville, Maine
Meriden, Conn • Mason, Ohio • Chicago

Copyright © 2018 by Clare Revell.
All scripture quotations, unless otherwise indicated, are taken from the Holy Bible, New International Version®, NIV®, Copyright 1973, 1978, 1984, 2011 by Biblica, Inc.™ Used by permission of Zondervan. All rights reserved worldwide. www.zondervan.com
Thorndike Press, a part of Gale, a Cengage Company.

ALL RIGHTS RESERVED
This is a work of fiction. Names, characters, places, and incidents either are the product of the author's imagination or are used fictitiously, and any resemblance to actual persons living or dead, business establishments, events, or locales, is entirely coincidental.
Thorndike Press® Large Print Christian Mystery.
The text of this Large Print edition is unabridged.
Other aspects of the book may vary from the original edition.
Set in 16 pt. Plantin.

LIBRARY OF CONGRESS CIP DATA ON FILE.
CATALOGUING IN PUBLICATION FOR THIS BOOK
IS AVAILABLE FROM THE LIBRARY OF CONGRESS

ISBN-13: 978-1-4328-5988-6 (hardcover)

Published in 2019 by arrangement with Harbourlight Books, a division of Pelican Ventures, LLC

Printed in the United States of America
1 2 3 4 5 6 7 23 22 21 20 19

For Ceryn, who has inherited
her mother's love of
everything disaster related.

GLOSSARY

Tender up for grabs — contract to be applied for

Balaclava — woollen mask worn over the face to hide it. Only the eyes are visible.

Butchers — cockney rhyming slang butchers hook meaning take a look

Knickers in a twist — get stressed or upset over something

Kibosh — wreck, destroy, ruin

Put paid to (something) — prevent you from doing it

1

After the brightness of the afternoon sun, it took Lou Fitzgerald's eyes several moments to adjust as she stepped inside the communications van on the far side of the archaeological dig. More than a little irritated that she'd had to break off what she'd been doing for this interruption, she tucked her sunglasses over her shirt pocket and strode to the desk. It had better be important, or the person on the other end of the phone would get the full force of her wrath. She picked up the phone, tossed her cap to the desk, and glanced at Bill. "Which line?"

The communications tech didn't look up from what he was doing. "Three."

Lou punched the button. Hopefully, this wouldn't take long. There was only one person she could think of who'd ring and declare it urgent enough for her to stop work. "Dr. Fitzgerald speaking."

"You're a difficult woman to get ahold of, Lou." A cheerful male voice echoed down the line. And definitely not the one she was expecting. "Did you lose your phone again?"

Lou grinned. "Jim, you know very well you're the one who loses phones, not me." She tugged over the computer chair and sat. Captain Jim Kirk, all joking about the TV program aside, was one of her best friends. She'd always hoped they'd end up together, that her teenage crush would be reciprocated and progress into something more, but that hadn't panned out.

The friendship however had remained, cemented by their teenage jaunt across the world.

"Hah," Jim snorted. "You still haven't answered yours in days. Did you drop it overboard a ship?"

"Again, I repeat myself, dropping phones overboard a ship is your habit, not mine. It's a good thing you joined the Air Force and not the Navy after all." She shoved down the giggle. "To answer your question, no, I didn't lose my phone. I know exactly where it is, and that's in my bag under the desk, thus out of my way on the dig site. Work's been hectic and I can't afford a distraction. I'm barely getting five minutes to myself these days, and I'd rather use those to catch forty winks. Besides, the phone signal out here can be rubbish at times."

Jim snorted. "You're in Wales, not Egypt. Hardly the back of beyond."

"And that makes a difference because . . . ?" Lou left the question hanging. "You know as well as I do that lots of things affect phone signal. Mountains for example, of which we have a plethora in Wales. The lack of phone towers. Distance between the phone and said phone towers. And I know you didn't call because I haven't written, because I know you too well." She glanced at her watch. "What time is it where you are?"

The line crackled and Jim yawned. "It's almost eleven at night. I'm about to go to bed. Paul is up to no end of mischief. You taught him well with that saucepan trick."

Lou chuckled. "It's what aunts do. And how is Ailsa?" Despite the fact Jim's affections had gone elsewhere, Lou was very fond of his wife.

"She's pregnant. Baby's due in five months. We're hoping to be back stateside for the birth, but if not, the base here will do just as well. She'd prefer to have Nichola and Mum around to look after Paul when she's having the baby." He paused. "And admittedly, as good as the Air Force docs are, I'd prefer to be back at home as well."

"Congratulations." A surge of jealousy flooded her before she tamped it down. She'd always imagined a family of her own by the time she reached her mid-thirties. But some dreams were never to be. Choices made early on in life put paid to that.

"Thanks. And speaking of Nichola — have you spoken to your mum recently?"

Lou shook her head, knowing he couldn't see her. "Not for a few days."

"You should give her a call while you have a signal."

"Sounds mysterious. Is something wrong?"

"She's just forgotten what you sound like."

Lou scoffed. "Yeah, right, of course she has. OK. I'll ring as soon as I get home tonight. Well, back to the hotel anyway. She should be up by then. Las Vegas is eight hours behind me. I get confused with the date line as to where they are compared to you. Is it strange not having Dad as your CO now?"

"A little, but most people agree that he's one of the best generals out there. People fight to get posted to Nellis these days."

A lot of noise came from outside, and Lou frowned. They knew she preferred silence on a dig. Rowdiness led to mistakes and precious objects being damaged. Running footsteps crossed to the van and the door flung open, letting the heat and light into the darkened room.

One of the archaeological team stood silhouetted against the sunlight. "Dr. F.?"

Lou glanced up. She'd long given up trying to stop the nickname and went with it. "What's up, AJ?"

"Sorry to interrupt. But we need you. You have to come and see this. Now."

His enthusiasm was catching. "Be right there. Jim, I gotta go. I'll leave my phone on tonight. Call me when you get up, and we can chat properly. Yes, there is a phone signal in town before you ask. Give Ailsa my love. Bye." She put the phone down and stood, tugging her cap on firmly. Reaching behind her neck, she tugged her long ponytail through the gap at the back of the hat.

She headed outside in several rapid strides, putting on her sunglasses. "So what's up, AJ?" She pulled her cap down over her eyes, the peak shading them from the bright sunlight.

"We found something you need to see." He set off at a trot towards the trench.

Lou hurried after him, grateful this prosthesis was a better fit than the last one she'd had, and she could keep up. No one on her team knew about the disability, and she intended to keep that information to herself. The last thing she needed was to be called Long-Lou-Silver or Hop-a-Long Louisa. Her stomach churned, and her mind whirled. There was an underlying current to the dig site that hadn't been there ten minutes ago.

Had they finally found what they were searching for?

AJ pointed to the trench. "Down there."

"This had better be good," she teased. Resisting the urge to jump, Lou climbed down the ladder, her breath hitching with every step. She crossed to the uncovered stones she'd been working on the past few weeks and dropped carefully to her knees. She pushed the last remaining earth away and stared in wonder.

Then she closed her eyes.

This was it. Her very own 'Eureka!' moment.

Joy bubbled through her, and it was all she could do not to leap ten feet in the air and punch the sky. "This is it," she whispered. Tears pricked her eyes. "We did it."

"You did it, boss." AJ grinned. "You were right."

Lou blinked hard. "Team effort, AJ. We

did it." She sucked in a deep breath, forcing herself to think logically through what would be the next steps. "OK. I want this whole area cordoned off and tented. It's essential we keep the place dry. I need my camera and case. We have to record everything. And someone get ahold of that local councillor, Jordan Brown. This should change his mind about developing the area."

An hour later, Lou scowled as someone blocked her light. "Do you mind?" she grumbled.

"No, actually I don't." Varian Sparrow's voice made her jump.

She glanced up to find her boss standing behind her. "It's nice to see you too, Varian. Your timing is impeccable. I planned to call you later. You should take a butcher's at this. It's amazing. It proves everything I've been saying."

"Lou, we need to talk. Is there somewhere we can go?"

"Sure, there is, but it'll have to wait. I need to get on with this while we still have daylight."

"This can't wait. I need to talk to you now."

Lou resisted the urge to roll her eyes. He may be her boss, but he sure knew how to pick his moments, and nothing he ever said

15

was that urgent. "So talk while I work. What's up?"

He jerked his head and held up a hand. "Not here. It's important."

"For this it had better be." She accepted his hand up and brushed the dirt off her jeans. "Fine, you can have ten minutes." She glanced at the other members of the team. "No one touch this while I'm gone."

Lou leaned back in her chair, glad she was sitting down. Her heart raced, cheeks burned and her stomach clenched. "You're kidding me," she finally managed past the huge lump in her throat.

"No. I'm sorry. I'm not kidding. I'm deadly serious." Varian certainly didn't appear sorry, and he definitely didn't sound apologetic. He both looked and sounded smug, as if this had been his plan all along.

"I can't leave," Lou insisted. "Didn't you hear me? We found it. Proof that I was right all along." She waved a file at him. "This is my work. My discovery. You can't just replace me."

Make that replace her *again* — the same way he always did, right when she was on the cusp on proving something or on the brink of another discovery.

"I'm sure your team is more than capable

of carrying on without you."

"Uh, no, they're not," she spluttered. Were they really having this conversation? "They need me as much as I need to be here."

"Are you saying you don't trust them?"

"No. I'm not saying that at all! I trust them implicitly. Well, most of them anyway." She sucked in a deep breath, her hands curling into balls under the desk. She tamped down her temper and tried to put a lid on her emotions. "I'm saying I've put years into this and I want to —"

"— be the one to finish it?" Varian completed her sentence in that annoying manner, which only served to irritate her further.

She scowled, fingers drumming on the desk. "Yes. Is that so wrong? It's my work, my paper, my blood, sweat, and tears, not to mention sleepless nights that have gone into this and you want to ditch me in favour of some up and coming lackey so you and he can take the glory? Again. It's not fair."

"Life isn't fair. You've got an hour to get your notes and files together before you brief us —"

"I don't believe I'm hearing this!"

"Then you leave and don't look back."

Lou scowled harder, wishing she could give him the "stink-eye" as Jim termed it when they were kids. "Who is he anyway?

This person you're replacing me with."

"Monty is coming down to . . ."

She almost yelled aloud in frustration, reining it in at the last second. Monty was Varian's son. It made sense he'd be the one taking over now that they were so close to a discovery that would make her name and put this corner of Wales on the map right up there with Stonehenge and the Grand Canyon.

Lou resisted the urge to hurl something across the portacabin. "What a surprise. You know, it's so nice to see that nepotism is alive and well and flourishing in Wales. The exact same way it does all over the country wherever the Sparrow Foundation can be found."

She paused, counting to five slowly. "Are you sacking me?" she muttered.

"On the contrary, I have a nice simple job for you."

"Tell you what. Send Monty to do your nice simple job. See if he can do that without messing it up. We all know what happened on the Tumbrel dig. How he was responsible for those deaths."

Varian's expression darkened, and Lou wisely shut up before he really did sack her. "Have you heard of Dark Lake?" he asked.

"Should I have?"

"It's a reservoir up in the Pennines. The villages of Abernay and Finlay were flooded in the first half of the last century to make the Aberfinay Dam, shortly before the start of the Second World War. It's now known as Dark Lake, as is the new village that sprang up next to it. The dam provides water for one of the large towns. It doesn't matter which one. The whole area is owned by an old family friend, Evan Close."

Her fingers drummed her irritation on the desk. "And? What does this have to do with the price of fish?"

"The water levels have dropped enough to see the church spire above the level of the reservoir. A few unusual artefacts have washed ashore. I want you to go up there and see what's going on."

"Why?"

"As I said the land is owned by a family friend. Neither of us wants this getting into the media. We'd prefer it be handled quickly and quietly. I can get you permission to dive once or twice. And arrange for a diving team to meet you up there."

"Can't it wait a few weeks?"

"No. It has to be done now."

"Send *Whatshisface* up there."

"Monty can't swim. You can. You have a gold medal to prove it."

Lou chewed her bottom lip. "That was a lifetime ago. I had to make a choice over careers, and I chose archaeology. I finally get my big break, and you're taking it away from me. When I've done all the leg work, all the research . . ."

Varian handed her a file. "I'd shut up about now if I were you. Assuming you want to keep your job. I'm sending you to Dark Lake. End of discussion. I'll see you in an hour."

Lou stood. Part of her wanted to quit on the spot, but the other part of her had more sense. "You know what? Brief yourself. These are all my files and notes. I'm sure my team can tell you anything else you need to know if you can't read my writing."

"Lou . . ."

"Don't you Lou me. I've spent the best part of ten years working for you, and this is how you repay me. Every. Single. Time." She stomped over to the door and slammed it hard behind her.

Tears burned her eyes for the second time in an hour. But for a totally different reason. She tugged her hat down firmly so no one else would see. She ignored AJ calling her name as she hurried to her car. He'd find out soon enough where she was going in such a hurry.

She had to go back to the hotel and pack. Then she needed to find out where along the Pennines Dark Lake was located. But first, she had to research Evan Close.

Slamming the car door shut behind her, Lou took several deep breaths before tugging out her phone and bringing up the search engine app. She tapped in Evan Close's name and images.

Wow. Her anger was forgotten as she gazed at the photo. He was a hunk. Tall and thin, rather austere features, with ice blue eyes and short dark hair that stood up a little on top.

Lou had to giggle despite herself as she realised she used the hunk scale she and Staci had invented as kids to rate him. He'd score seven and a half, maybe even an eight, just on looks. No man ever rated a ten as that was perfection and wasn't possible.

It was time to get this show on the road. The sooner she got up there, the sooner she could meet the bloke and do what Varian wanted her to do, whatever that was, and the sooner she could go home. He'd been more than a little vague. Maybe once she stopped being mad at him, she'd be intrigued.

But right now, as she started the car, she was too annoyed for anything else. She dropped her phone into her bag and shoved the gear stick into first, wincing as the gears ground in protest. She leaned her head against the steering wheel, forcing herself to calm down. Crashing the car, or being stopped for dangerous driving, would only inflame her already stretched nerves and wouldn't help one iota.

2

Evan Close eased back onto the plush red leather sofa in his London office and lifted the glass of whisky from the silver tray on the side table. He had very few vices, but this was one of them. The amber liquid sparkled in the late afternoon sunlight. His nerves had been on edge since the phone call after lunch, and now he was tauter than a violin bow.

He had spent years building up Xenon, his civil engineering company, and had finally begun to reap the rewards from years of hard work. And he now stood on the cusp of losing everything.

Thanks to Varian Sparrow. There was a family connection somewhere in the past. He and Varian were cousins several times removed, but he didn't pay any attention to that. The less he and Varian had to do with each other the better, as far as he was concerned. Especially now Varian was sending a woman to dig into a past he needed kept buried.

He could have done the research into this woman by himself, but that was why he paid other people.

Besides, he'd had work of his own to do. A new tender was up for grabs, and he had to polish his pitch and make sure his offer was better than anyone else's. Files were spread out over the table in front of him. Facts, figures, running costs from his other projects, including the jewel in his crown — the Thames Barrier.

The tap and the door opening occurred simultaneously. He glanced upwards. Only one person had the authority to do that. And it wasn't his secretary either. He nodded to the tall, dark haired man standing opposite him. "So, what do we know about her, Ira?"

Ira Miles, his head of security, opened the file and handed Evan a photo. "Quite a bit."

"Take a seat." Evan studied the picture as Ira folded himself into the chair on the other side of the coffee table.

The woman in the photo was pretty. Long black hair, sparkling blue eyes, dimples in her cheeks, and perfect teeth that shone. She appeared young, but he didn't suppose she was.

"Her name is Dr. Louisa Willow Benson Fitzgerald. She's thirty-two and was born in Southampton. She won swimming gold in the Para-world championships thirteen years ago in the four-hundred meters free-style, setting a new world and common-wealth record in the process. She gave up swimming to pursue a career in archaeology. B.Sc., M.Sc., Ph.D., ending up as one of the top archaeologists in her field." He paused and looked expectantly at Evan.

"What did I miss?"

"Archaeologist . . . field . . . digging . . ."

Evan groaned. "That's a terrible pun. Even by my standards. Go on."

"Her father, Robert Benson, died when she was twelve. Her mother, Nichola, was remarried five years later to an American pilot, Jack Fitzgerald. He's now the General in charge of Nellis Air Force Base. Dr. Fitzgerald has two siblings from that mar-riage, a brother, Robert, aged fourteen, and a sister, Emily, who is twelve. She took her stepfather's surname when he adopted her. Before that, she and two friends ran away. According to what I discovered they sparked a worldwide search after they left South-ampton on board a cabin cruiser. They were finally found seven months later on Agrihan where they'd been shipwrecked."

Evan raised an eyebrow and snatched the offered paper as he snorted in disbelief. "Really? And Agrihan is where exactly?"

"It's part of the North Marina Islands in the Pacific. That's a distance of around seven-thousand, two-hundred and twenty miles from where they set off. And that's going as the crow flies east to west. Though I imagine they'd have gone west to east, so the mileage could be out by a fair few miles."

"Hmmm. And these kids were how old?"

"Dr. Fitzgerald was fifteen; her friends Jim and Staci Kirk were seventeen and thirteen respectively."

Evan tossed the paper to the side, discounting the story as totally implausible. "Yeah, right." He swallowed a generous sip of the whisky and waved a finger over the top of the glass. "Go on."

"She has a prosthetic left leg due to injuries received when she ran away. No more details on that. She's sidestepped the question on every interview she's ever given. If it is a matter of public record, it's been well and truly sealed. Her reputation as an archaeologist is formidable. By all accounts, she's like a dog with a bone, as the cliché says. Once she starts uncovering something, she keeps going until she's found all the answers. There is a list of her papers and so on attached to that document I gave you."

Evan shifted on the sofa, a gnawing starting in the pit of his stomach. "Is she a threat?"

Ira shook his head. "She is ambitious, but a threat? I'm not sure. We'll need to keep a close watch on her."

Evan drained the whisky and held the glass up to the light. "Why send her?"

"Sir?"

"It's a rhetorical question. I was wondering why Varian would send her when it's in his interests to keep the past buried. It's something we need to address in the not too distant future." He rose and set the glass down. Crossing to the large picture window, he glanced at his reflection, pushing his fingers through his hair. Then he gazed out at the streets of London several stories below him. The Thames glinted in the sunlight. "I need to get up there. I'll take the jet. Pack for several days, and I'll do the same. Make the usual arrangements for us to be met at the airport and leave the file with me. I want to read it."

Ira nodded, placed the folder on the desk, and headed to the door.

Evan crossed back to the desk and held down the intercom. "Janet, I'm heading up to Dark Lake for a week or so. Can you arrange to have the jet on standby? And ask the manor staff get the house ready. I'll be there first thing."

"Yes, Mr. Close."

Evan released the intercom, and then grabbed his briefcase and placed it carefully on the desk. He'd paid good money for the black leather with gold trim and didn't want to damage it. He strode to the filing cabinet and drew the key from his jacket pocket.

He ran over the files until he reached *D*. Then he removed every file pertaining to Dark Lake. What was Varian Sparrow playing at? Yes, the water levels in the lake were low. But that had happened before and would happen again. Just like at the Ladybower Dam several years ago. It didn't mean anything. Did it?

He couldn't take the risk. The secrets of Dark Lake had to stay buried in the past where they belonged. The problem was, this archaeologist, this Dr. Louisa Fitzgerald, dug up and exposed the past for a living.

She had to be halted, one way or another.

If it was the last thing he did, he had to stop her.

3

Lou eased herself from the car, stiff and aching after the long drive across the country. At least there was a motorway connecting Wales and the very north of England, so far north she was only a few miles shy of Scotland. Perhaps after this was done, she should pop over the border to visit some friends in Lockerbie.

Having spoken to her parents and Jim the previous evening, they all told her the same thing, which basically boiled down to "go where the boss tells you and lump it." They didn't get her point. The discovery in Wales was hers. It proved the link between Stonehenge and the stone circle she'd been excavating. Publishing the paper and speaking to news broadcasters would have made her career. As it was, someone else would get the glory, the acclamation, and the huge pay bonus that went with it.

She'd even told them about the university

job — combining field work and teaching. She'd suggested it was time for a change, but again they'd told her not to do anything while she was angry. That just inflamed her temper further.

She'd been too mad to drive the previous night, so she had attempted to sleep and failed miserably at that. Instead, she'd logged onto the company server just after midnight. She first downloaded, and then deleted all her old files that weren't related to Llaremont — making sure they weren't recoverable by anyone. Not even the best IT bloke the Sparrow Foundation employed would be able to recover them once she'd finished. Varian would notice the Llaremont files were gone, whereas her old stuff wouldn't be missed as quickly. Having done that, she'd changed all her passwords and logged out of the system.

She'd checked out of the hotel before dawn and hit the motorway still fuming, covering the distance in a little under five hours. Her resentment had grown with every passing mile. Her hands shook as she tugged open the boot and yanked out her case.

Varian had no right to do that to her.

Not after all the years she'd given him. Once this was done, she'd quit, go work for another firm. She'd been head hunted a month ago by a university. OK, the money was a lot less than she was currently being paid, but she could stay in the same place for more than a few weeks at a time. Finally put down roots, something she'd longed for but was unable to do. More importantly, she would hopefully be working for someone who wanted and appreciated her.

That was more than Varian did, and he didn't deserve her talents anyway.

Lou slammed the boot, her mind made up. There was a much better solution. The university was only a fifteen-mile drive from Dark Lake. She'd call them to see if the job was still available before heading over to visit. Show them how interested she was. Even if they didn't want her, this was the last time Varian would make a fool of her.

She fully intended to tell him what to do with his job, but not yet. Not in the heat of the moment when she'd only say something she'd regret. She'd quit first thing on Monday morning. That would give her a week to get her feet on the ground here. At least she assumed it was Tuesday. Or maybe it was Wednesday?

Lou closed her eyes, inhaling a deep breath of the clean, fresh air. She let it out slowly, letting go of the anger and stress at the same time. One of the tricks the shrinks had taught her years ago that actually worked.

She glanced at the hotel — like the stone built houses that made up the rest of the small, yet pretty village. The buildings all had grey stone walls, slate roofs with chimneys, and tiny walled gardens with flowers and wishing wells. The hotel was built on the main road and right next door to the local village pub — The Wolf Pack. According to the guidebook it had a maze, something she definitely needed to check out at some point.

The inside of the building was simple, but smart. A smiling desk clerk gave her a key and directions up to her room on the second floor. Lou would have preferred ground floor, but at least there was a lift. The room itself was small, but cosy. A pine bed filled most of the floor space, with a chest of drawers and wardrobe along the opposite wall. The usual large screen TV and tea/coffee making accoutrements crowded the top of the chest. The bedding and curtains were matching green gingham.

It reminded her of the set she'd had when she was ten.

She crossed the room to check out the view, noting the fire escape right outside her window. That was a good thing. Being trapped in a fire was one of the things she dreaded most, right along with drowning. Both were hardly surprising given her past.

Her room overlooked the main road, but the village didn't have a night club or much traffic, so noise wouldn't be a problem. Well, maybe when the pub turned out, but after that, it should be fine.

Lou flopped down on the bed and bounced, testing the springs. Not bad. Reaching into her bag, she tugged out her phone and quickly brought up the e-mail the university had sent. May as well call now while she thought of it; she'd only forget if she didn't. Or she'd wimp out, as Jim so eloquently put it. She found the number and dialled. Fingers tapped on the bed-spread as she waited for the call to connect. "Hello, this is Dr. Lou Fitzgerald. Could I speak to Professor Cunningham please?"

Absently, she rubbed her knee as she spoke. Some days she could still feel pain, even though there was nothing there.

"Tobias Cunningham speaking."

"Professor Cunningham, this is Dr. Fitzgerald. I'm calling in connection to the post you offered me a month ago. I was wondering if it's still available, because if it is, I was wondering if you'd consider allowing me to change my mind? I'd really like to take the job, if it's still going." Lou held her breath, waiting for a response. She was prepared to do whatever it took: grovel, beg, take an even bigger pay cut, teach more classes than she originally intended.

"May I ask why you've changed your mind? Last time we spoke, you were full of enthusiasm as to where your latest project was taking you and didn't want to leave."

"Let's just say I've been royally done over as far as that is concerned."

"In what way?"

She closed her eyes. "I shouldn't complain to you, but my boss allowed me to do all the work and right when my theories were proven correct, he replaced me with someone else. Believe it or not, with his son."

"I see. So you're resigning in a fit of temper, and we're your back-up plan."

"Not really. More like I've come to my senses as this isn't the first time they've done this. The post you're offering involves teaching, doesn't it? I want to pass on my knowledge and try to enthuse the next generation, as well as doing field work and apply for research grants. I'm resigning at the start of next week anyway, but thought as I'm in the area, I could maybe come and visit, talk things over, try to persuade you to take me on."

A dry chuckle echoed over the phone. "Very well. Yes, the post is still available. We'll have dinner and talk, but I'm making no promises. How about Friday? Say seven thirty at The Wolf Pack. It's a pub in Dark Lake about fifteen miles from here."

Lou's heart leapt and a huge grin covered her face. Was this meant to be? "That's brilliant. Thank you very much for agreeing to meet with me. See you then." She scribbled down the date, time, and place on paper she found on the chest. She drew the file from her bag and searched for the phone number for Charlie Bramston — the local historian. And she may as well drive over to the dam and meet the bloke in charge up there, a Jasper Steele, according to the file, and get the ball rolling, before she hunted down Evan Close.

Evan sat in the back of the car and watched the countryside as Jock drove past the entrance road to the manor house his family had owned for generations and through the village before taking the route leading to the dam. He didn't use the chauffeur all the time, but as he didn't leave the car at the airport, this morning it was a necessity.

When they reached the entrance to the

dam car park, Evan leaned forward and tapped the driver on the shoulder. "I'll walk from here, been cooped up for far too long. I'll also find out what Jasper knows about this new dig they want to do." He glanced at Ira. "I'll see you back at the house."

The cold wind blasted through him as Evan opened the car door. He stepped from the vehicle and tugged his coat collar up against the chill air. He'd always found it amazing that one part of the country could be sweltering hot while another part was cold, dismal, and wet. That seemed to be par for the course here in Dark Lake.

Evan began walking, his sizeable paces effortlessly covering the ground. Despite the history of the Aberfinay Dam and the sorrow surrounding Dark Lake, he had always liked it here. It was a shame such beauty hid such a sordid secret. Did it taint him, too? How far did the proverbial sins of the fathers go before they were absolved?

Long strides carried him from the entrance of the car park to the dam. The levels in the lake were much lower than he'd been led to believe. Most of the church spire was now visible. A huge hole gaped in the side. The blackened stone beneath hinted at the fire that had raged in the days and hours before the flooding began. No one had ever really spoken about that day or of the fire, but Evan had found the journal his great-grandfather kept and had learned enough from that to know the secrets of the lake had to stay buried.

Two people stood farther along the dam. The black man with the clipboard Evan knew: Charlie Bramston, a close personal friend of Varian. He was the local history buff and self-proclaimed custodian of the reservoir, who liked to think he knew everything. Of course, what he did know was the edited and sanitized version invented for public knowledge.

One of the little known facts about history was it was either written by the victorious or the survivors. Thus, the slant depended on who wrote it, not on what really had occurred.

Evan recognized the woman with Charlie from the photos in his files. Dr. Louisa Fitzgerald. Her long dark hair was tied back in a ponytail, sun glasses perched on top of her head, while a long mac obscured her figure.

Their body language and gestures indicated a disagreement between them long before he strode into earshot.

"And I'm telling you, Dr. Fitzgerald, we won't get permission to dive, and if we did the buildings are too unstable."

"We'll see about that. Varian assured me he'd sort it. Where can I find the dam foreman?"

"Jasper Steel's office is right over there. He'll tell you the same —"

"He's in there now, I assume?" She swung on her heel and started to walk away.

Evan sped up. "Can I help you?"

The woman spun to face him. Her eyes narrowed in what could be recognition, and her brow furrowed for an instant. "Only if you're Mr. Steel, but I don't think you are."

Evan held out a hand. He had to play it cool despite the way his heart was thumping and threatening to burst free from the confines of his chest. She was merely a woman, an obstacle to be dealt with. Nothing more. "No, I'm not. My name is Evan Close. I own the land and the dam. As well as the contracts for the upkeep of said dam. I run Xenon."

"Then perhaps you can help me." She seized his hand; her fingers cool and her touch light. "Dr. Lou Fitzgerald, head archaeologist for the Sparrow Foundation. I'm here to check out your lake."

4

Evan held her gaze. "I know who you are, Dr. Fitzgerald."

She raised her brows and dropped his hand as if it burned her. "Does my reputation precede me?"

"Varian Sparrow and I go way back. He told me you were coming."

"I see. Well, then, as you know why I'm here, I'd like permission to dive in the lake. Explore the ruins. Take photos. That kind of thing."

"Why?"

Lou frowned, confused. "You said you knew I was coming."

"Yes, but why the sudden interest in a lake that's been there so long? After all, it was constructed before World War II."

"History is buried down there." Dr. Fitzgerald spoke slowly as if explaining the basics to a small child. "Varian wants the ruins catalogued before they vanish for good. He insists that with the levels in the lake this low, now is the best time to do it."

"I'd say you're several years too late for that. Everyone connected with the lake, the building of the dam, and flooding of the village is long dead."

"Ah, but in my line of work that's always the case. It's surprising what you can learn from what people left behind, Mr. Close." She tugged a folder from the case in her hand and removed a sheaf of photos. "Look at these."

Evan snatched them and flicked through them. His stomach sank further with each photo. How had she gotten hold of these? And why was he only seeing them for the first time now? What kind of a game was Varian playing?

He glanced up. "And this proves what?" Somehow, he managed to keep his voice on an even keel, despite the turmoil surging within him.

"That something is still down there. Those photos are of items washed up along the shoreline over there. The church is proof some of the buildings are still intact. Three weeks is all I'm asking."

Evan paused as he considered the idea. Three weeks was an eternity. Three days would be too long. "I really don't see —"

"Mr. Close, that" — Dr. Fitzgerald interrupted him as she jabbed at a photo — "is the burned femur of a child."

"You don't know that. It could be anything. An animal or . . ."

"I can assure you it's not an animal bone. It's a child, aged around seven or eight." She cut him off. "It's my job to know that. I also happen to know that there are no death certificates for burn victims in the area in at least the last one hundred years. Now, either you let me dive or my office sends the photo and the bone to the police, and this whole area becomes a crime scene." She stared him down, her face firm and her jaw set. "It's your choice."

Choice? Yeah, right. What choice did he have? He narrowed his eyes. "It sounds more like blackmail to me, Dr. Fitzgerald."

She tilted her head, her gaze never leaving his face. "Not at all. Simply stating facts. Not to mention that the press would also have a field day with these photos."

Evan sucked in a deep breath. This woman had the means to be an irritating thorn in his flesh. "Ten days," he said firmly.

That would give him more than enough time to negotiate with the river authorities and tidal control and have water diverted long enough to refill the reservoir, essentially re-flooding the valley. The soonest he could organize that would be a just under a week. If it happened sooner, before she finished, it would hardly be his fault.

Dr. Fitzgerald shook her head, her ponytail whipping from side to side. "That is nowhere near long enough."

"That is all the time you can have," he reiterated firmly.

"In that case I shall do as many dives as I see fit. Night time ones, too, if needed. I'll also require unlimited access to the dam, lake, and surrounding land."

He hesitated before giving her a curt nod. "You've heard the rumours?"

"That this place is haunted?" She rubbed the back of her neck, a smirk on her lips. "I don't believe in ghosts, Mr. Close, nor am I afraid of them. I prefer working when no curious onlookers are around, so the ghost stories will be a great deterrent." She held out her hand. "I'm sure I'll see you around."

He captured her hand, only instead of shaking it, he raised it slowly to his lips and kissed it softly, never once breaking eye contact with her. He noted with satisfaction that her eyes glistened and her cheeks flushed. Her skin was as soft as he'd imagined. He'd thrown her off balance and that was exactly what he wanted. He smiled.

"I'm sure we will meet again. Dark Lake is a small village." He inclined his head. "Dr. Fitzgerald, Charlie."

He spun on his heel and headed towards the office to find Jasper. He had many things to put in motion and very little time to do it.

Lou watched Mr. Close walk away, shock-waves rippling from the back of her hand to her core. She could still feel the imprint of his lips, fire burning there as much as on her cheeks.

Talk about taking her by surprise. She hadn't expected him to act like a gentle-man. Kissing the back of one's hand was so old fashioned. Only found in the Jane Austen novels she'd read, not that she'd admit to reading them if anyone asked. She also read contemporary romance, as well as some of the grittier ones — preferring the suspense genre to straightforward love stories. She read a lot for relaxation. She needed to in her line of work; otherwise, she'd never switch off.

Plus, reading helped on those nights she couldn't sleep. When the memories hit her head on, forcing her to relive over and over things she'd rather forget. And diving wouldn't help that one little bit. In fact, it'd probably make things worse for a while. Not that she needed that on top of everything else.

A touch on her arm brought her back to the here and now. She shook her head and sighed. "Sorry. My mind went off on a tangent for a moment."

"It's fine. I asked if you wanted to go and hire the scuba gear," Charlie asked.

Lou nodded. "Yes. And I need to brief the rest of the team Varian said he'd arrange."

Charlie frowned. "What team?"

She raised an eyebrow. "He said . . ."

"You should know by now, girlie, what Varian says and what Varian does are two totally separate things. There is you and me and a couple of blokes from the pub who know how to dive. That's it."

"Great," she muttered, tempted to correct both his grammar and the use of the word girlie, but really couldn't be bothered. For a second, she wondered if she should turn around and go home. Forget the whole thing. Then again, she'd just gone to bat with Mr. Close and fought for the right to do this. "Fine, OK. You ring them and get them here. I'll call Varian and find out what game he thinks he's playing."

As Charlie left, Lou leaned against the parapet, gazing out over the water at the church spire. The stone work at the base, right above the water level, appeared to be blackened. Had there been a fire at some point in its history? It would explain the burned bone, but not the lack of records anywhere.

She tugged her phone from her pocket. Taking a deep, calming breath, she rang Varian.

"This is Varian Sparrow. Leave a message."

The calming breath evaporated. She glowered. "It's Lou. And I'm not surprised you don't have the guts to answer your phone. This is a shambles, Varian. Shambles with a capital S, H, A, M and every other letter in the word. There is no team. There is no permission to dive or anything else, for that matter. You are jolly lucky I'm not resigning on the spot. You send AJ and Clara up here on the double, or I *am* quitting. In fact, they'd better be here by morning, or I hand those photos to the cops and walk."

She shoved the phone into her pocket, spun around, and walked back to the car. Easing into the vehicle, she made several more calls, the first to the scuba diving company to arrange the equipment hire. She charged that and everything else to the company credit card without any hesitation.

Finished with the remaining calls, she leaned back in her seat and closed her eyes for a few seconds, trying to regain her equilibrium. Every part of her was screaming to leave, let someone else do this. But she wasn't a coward. If she were, she'd have given up long ago.

Lou rubbed her hands over her face. She didn't have time to sit here and let Varian wind her up further. She started the car and drove back into the village, parking once again in the small hotel car park.

She wandered along the single street of shops. She checked the small estate agents in the hope there would be a holiday home or short term let she could rent as she was sick of hotels. But there was nothing. As she went back onto the cold, grey street, her phone rang.

Lou grimaced as she read the name on the screen. At least he'd had the decency to return her call before the day was out for once. She stood to the side of the pavement, not wanting to either walk and talk, or get in the way of other pedestrians. "Varian, how lovely of you to call me back. How are you?" Somehow, she managed to inject a half-hearted attempt at sarcasm into her voice.

"Busy. I've arranged for a supply of diving

gear, tanks, valves, and so on to be delivered to the dam for you. You won't need to order anymore off your own bat, so don't even think about doing so. You can have AJ but that's it. Clara stays here and works with Monty." His terse tone annoyed Lou further.

"Excuse me?" For a nanosecond, Lou wasn't sure she'd heard Varian correctly. "I thought you said I could only have AJ."

"That's because I did say that. I need Clara here."

"If you want Dark Lake excavated properly, then I need help to do it. A local know-it-all along with two blokes from the pub with questionable diving experience, does not an archaeological team make. It doesn't cut it. I need people I can trust, especially under water with potentially hazardous debris all over the place, not to mention people who know what they'd be doing, and they certainly can't know how I like things done. Mr. Close has given me ten days to do this, and that was grudgingly. I meant what I said about quitting. You can find someone —"

The line went dead, and Lou growled in frustration. "Fine. Hang up on me. I'll resign by e-mail."

"The service probably dropped." A deep

47

voice spoke behind her. She'd only heard it once, but she recognized it. "It does that quite often up here. Something to do with the weather or something."

Lou turned around to face him. "Hello, again, Mr. Close."

"You seem stressed, Dr. Fitzgerald. Is everything all right?"

"Just peachy," she murmured. Then she breathed out her frustrations and shoved her phone and hands into her pockets. This wasn't Mr. Close's fault, and she shouldn't take it out on him. "No, not really. Everything is about as far from all right as it's possible to get. But that is just par for the course, right now. You own all this land, right?"

He nodded. "Yes."

"I don't suppose you could tell me some of the history, could you? Background information and so on."

Hesitation, or was that reluctance, flickered in Mr. Close's eyes. "All right."

She nodded. "Thank you. I'll buy you coffee. That is if I can find a coffee shop. I'm still finding my way around here."

"I can go better than coffee," he said. "We'll have lunch. It can be my treat for boring you rigid with the village history." He waved a hand. "This way."

48

5

Evan ordered the food at the bar and paid. Then he picked up the drinks and carried them back to the table where Lou sat. The Wolf Pack did decent food for a pub, and unless they were really busy, which hardly ever happened, the meals were always delivered quickly.

Why had he agreed to this? Was he that desperate for company — for female company — that he'd put himself in danger of betraying everything? Or was it a simple desire to spend a little more time in the company of someone who wore her emotions on her sleeve and wasn't afraid to make her feelings known about her boss, even if that could get her fired?

Whatever his reasons for inviting her to lunch, the woman had calmed down considerably since she'd left the dam and that had to be a good thing.

He set his pint down on the table and then

placed Dr. Fitzgerald's down in front of her. "I've never come across a woman who drinks beer before. At least not by the pint."

"Then you must not get out very often. Or gone to the same university I did. Although, I must admit I have picked up the American habit of drinking it cold."

He smiled. "Likewise." He shrugged off his overcoat, laying it carefully on the back of his chair. "So, what can I tell you?"

"I'd like to learn the history behind the village and the dam. Something to tell me why a dig here is so important to my boss that he yanks me off my project and sends me a couple hundred miles north at a moment's notice."

She studied him, and he glanced down, wondering if he'd spilled something on his blue suit. Satisfied he hadn't, he undid the jacket and eased back into the seat. "Can't the Internet tell you that, Dr. Fitzgerald?" he asked.

"It can, and it will, but only the bare facts, not the emotions or the little details that make a dig like this come alive. For example, the Internet can tell me that Joe Blogs lived at 54 Main Street and protested against the flooding of the village by chaining himself to the railings outside 10 Downing Street, but it won't tell me what made him do it.

Did he simply object because everyone else did, or was there more to it than that?"

She winked. "Was he a mass murderer who hid all the bodies in the church crypt? Or was he a smuggler and stashed all the loot there? Or was he the local graffiti artist and didn't want all his work lost forever. And yes, he probably kept his paint in the church crypt along with everything else."

Evan chuckled, despite the way her words needled. "In that case, I suggest you check out the church crypt for bodies, loot, and spray paint as soon as you can. Seriously though, I didn't live through it. My great-grandparents died before I was born, and my grandfather never really talked about it. They lived in Abernay, about a stone's throw from the church before they moved to the manor after the flooding."

"The church is the one we can see?"

He nodded, running his finger along the rim of the glass. "Abernay was this end of the reservoir. Finley the other."

"Was your great-grandfather the man in charge of the project?" She glanced at the notebook. "David Close?"

Evan nodded. When had she started taking notes? "Yes. Although that was in name only from what I learned. Other men built the dam." He paused as the plates of food

51

came. "Thank you." He took a deep breath. "This is one of my favourites, a house specialty."

Dr. Fitzgerald picked up her knife and fork and freed them from the serviette. "Looks like Lancashire hot pot."

"Similar, but with a Cumbrian twist." He added salt and pepper to his before opening his knife and fork. He laid the serviette on his lap. "My great-grandfather got a lot of stick for working on the project."

"I bet. Why did he do it? If you still own the land, then he can't have sold it."

"Only part of the land was sold." The whole topic made him uncomfortable. Why on earth had he agreed to this conversation? "They force sold the houses in both villages, evicted all the occupants, both tenants and owners alike, before rehousing them all in large towns elsewhere. The villagers even protested in London, but to no avail. My great-grandfather lost just as much when the flood came."

Dr. Fitzgerald ate hungrily. "This is good. Your great-grandfather didn't live in the manor house at the time of the flooding then?"

Evan's stomach pitted. "I'm sorry?" he asked, somehow making his voice remain calm.

"You said he lived by the church, yet your family have owned the manor house for eight generations, and it obviously wasn't rebuilt or part of the deal to sell off the land." She held his gaze. "Varian gave me a file with a few briefing notes. Brief being the operative word."

"Then why are we having this conversation?" He frowned. Personal family history wasn't part of the deal.

She paused, a forkful of meat part way to her mouth. "As I said, the public records only tell half the story."

Ain't that the truth? His great-grandfather's journal put a whole different slant on the entire affair. "His father was still alive and living there. Great-grandad never saw eye to eye with him."

He paused. How much should he tell her? Maybe he'd tell her enough to shut her up, to appease her curiosity, and no more. He chewed slowly then spoke. "His parents thought Great-grandma was beneath them. She was, how do I put this, the scullery maid."

Dr. Fitzgerald grinned and then chuckled. "Your great-grandfather married the scullery maid? It sounds like something from a book or a TV show."

He bristled, hackles rising and defences

53

going up. "It's no laughing matter, Dr. Fitzgerald. Things were different back in the nineteen twenties and thirties. Class mattered. There were certain lines you didn't cross. Just like today, in some respects, but not quite so much. Anyway, going back to the subject of the dam, the protest failed. The dam was finished, everyone moved out, and the villages were flooded. Great-grandad oversaw the work and building of the new village. None of the original residents moved in. People didn't stay long at first, but after the war, things were different. People needed housing, so they stayed. It's taken a long time to build the place up to what it is today."

She nodded. "What about the church fire?"

Evan choked. He grabbed his glass, swallowing quickly. "Church fire?"

"The stones visible on the spire are blackened. The only thing that could cause that is a fire. And a pretty big one."

"Oh, right. Again, I wouldn't know for sure, but local folklore says bomb damage."

Dr. Fitzgerald shook her head. "As far as I know, the flooding occurred in 1934 or '35. Well before the war."

"September 1935. It's the anniversary next week. And I said bomb not blitz."

"Terrorists in the middle of Cumbria?"

Evan shrugged. "It could have been a case of you're not taking this from us, we'll destroy it. Or it could have easily been a lit candle catching an altar cloth. Or something."

"I imagine it's documented in the library."

"Probably." He reached for his glass again, taking several long swallows.

Dr. Fitzgerald finished her meal. "That was delicious. How much do I owe you?"

"Nothing."

She wiped her lips on the serviette. The simple movement captivated him. What was it about her that distracted him? He was instinctively drawn to her like a moth to a candle flame, and that never ended well. She folded the paper napkin and laid it on her plate.

"Mr. Close, really I can't accept that."

Evan came within a hair's breadth of asking her to call him by his given name. Then common sense prevailed if only for an instant. "You can pay next time." The impulsive words were out before he realised, but there was no taking them back. They hung between them like an insurmountable cliff face.

"Next time?" Her eyes twinkled. "That's a little presumptuous, don't you think?"

"Not really," he said, covering quickly. "I've told you my story. It's only fair that you tell me yours. How about dinner tomorrow?"

"Your story? You've hardly told me anything. A little about your great-grandparents, but nothing about you."

"All the more reason for dinner tomorrow night." Why was he pushing this? He should let her go, back away, keep his distance, and things might be OK.

"Thank you for lunch, but I need to go. I have a lot of work to do in a very short time frame." Dr. Fitzgerald slid into her jacket and grabbed her bag as she stood.

Ever the gentleman, Evan rose. "A word of warning, Dr. Fitzgerald. Whether you believe the ghost stories or not, it isn't safe by the lake after dark." He seized her hand and ran his thumb over the back of it before kissing it. Just as before, sparks zipped through him. "I mean it."

"OK."

"You never did say whether you'll have dinner with me tomorrow. And yes, that is the fourth time I'm asking. Please don't make me ask a fifth."

She caught her breath, colour flaming in her cheeks again. She left her hand in his, as if she enjoyed his touch, or perhaps she could feel it, too. The instant attraction, the spark that flowed through him, was setting each nerve ending aflame with . . .

Passion? Was that what he was feeling? He wasn't sure. All he knew was that at this precise moment, his entire being was off kilter, and he didn't like it. He had to be in control, all the time.

The pretty archaeologist inclined her head. "OK. Dinner tomorrow."

He smiled. "Then I'll pick you up at seven and we'll eat at the manor. I can show you around the place, tell you more of the history. Show you the family portraits and so on."

A slight frown crossed her face. "I thought the agreement was you paid for this, and I will be paying for dinner tomorrow."

"You can owe me one." He finally let go of her hand. "Good afternoon, Dr. Fitzgerald."

The frown vanished, replaced by a faint smile. "Have a good day."

He lingered as she left, his gaze following her across the pub to the door. The way she walked and moved was mesmerizing, to put it mildly. Shaking his head, he sat down and picked up his glass to finish his beer slowly.

Ira Miles slid into the seat Dr. Fitzgerald had vacated. "Keeping your enemies close?"

"Something like that. It's a case of having to do so. Just make sure the library is kept locked at all times and that CCTV is on in all the rooms in the manor. Dr. Fitzgerald is joining me for dinner tomorrow. I don't want her going off and exploring on her own."

6

Lou spent a frustrating afternoon in the library. The history section contained hardly anything of any use to man nor beast. She tried the tourist office, but that proved utterly fruitless. Charlie wasn't answering his texts, but she'd try him again later. It was almost as if all records for the area had been wiped the day they flooded the valley and the villages died.

Heading back to the hotel seemed the best option. The scuba gear wouldn't be available until tomorrow, and dusk was falling.

Lou settled onto the bed with her laptop and hit the Internet search engines. A village had existed on the site of Abernay since the Roman invasion in 71 AD. A monastery had been built as early as 685, but that had been destroyed when the Vikings invaded in 875. It was left abandoned during the intervening years, finally being rebuilt in 1154 until destroyed again during the dissolution of the monasteries by Henry VIII in 1540. All the stones were removed and used elsewhere.

Several battles ensued over the years; the most noted one during the civil war in 1645, where the death toll rose to over a hundred. The village was ostracized for its part in the Pilgrimage of Grace in 1536.

There was a small mention of the protest about the building of the dam, but nowhere as much as she'd hoped or expected. A few photographs, including some aerial ones, of the village before and after the flooding completed all she could find.

She leaned back on the pillows. Not much for a place that had been there so long.

No mention of ghosts or anything else. Not that she'd expected to find any. She'd need to call up urban legends for that. Going back to the search engine, she began typing. Only to be distracted by her phone.

Yawning, she picked it up and read the message from AJ.

HEY, BOSS. WILL BE LEAVING FIRST THING. SHOULD BE THERE BY ELEVEN. NEED ME TO BRING ANYTHING? I CAN RAID THE OFFICE ONCE V AND M GO HOME. I KNOW WHERE THE BOSS KEEPS THE SECRET CHOCOLATE STASH.

Lou grinned. AJ was a card. A total twit at times, no sign of respect for authority, but a great bloke to have around in a crisis. His way of thinking outside the box had got her out of a jam on more than one occasion.

No one knows that unless they have been Sneaking in my drawers and locked boxes She replied.

Hah. I know every-thinggggggggg. Seriously? You need anything . . . chocolate?

She thought quickly, then tapped out a reply.

Yeah, I left my trowel and other bits in my bag under the desk, along with my diary and Filofax. Meet me at the dam in the morning. I'll book you into a room in the hotel here. Is C coming?

Ask me another, Dr. F. She and M are as thick as thieves. Wouldn't be surprised if he is living with her after what I saw in the office earlier.

Lou snorted. *Thieves* was so the right word. And Monty and Clara being involved with each other would fit why she wasn't coming as well. She sent one final text.

At least with AJ here, she'd get something done. Either way, whether she got the university job after meeting with Professor Cunningham or not, she would be quitting as soon as she possibly could. The only question was how much notice did she need to give and would it be better to resign now or once this dig was over?

She stood and crossed to the window to close the curtains. Thick fog had descended, making street lamps glow eerily. Not a single sound came from anywhere. She closed the curtains with a swish and grabbed the TV remote. Nothing caught her fancy, and she switched it off. The room phone rang, but when she answered, no one was there.

Maybe she should go find something to eat. Not that she was hungry, but her blood sugar was starting to dip. And a walk would do her good.

Lou slid into her coat and clutched her bag and room key. She took the lift to the ground floor. The reception desk was empty, a steaming mug of coffee sitting on it. The restaurant bore a sign saying *closed*. So much for getting something to eat there.

She peeped into the hotel lounge, but that, too, was empty. Magazines and cups lay scattered about as if they were in use, simply lacking the people. It reminded her of the story of the *Marie Celeste*. The fog came down and everyone vanished, leaving things as they were. Her mobile rang. "Hello?"

Again, like the room phone, no one replied.

She shook her head. She was letting herself be spooked by ghost stories and a lack of people. She'd walk the few yards to the pub, get something to eat there, and come back. Five long strides brought her to the door. The frigid air stole into her lungs, taking her breath away.

Lou tugged her collar around her neck and shivered. The swirling fog was thick and yellow, reminiscent of the pea-soupers London used to get, the ones she'd seen on the Internet. She couldn't see a thing.

"I'd stay in if I were you, Dr. Fitzgerald."

Lou jumped and twisted around to find Charlie Brampton inches from her face. "Evening, Charlie. I didn't hear you creep up behind me. And why should I stay in?"

"It's safer." He nodded to the fog. "Nights like this, the spirits walk."

"Seriously?" Lou scoffed. He had to be kidding, surely. "You do know there are no such things as ghosts."

Wide white eyes stared at her from his

63

dark face. "Nights like this, the fog and dead rise. Mark my words, Dr. Fitzgerald. This is not a natural fog; people go out, and they never come back."

She shivered again, although whether from the cold or the way her mind suddenly ran rampant, she couldn't tell. A muffled siren began to rise and fall, the sound muted by the fog. "What's that?"

"Ghosts," Charlie intoned. "That's the siren warning that the flooding is about to start. Goes off a lot this time of year, just like the fog. The fog rises and with it the drowned folks rise to seek revenge."

"Charlie, that's enough." Mr. Close's firm, steady, and somewhat calming voice came from behind them. "I don't want you to go scaring Dr. Fitzgerald with your stories. It's not friendly, especially on a night like this."

Lou tried not to react visibly as she twisted to face the second person to have crept up on her unawares. Seriously, were they all out to give her heart failure tonight?

Charlie shrugged. "Merely telling it how it is, Mr. Close."

"In this case, Dr. Fitzgerald, it's merely the Tanmoor sirens."

"Tanmoor?" She peered at him.

"The loony bin," Charlie inserted.

Mr. Close shot him a glare. "Tanmoor is

the hospital for the criminally insane fifteen miles away from here. It's similar to the Broadmoor institution in Berkshire. They test the sirens every Monday morning at ten."

Lou shivered. "But it's eight thirty Tuesday evening."

Mr. Close nodded. "Then it means someone has escaped. On this occasion, Charlie may be right, and it's safer to stay inside."

"I was going to the pub for something to eat," Lou said. "Purely because the desk and lounge are deserted, and the restaurant is closed."

"Not tonight. I'll find someone. Come back inside where it's safe."

Feeling very much like a naughty child being sent to her room, Lou did as he asked. As an afterthought, she peered at him, trying to see him as something other than a very handsome man. An extremely tall, handsome man, who had at least a foot in height on her. "So, if it isn't safe out there, how will you get home?"

He smiled slowly, the smile never quite reaching his eyes. "I have a car and a bodyguard. I'll be perfectly safe."

Lou did a double take. "You have a bodyguard?"

He nodded. "And Mr. Miles is a very

good shot. He never misses."

Not sure how to respond, she twisted and headed inside. Why would the bloke need a bodyguard? Never mind one who was an excellent shot. What exactly was he hiding, and what was going on here? "The desk is still empty."

"I'll see if I can find someone," he said.

"It's fine. Don't trouble yourself on my account. I'll try the desk a bit later, and see if I can get room service. G'night." She headed back to the lift and sighed as the doors closed. A minute or so later, she reached her room and opened the door.

The window was wide open. Fog swirled in, churning around the room and reaching for her with long tentacles. Cold oozed into her, piercing her. Moving quickly, she left the door open and reached the window in five strides. She could see Mr. Close and another man standing under the streetlight looking up at her window. She nodded to him, slammed it shut and double checked the catch. She hadn't left it open. She knew that for certain.

At that moment, Lou caught sight of a man's reflection in the glass. He stood behind her, a knife in his hand, balaclava over his face. She spun around, screaming as he tackled her, tucking her against him.

Panic overwhelmed her. All the moves she'd learned in self-defence classes left her. Metal touched her throat. She tried to swallow, fear making it impossible.

Was this it? Had she overcome everything life had thrown at her to die in a cold, foggy hotel room alone?

No. She hadn't. Sucking in a deep breath, she pushed her head back, trying to hurt her assailant. At the same time, she brought her leg up backwards in an attempt to kick him. However, he'd apparently anticipated this, as his foot promptly swept her false leg out from under her and she wobbled. She would have fallen if he wasn't holding her so tightly.

"Don't do that again," he hissed.

"What do you want?"

"You." The knife dug a little deeper, and he began pushing her across the room.

She hit the wall with a thud, breath forced from her lungs.

"Let her go." Mr. Close's strong voice echoed from the doorway.

Lou glanced over. She'd never been more pleased to see someone. "Mr. Close . . ." She broke off as she realised the man standing beside him was aiming a gun at her. "Wait —"

The gun fired.
Lou screamed.

7

As Dr. Fitzgerald screamed, Evan moved quickly to her side, afraid that Ira had missed and shot the wrong person. Despite his confidence in Ira's abilities, this one had been a little close. "It's OK, Dr. Fitzgerald. You're safe now. Ira, call the police."

He led her to the bed and set her down on the edge of it. "It's OK. It's over now. I did tell you that Mr. Miles was a good shot." He drew the blanket from the bed, and wrapped it around her shaking shoulders. "Are you hurt?"

She shook her head. "I'm OK. W— what are you doing here?"

"As you shut your window, we could see a man wearing a balaclava behind you. He was obviously up to no good. We were coming to investigate."

"G-glad you did."

"You're bleeding. Let me see." Tugging his clean handkerchief from his jacket pocket, he pressed it to the wound on her neck.

Dr. Fitzgerald flinched and bit her bottom lip but made no sound. She appeared almost embarrassed, even though there was no need. Her gaze flickered past him to the man on the floor. "Is — is he dead?"

"No, but he won't give you any more trouble." Evan glanced over at Ira, who still held the gun on the man, despite the fact he was now tied up. "Will he?"

Ira shook his head. "No, it's only a leg wound. The police and paramedics are on their way."

"Thank you. Can you also call another ambulance for Dr. Fitzgerald?"

"I'm fine. It's only a scratch. Please, I don't want a fuss. I've done worse in my time than a simple cut."

Peering under the handkerchief, he was dismayed to discover the cut was still oozing blood. "Then allow me to administer first aid. This needs a dressing on it."

"OK. There's a first aid kit in my pack. It's a field one, so it's quite comprehensive."

He nodded. "Hold this for one moment." He placed her hand over his makeshift dressing. "You will need to press quite firmly."

Dr. Fitzgerald held his hand briefly.

"Thank you, Mr. Close. If you and Mr. Miles hadn't arrived when you did, I . . ." her voice faltered, and she shook harder.

Evan patted her hand, aware of Ira talking on the phone in the background. "I'm just glad we got here." He moved over to her pack and undid it. Fortunately, the first aid kit was near the top. She wasn't kidding about the size of it. "And I think we're past the Mr. Close formalities now, don't you, Dr. Fitzgerald? My name is Evan."

She held his gaze. "Louisa. But my friends call me Lou. In fact, most people do, apart from when I'm in trouble. Then Mum uses my full name."

He smiled. "My mother does the same. How many names do you have?"

"Four."

"Four?" he repeated, knowing full well that she did.

"Yes." She paused. "You don't seem that surprised, but then I guess you've checked me out on the Internet the same way I have you."

A slight smile crossed his lips. "Guilty."

She nodded as he crossed back over to her. "It's quite a mouthful. Fitzgerald is my stepfather's surname. I kept my original as a middle name when he adopted me."

Evan put the first aid kit on the bedside

unit and opened it. "You must care for him a lot."

"Yeah, I do. He's always there when I need him. It's as if he knows instinctively somehow." Lou nodded. "He literally saved my life many years ago. Then when he married Mum and adopted me, it only seemed right." She paused. "I don't make it a habit of needing to be saved."

"I wasn't making that assumption. Let me see your neck." He peeled back the handkerchief and frowned. The wound was no longer gushing but he suspected it wasn't as superficial as she'd tried to make it out to be. He glanced at the first aid kit, noting the steri-strips in the top compartment. He'd make use of them. "I need to clean it up a little first. Hold this again."

Taking some cotton wool from the box, he headed into the small bathroom to dampen it under the cold tap. Her toiletries were arranged on the glass shelf above the sink in a neat row: shampoo, conditioner, shower crème, and shaving foam all lined up with labels outermost, with toothpaste, toothbrush, and a razor in the glass at the end.

As he came out of the bathroom, there was a knock on the door.

Lou started to get up.

"I'll get it. You keep still, and don't let go of that hanky."

Evan strode to the partly closed door and opened it. Two uniformed officers, a couple of paramedics, and a rather agitated hotel manager stood there. "Sergeant Drake, do come in. I'm afraid the suspect will need medical attention as it was necessary to shoot him in order to save Dr. Fitzgerald. It is a mere flesh wound; he is in no immediate danger of dying. Now, if you'll excuse me, I will tend to Dr. Fitzgerald's injuries while you speak to her."

He tuned out the two officers and shifted his concentration to Lou's neck, trying not to let his mind run rampant. His fingertips burned as they grazed her skin as he worked to gently clean the wound. He applied the steri-strips, finding four were ample. He took his time, each gentle touch sending powerful surges of electricity through him, making his taut body react in a way he didn't expect or want.

Something akin to relief surged through him as he finished attaching the small dressing to her neck. Touching her shoulder briefly, he smiled. "All done."

"Thank you."

"Welcome." He went into the bathroom to wash his hands. He caught sight of Ira in

73

the mirror watching him. "Before you say anything, I'm being careful. And thank you. Your aim, as always, is excellent."

Ira nodded.

"Bring the car around. Dr. Fitzgerald will be staying at the manor house for the duration of her time in Dark Lake. This place isn't safe."

"And the fact you can keep a close eye on her —"

"Will be an advantage," Evan finished. "I know what I'm doing. Trust me."

Ira hesitated as if he were about to say something, then changed his mind, and nodded. "I'll go and get the car."

Evan dragged his gaze away from the woman and dried his hands before heading back into the other room. He moved protectively to Lou's side, but didn't sit.

Sergeant Drake put his notebook away. "We'll be off, Dr. Fitzgerald. It all seems fairly cut and dried, but if we need you again, we'll let you know."

"Who is he?" Evan asked, noting that the intruder was no longer in the room.

"Bart Manchester. He escaped from Tanmoor in the laundry van this morning."

Lou frowned. "But the sirens only just went off."

Sergeant Drake shook his head. "They

went off this morning."

"But we heard them only a short time ago in the fog." She shifted her gaze to Evan. "You said that's what they were."

"I must have been mistaken. Perhaps it was a fog horn from somewhere."

The two officers left as the hotel manager spoke for the first time. "I'm really sorry about this, Dr. Fitzgerald. We'll move you to another room."

"There is no need," Evan told him in a no-nonsense tone. "Dr. Fitzgerald is coming to stay with me."

Lou shook her head. "Evan, that's very kind of you, but you don't have to put yourself out on my account. I'm perfectly fine here."

He shoved aside the thrill he got from hearing his name fall from her lips. "I have to disagree. There is every need and you are quite evidently not fine. Besides, the manor is closer to your work, and I won't be charging you exorbitant rates for somewhere that isn't safe."

"I have a colleague arriving tomorrow. He'll be here mid-morning."

"Then he is more than welcome to stay as well. It's been a while since I've had guests. We'll collect your car in the morning rather than you getting lost in this fog. I'll help you pack your things. Ira is waiting out front with the car."

"I really . . ."

"I insist, Lou. I wouldn't sleep tonight knowing you were here alone."

Not giving her time to object any further, Evan turned his attention to the hotel manager. He tugged out his wallet and handed the manager three twenty pound notes "This should cover this evening. Even though I'm sure you weren't going to charge Dr. Fitzgerald for tonight after this. However, you will need to get the room cleaned and blood can be very difficult to remove."

The manager pocketed the money and left.

Evan gave Lou his full attention. Her eyes had narrowed and her lips pursed into a thin line. She wasn't happy about this arrangement. He held up a hand. "Let me guess. Your mother told you never to sleep with someone you hardly knew."

"Well, I wouldn't put it like that." Colour tinted her cheeks, and it was all Evan could do not to smirk.

"Let me assure you, sleeping with you isn't on the agenda now or later. At least, not until after marriage. I do have some morals after all."

"Married?" she spluttered.

"A turn of phrase," he insisted. "My mother always told me to keep myself pure for my future wife and that is what I intend to do. Whether you eventually become the aforementioned wife or not, only time will tell. But right now, what I'm offering is a place to sleep where no one will break in and try to kill you. Or worse."

"What could possibly be worse than being murdered?" she demanded, sticking her hands on her hips.

"My, my, you're pretty when you're angry." He raised an eyebrow. "You really wish me to go into detail as to what a serial rapist, who tortures his victims for hours at a time, might have planned for you?"

He noted her squirm. "I didn't think so. Now, I'll help you pack up and then take your case for you. Ira will be waiting."

8

Lou sat in the car, Evan beside her. Half of her was glad to be out of the hotel and somewhere there would be an armed guard. The other part of her, the daring, do-it-alone part, reminded herself of her childhood and what they'd done without adult supervision and survived intact. Well, more or less intact.

Every part of her agreed on one thing. What she objected to was the strong-arm tactics Evan had used and the way he'd made the decision and didn't give her a choice to say otherwise.

She glanced at his profile, but it was too dark to see him. The power had gone out as they'd left the hotel, plunging everywhere into a thick choking fogginess. The miasma ahead glowed yellow in the headlights as the car crawled along the road.

Lou rubbed her throat gingerly. It hurt, but not as much as she expected. She could still feel Evan's touch, the gentle way he'd calmed and treated her. She hadn't expected that, given his offhand way of speaking and the way he'd talked to her before.

"We never did get you any dinner," Evan said. "I'll ring the house and get Mrs Jefferson to rustle something up."

"Please don't disturb her at this hour." Lou had lost any appetite she may have had long ago. "A cup of tea will be fine."

His fingers ran over the top of her hand, setting her nerve endings on fire. "Nonsense. You need something more than tea after a fright like you've had. How about hot chocolate and a slice of whatever I can find in the cake tin? Mrs Jefferson's cakes are the best."

She smiled. "Thank you. That sounds good. I don't mind the sofa tonight."

"Nonsense. Ira rang ahead, and Mrs Jefferson will already have made up a bed. She will organize one tomorrow for your colleague. Assuming you want separate rooms."

Lou snorted. "Too right I do. He's not my type. And I am most certainly not his type."

"I see. Does he prefer — ?"

"Blondes." She cut him off before he could develop that thought. "He prefers blondes. One in particular. In any case, he's not the type to get involved with a co-worker or his boss."

"I see. And you? What do you prefer?"

"I don't know really. There was someone I liked a long time ago. But he thought of me like a sister and never returned the feelings I had for him. He married someone else ten years ago now. We're still friends, always will be. We talk a couple times a week when he's not deployed somewhere remote and silly."

The dull swish under the tires was replaced by a crunch of gravel, and Lou assumed they had arrived at the manor house. The car halted a few seconds later, and the engine fell silent.

"We're here." Ira spoke from the front, before getting out and opening the door for Evan.

"Stay here," Evan told her as he climbed out of the car.

Not wanting to wait, Lou tried to find the door handle but couldn't. Panic set in for an instant before Evan opened the door for her. She got out, shivering in the cold, clammy fog.

His hand touched the small of her back protectively, and a torch shone at their feet. "Let's get you inside."

The huge hall was cavernous, lit only by paraffin lamps and a few candles. Obviously, the power was out here as well. A rather tall, well built, forebidding lady, dressed entirely in black, appeared carrying a candle. "Good evening, Mr. Close. I made up the blue room for your guest."

"Thank you, Mrs Jefferson."

"Will you be needing anything from the kitchen or anything else?"

"No. I'll make myself and Dr. Fitzgerald a drink before I go up."

"I don't mind doing it."

Evan shook his head. "We've kept you up far later than usual as it is. Besides, I'm more than capable of boiling some milk and raiding the cake tin. Oh, before I forget, Dr. Fitzgerald's colleague will be joining us tomorrow. Perhaps you could make up the green room for him at some point in the morning before midday."

Mrs Jefferson nodded. "Very good, sir."

Evan picked up a candle from the hall table and handed it to her. "This way, Lou. Ira will already have taken your bags up for you." He took another candle for himself and headed to the stairs.

Lou followed him, hoping there was nothing on the floor she could trip over. She wished she could stop and take in the décor and paintings. Maybe tomorrow in the daylight.

"The blue room overlooks the gardens and the maze. It's meant to be better than the one at the hotel, but I couldn't swear to it."

"Really? I'll have to try it," she replied. "Not in the dark, obviously. Or the fog."

"That wouldn't be a wise move. No one has used the maze in a long time. I should probably get the gardener to clear the paths."

"Why mention it if no one uses it?"

"Because you'll see it in the morning when you open the curtains and are bound to ask about it."

"Have you been in it?"

"Not since I was eight. I got lost in there. It was dark before someone found me. I was told that I'd been there all day."

"Must have been scary."

Evan stopped in front of a wooden door. "I remember being very scared and very alone." He opened the door. "This is you." He lit the lamp on the table by the door.

Yellow light glowed in one corner of the room. "There are more matches and candles on the side. As you can see, we're used to the power going out here. The bathroom is across the hallway. Give me ten minutes, and I'll bring that drink up for you."

She yawned. "That's very kind, but honestly I'd rather sleep. My eyes just don't want to stay open any longer. I'll see you in the morning."

"Breakfast is at eight. I'll knock for you on my way downstairs. Good night, Lou."

"Good night, Evan." She sank onto the bed as he shut the door. Was this really such a good idea? Muffled voices came from the landing and she crept to the door to hear better.

"Is the library locked?" Evan asked.

"Yes, sir." That was Mr. Miles, the security man/bodyguard. "Here's Mrs Jefferson's key from her set. She wasn't happy about handing it over. She wanted to know who'd be cleaning in there. All your papers are in the safe. Along with the journal. The cameras are also on in the hallways and common areas."

"Good. And I'll speak to Mrs Jefferson in the morning about cleaning."

The voices faded along with the footsteps, and Lou twisted back towards the centre of the room. A long-muted whistle from outside made her jump. But nothing happened, except the manic racing of her heart. She shook her head and unpacked her few things.

She sat on the bed and removed the prosthesis then rubbed the stump, for an instant feeling her toes itch. She'd expected the phantom pains to stop long ago, but every so often they'd come back to haunt her. Literally.

She lay on her side, her mind whirling. Had it really been a random attack back at the hotel? Surely, she'd simply been in the wrong place at the wrong time. Why was the library locked and the key hidden? And why the need for CCTV? Was it for her benefit or did Evan have something to hide? Maybe he was just naturally paranoid — he did have a bodyguard after all.

It was like a jigsaw puzzle with several pieces misplaced. And if there was one thing she hated, it was a puzzle with a bit or three missing.

9

Lou woke and sat bolt upright in the same moment. She stared across the pale grey morning lit room, her heart pounding. Sweat sheened her body, her damp nightgown sticking to her skin. The same dream once again, swallowing her whole each night.

What had woken her? It hadn't been the alarm she relied on to wake her as that hadn't gone off yet. She glanced around. Nothing seemed amiss, not that she'd really seen the room in the dark the night before. She glanced at the clock on the bedside table and then shook her head. Of course, it was flashing. At least that meant the power had been restored. Dawn seemed to be coming later and later, and the clocks had yet to change.

A knock came from the door. Was that what had woken her?

"Just a minute," she called. She twisted

her leg out of bed and reached for the prosthesis.

"No rush," Evan replied through the door. "It's seven thirty. I'll come back a few minutes before eight."

"OK. Thank you." She rubbed her hands over her face, the nightmare still on the edges of her mind.

Twenty-five minutes later, she was dressed and ready when Evan knocked on the door again. His intent gaze ran the full length of her body, and when he glanced up she saw appreciation in his eyes. She wasn't sure why. It was only jeans, a shirt, and sweat-shirt.

He wore black from head to foot, with the exception of a white shirt collar peeping over the top of a cable knit jumper. He smiled, smelling of toothpaste and cologne. His beard had been neatly trimmed and his short hair was either not brushed or gelled into place standing up. "I trust you are well rested."

"I slept no worse than usual. Same night-mares, but then I expected that."

"You get nightmares a lot?"

She closed the door and began to walk with him along the corridor to the stairs. "This time of year I do. Especially when my work involves swimming of any kind."

"Ah. You are diving the lake this morning?"

Lou nodded, taking in the gilded paintings as she passed them. The stairs were far more ornate than she'd expected. A centre carpet protected oak boards edged by a wide bannister. "Yes, and every day until I'm done here."

"I thought you enjoyed swimming. You do still hold the world record."

She sighed. "It's a long story."

"Perhaps you will tell me some time."

"I'm sure you already know if you knew about the world record."

Evan smiled as he reached the foot of the stairs. "That is a matter of public record. And as you said, the Internet can sometimes tell you the how without mentioning the why." He showed her into the dining room. "Food is on the side. Help yourself. Tea and coffee are on the table."

"Thank you." She picked up a plate and stared in awe at the vast selection of food. Was this really only for the two of them? She could have fed four people for a week on this one meal alone. She took some of the eggs and sausage and a slice of toast.

She pivoted and tried not to gasp at the size of the table. It virtually filled the wooden panelled room. Only two places had been laid, and she took the seat to the side, assuming the one at the head of the table was for Evan. She set down her plate and then slid into the chair.

While she waited for Evan, she poured some tea. It was too early in the morning for coffee, despite the fact her American stepfather lived and breathed coffee. Besides, she had to be able to think straight today, and coffee wouldn't help on that front. She found coffee only served to addle her brain if she drank it first thing — way too much caffeine for her.

Evan piled his plate high with food. How could he eat that much and stay in such good shape? It really wasn't fair. He glanced over at her. "So, what are your plans for this morning?"

"I need to pick up my car and hope the dive gear is delivered to the dam by ten. Then I start work. Alone, as I don't fancy a team of two blokes from the pub who may or may not have diving experience."

Evan sat down. "Please, eat. Don't let it get cold."

Lou nodded and picked up her knife and fork. "Charlie is organizing a boat, so that's one less thing to do. I take the boat out and dive."

"You aren't planning on diving alone, I

hope." He frowned.

She shook her head. "I told you my colleague is arriving this morning. I have other things I can do before he gets here. He'll be partnering me on all the dives. It's one of my unbreakable rules."

"And a very sensible one, too."

She watched in amazement as he smothered his food in tomato ketchup. "It's much safer that way. I know how unforgiveable water can be. I found that out first hand."

"Oh?"

"Few incidents whilst sailing several years ago," she said evasively.

"Do tell."

"Big storm, well, to be honest, it was a hurricane. An explosion in the docks where people died. Shipwreck." She paused, rubbing her leg. Her toes itched again. The anniversary of the attack was fast approaching, and that made things worse.

"Is that how you lost your leg?"

She shivered. "How did you know? Oh, that's probably public record, too. The disabled swimming world record holder turned archaeologist."

"Forgive me. I didn't mean to pry." Contrition furrowed his brow.

She shook her head. "It's OK. No, it was a swimming accident, but not anything I mentioned just now."

The door opened. "I'm sorry to bother you, Mr. Close," Mrs Jefferson began. "But you have a phone call from the United States. A Mr. Taylor and he says it's urgent."

He sighed and glanced at his watch. "It must be for him to be ringing at this hour. I'll take it in the study. Could you have the car brought around for Dr. Fitzgerald, please? She'll need a lift back to the village to collect her vehicle."

Mrs Jefferson straightened the keys on her belt. "Of course."

Evan stood and picked up his plate. "I apologize, Lou, but this could take some time. Phil could talk the hind leg off a donkey and then convince it to run a marathon immediately afterwards." He paused. "I'm sorry. That's the wrong expression to use."

"It's fine. I'm tired of people hopping on egg shells before leapfrogging over the elephant in the room." She winked. "See, I can make bad one legged jokes as well."

His face lit up slightly. "If you'll excuse me, I will see you later."

Lou nodded and dropped her gaze to her plate. She finished her food and headed into the hall to find a man in a chauffer's uniform waiting.

"I've been asked to drive you into the village, miss."

"Thank you. I'll grab my bag and I'll be there."

Three hours later, Lou was finally ready for the first dive. Her stomach writhed and churned in a tormented mixture of fear and exhilaration. She was anxious to see what was down there, to find out how much, if any, of the village was left intact after so many years below the waves. But the rest of her was afraid. What if something went wrong? What if she had a full-blown panic attack and couldn't make her way back to the surface?

The longer she procrastinated, the more reasons she came up with to accept a desk job, or one that didn't involve diving and swimming at all.

The lake was murky, cold, grey, and uninviting. It lived up to its name perfectly. Aberfinay dam towered over it, casting a shadow despite the lack of real sunlight. A cold wind blew, rippling the water and making white horses on some of the waves by the shore. Lou shivered. What was she doing? Was she mad? She should call Varian and resign this minute. Let AJ take over and have him insist on Clara joining them.

Then her gaze fell on the church spire, and a longing to explore kicked in. She'd be the first person to 'walk' those streets, to be in that church in decades. There was only one fly in the ointment. AJ hadn't shown up, and it was almost twelve. She was wearing her wet suit under her tracksuit, her prosthesis strapped over it for now and the dive gear was in the boat, and it would be a waste of effort if she didn't get in the water at least for a few minutes.

"How much longer will you wait for him?" Charlie asked. "It's not too late to get those blokes from the pub for you."

Lou shook her head. If she didn't go now, her nerve would fail her. She at least needed to get out on the water and touch the steeple. "No. I want you to stay here in case he does turn up. I'll take the boat myself. I'll find some way of fixing it to the steeple. I'm not diving just yet. I want to get a feel for the place from the lake." She leaned against the wall, unzipping her jacket.

A car door slammed and she spun, hoping to see AJ and ready to give him five minutes to get in the boat. But it wasn't. "Evan . . . I wasn't expecting to see you."

Evan smiled, sliding his hands into his overcoat pockets. "I was passing." He watched as she removed her tracksuit, his eyes widening as he took in the prosthesis. "How do you swim with that on?"

"Easy," she teased. "The same way anyone else does. Seriously, the leg comes off — see the straps? The wet suit is specially made to go around the stump. Care to join me?"

"Not today. I left my wet suit at home. But I thought you had an unbreakable rule about diving alone."

She grinned, unable to resist teasing some more. "I'm taking my invisible friend."

"Lou . . ."

She held up a hand. "I'm going out on the lake for a start. Take photos of the church spire. Pluck up the courage to stick my foot in the water." She paused. "Foot, not feet." She waited for the reaction that never came. "If all else fails and AJ doesn't show in the next hour or so, then I guess I have to consider my unbreakable rule broken. I won't have a choice. Not if AJ isn't here and you don't want to come." She paused. "Besides, the local landowner only gave me ten days, and I can't afford to waste a whole day."

"By all means, blame me." His tone was light, and he raised his hands and winked to indicate teasing. "And that joke was awful."

She laughed as she climbed into the boat. "I'll see you later." She started the engine and untied the rope before deftly guiding the boat out towards the middle of the lake.

10

Evan stood on the dam watching Lou sail across the grey water. This was a mistake. Who knew what she'd find down there? What evidence still remained after all these years? How long would all this take? Maybe he should stop hiding the past. It wasn't his fault, after all. All those involved were long since dead.

A car pulled up, a door slammed, and footsteps clunked across the tarmac towards him. Black suited arms leaned on the parapet. "Evan. You're a hard man to track down."

His heart sank. "Varian. Obviously not hard enough, as you managed it." He glanced sideways. "What can I do for you? I was under the impression you weren't coming."

"We need to talk in person."

He leaned his back against the parapet and spread his hands. "So talk."

"Not here. She'll see me, and I can't have that yet. We'll talk in the office."

Evan shrugged and walked with him. "Is this because you're not in her good books, right now?"

Varian glared at him. "What's she been saying?"

"She hasn't said much, but I can tell. This is a little mean and underhanded even for you. Taking her away from her big discovery and putting her here in the back of beyond."

Varian slammed the door shut behind them, making Evan jump. "That is none of your concern."

Evan narrowed his eyes. "I want to know what you're playing at."

Varian glowered. "You know what happened here as well as I do. Your family was just as involved as mine."

"Precisely. By sending her down there you risk exposing everything." He sucked in a deep breath. "She's already asking about the fire."

Panic flittered in Varian's eyes. "How did she know about that?"

"The church spire is blackened. Anyone with a decent pair of binoculars can see that. And once she dives, she'll know how extensive the fire was." He raked his hands through his hair. "You know Great-grandad left a journal?"

Varian's gaze flicked back and forth. "No, I didn't."

"Oh, don't fret, Varian. I have it locked away in the safe."

"There's a reason I'm doing the Dark Lake dive and no one else is. I can control what information gets out and becomes public knowledge."

"And if more bodies wash up? She showed me photos of a bone. A charred bone, I might add."

"The report will state it came from the graveyard by the church. If she uncovers too much, the report will be lost. Nothing will ever be published. Don't worry."

"That's easy for you to say. You're not living with the woman."

Varian raised his eyebrows. "I'm sorry?"

"She was attacked in the hotel last night," Evan said. A horrid feeling crept into the corner of his mind and spread like wildfire through his body. "I was there, rushed in, saved her life, and offered her a safe place to stay."

"I see. That was Bart Manchester, I assume?"

The rush of realization set off alarm bells. "Did you plan that?"

Varian glanced away. "What if I did?"

Evan wasn't fooled for an instant. "What if I hadn't seen him from the street, run to her room just in time, and he'd hurt her more than he did?"

"He was told to rough her up a little." Varian shrugged and peered through the window at the boat moored by the church spire. "Just scare her away. At which point I release a statement saying there is nothing of consequence left under the waters of Dark Lake."

Anger speared Evan, and he clenched his hands into fists. "Good grief, man! The bloke you sprung from the loony bin is a serial rapist who tortures for fun. The only reason he wasn't in a proper prison is he pleaded insanity and got away with it. He knows exactly what he's doing. I thought Lou was a friend of yours."

"She is."

"Remind me never to become an enemy if that's the way you treat your friends."

"That's rich coming from you. And since when have you and Dr. Fitzgerald been on first name terms?"

"So what if we are?" He bristled. "As you asked so nicely, ever since I saved her life. I didn't set her up the way you have. Or treat her the way you did."

"No, you're just lying to her."

Evan jabbed his finger irately at Varian. "I'm not lying as such — merely not telling her everything I know up front. Maybe I'm tired of the cover up. Great-grandad was following orders. Your grandfather's orders to be precise. Perhaps it's time the truth did get out."

Varian grabbed his arm. "A word of caution. Burn the journal. Let the past stay buried. I'll give her a day or two and then shut this down due to nothing further found down there. She'll be laid off, and if she creates a stink, I'll have all her work discredited. She'll never work in archaeology again. This whole thing will go away and be forgotten."

Evan tore himself away. "And if she finds anything?"

"I'll take the paperwork and burn it. Any artefacts she finds will be destroyed. You keep quiet. Do I make myself clear?"

Evan faced him down. "And if I don't?"

"You'll regret it." Varian spun on his heel and left, closing the office door behind him.

Evan glowered. No one threatened him and got away with it.

Ever.

As she sailed across the lake, Lou had decided to use the church as a marker and

99

was pleased to find somewhere to tie the rope to the steeple. She'd spent half an hour or thereabouts taking photos of the shoreline where the bones and other artefacts had washed up, trying to determine where in the lake they could have come from. Then she took photographs of the spire and the damage to the brickwork. Scrapings of the burnt areas went into her bag. She wasn't expecting much from that, but there was always a chance.

Finally, she could put off the moment no longer. She wasn't much for praying these days, but the telegram prayer for safety shot heavenward anyway. She checked her air tank before putting it on and fixing the rest of her equipment. Satisfied everything was ready, she fitted her mask and mouthpiece. Then she unfastened the prosthesis and slid backwards into the water.

Momentary fear surged as the cold water engulfed her. She closed her eyes and tried to remember the breathing techniques she had learned from the therapist and coach. After ten terrifying seconds, she had things under control enough to open her eyes. She flicked on the wrist torch and began swimming slowly down the church walls. It was in good condition considering how long it had been underwater.

Her torch illuminated the walls, as she took photos of the windows and stone work. Fish swam past her as she worked. The stones were definitely blackened. There was no evidence of a bomb. That would have destroyed the building completely.

She reached the floor of the lake. Gravel and stones mixed with sand and mud. Grave stones stood as reminders of the past. She frowned. Shouldn't the dead have been exhumed and moved elsewhere before the village was flooded? She took photos to remind herself to research that tonight. The church towered above her. Her torch picked up the remains of a huge wooden door, the evidence of a fire very much here as well as on the surrounding stonework.

The door hung open enough for her to slide though. It was more than a little eerie to say the least. A massive fire had raged through part of the building; that was indisputable. Glancing up, she could see the roof had gone. Some of the pews were intact, others weren't. The pulpit stairs led up to nothing, the brass warped by the intense heat. It really must have been some fire. Torch light glittered off of a few of the remaining stained glass windows, but most were broken.

Lou slowly swam towards the front of the

church, her light illuminating a plaque on the wall, dedicated to those village soldiers who had died in the First World War. She swung the torch across the pew and jumped as it lit up a skull, which sat transfixed as if listening to a sermon. Trouble was, what was left of the ropes obviously used to bind him into his seat told a different story. He wasn't there by choice. The fellow's jacket swung gently as the water moved, and as Lou shone the light on his face, he winked at her.

Her heart almost leapt from her chest, and terror swamped her right before common sense prevailed and a fish swam from the eye socket. Lou shook her head. She was letting her imagination run away with her. She took several photos as she wondered who it was and what he was doing here. Why hadn't he left with everyone else? Had he been caught in the fire and, therefore, left here?

She shone the torch further up the line of pews. At least three more figures could be seen. Lou swam up to them, photographing bodies and the ropes securing them in place. She aimed the torchlight onto the floor. Moss grew between the flagstones. Weeds moved gently in the water. She photographed everything. This job was going to take longer than she had, but her interest had been piqued. She had more questions now than when she'd begun.

Something dropped onto her shoulder. She almost burst out of her skin, her already taut nerves shifting into overdrive. She whirled around, eyes widening and mouthpiece falling from her mouth as total panic set in.

11

Lou surfaced rapidly. Her heart pounded like a pneumatic drill, her vision blurred and each breath was a struggle as she searched for the boat. She shouldn't have come. She needed to be somewhere safe, somewhere far away from water.

Something black and pointed surfaced next to her, and she cried out in fear. Then the shark removed its face mask and AJ grinned at her.

"Hi, boss. Did I scare you?"

Lou scowled. "Not funny. Not funny at all." She moved her arms to stay afloat, trying to calm her shattered nerves. "You're an idiot, and you're fired."

"You can't fire me."

"I just did." She sucked in a deep breath. "I could have drowned."

AJ laughed. "No, you wouldn't have. You're simply being a drama queen. Purely because you had one bad experience when you were a kid, doesn't mean you'll drown now." He did his best to appear contrite and failed miserably. "I'm sorry. Have you found anything down there?"

"Yes. And yes, you *are* fired. You don't mess around on a dive. Ever."

"OK, OK. Don't get your knickers in a twist." He rolled his eyes. "I said I'm sorry. What more do you want?"

Lou shook her head and refitted her mask. Glad the camera was attached to her wrist and she hadn't lost it, she plunged below the surface again. She was aware of AJ diving beside her. Right now, he could make himself useful, but she was serious about firing him — but not yet. She needed him for the next couple of weeks. Besides, she was quitting and, therefore, it didn't really matter what she did anymore.

This time, she focused her attention on the cottage opposite the church. If she was right, it should be the cottage belonging to Evan's great-grandparents.

The roof and windows were long gone, but the walls were still intact. There was no door. Her torch illuminated a plaque on the wall by the entrance. Rubbing some of the green gunk off it, she could read the name. Dr. David Close. Definitely the right house. Again the blackened and scorched brick and stonework indicated a massive fire.

Lou swam inside. Another body floated against the far wall. She photographed it, along with the interior of every room. Not much remained in the way of furniture. What little the fire had left, the water had seen to over the intervening years.

Her tank beeped, and she tapped AJ on the shoulder, pointing upwards. He nodded, and they surfaced. Dropping her mouthpiece, Lou swam to the boat and hauled herself over the side. She unclipped the tank and pushed back the hood of her wetsuit.

Covering her face with her hands, she took a moment to sit in silence, trying to process what she'd seen.

After a minute, AJ gazed up. "OK. I'll say it. There's a body in that house."

Lou nodded slowly. "There's at least four in the church, as well."

"And a fire. A big one if the church is anything to go by. I mean, look at the height of the burned stone. Way beyond anything you'd expect. I can see why Varian wanted this place checked out. It's fascinating."

"Yeah." She examined her air tank. "This shouldn't be empty already. Not been diving anywhere nearly long enough."

"How long have we got for this dig?"

Lou reached down and picked up a new tank and checked it. "Ten days. Nine by the time we have new tanks. Tell me what's happening at Llaremont?"

"What do you mean?" AJ's face clouded, and his tone grew cagey.

"At the dig." Lou glared at him, watching him squirm. "You remember the one in Wales I got kicked off of the day before yesterday."

"Oh, right. Not much."

"Don't give me that," she snapped. "It's the biggest find since Tutankhamen's tomb and you reckon *nothing* is happening. Just level with me. I deserve that much."

AJ sighed. "Well, Monty and Clara are cataloguing and photographing and writing the reports. Bill is running around like a headless chicken preparing everything for the TV news cameras, which arrive on Friday. And they are writing an article for *History Today*."

Lou deflated as if someone pricked her with a pin. "What? That's the biggest publication out there."

"Yeah." AJ met her gaze for the first time since they got back in the boat. "Monty and Clara are getting co-writes."

Lou grimaced and cast her gaze downwards. Her stomach clenched and her heart broke. She wouldn't even get a mention. Years of her life and all that hard work, for nothing.

AJ touched her hand. "But I did pick up everything you asked for and more, including all your notes and files. Monty had already copied them all and shoved them on a flash drive. There was however an unfortunate incident last night before I left."

She raised an eyebrow as she put the tank down. "Oh?"

"Yeah, there was a massive computer failure. They may have lost several files and stuff. Oh, and the flash drive went missing. Along with all the paper copies of everything." He winked. "I kinda pressed the wrong button as I shut the thing down, and I might have picked up said flash drive with your stuff. It's all locked in the boot of my car. I figured you could file instead."

"Thank you. I could hug you. That's a brilliant idea. You're unfired." Lou gave the remaining three air tanks on the boat the once over. "Once we get back to shore, I need you to hit the local archives here and find out what you can about the fire. Your first port of call should be the local historian, Charlie Bramston."

"Sure. Where are we staying?"

"With the landowner, Evan Close, in the

manor house. There was an incident at the hotel last night. He offered us rooms at his place, and I took them."

"What sort of incident?" AJ tilted his head, concern flickering in his gaze.

"I was attacked." Lou moved back the collar of her wetsuit, showing him the steri-strips. "It could have been worse."

"How? You have stitches."

"Just trust me on that one. I could be dead, for a start. And they're steri-strips, not stitches."

"Worse than dead exists? What did the doctor say? Should you even be diving?"

"I didn't see one, and you fuss far too much. I'm not letting anyone chase me off this dig. Change your tank for a new one, and let's go again. I want the entire village mapped and photographed before nightfall. Tomorrow we'll do Finlay."

"What's the rush?"

"We only have ten days and there's a lot of ground to cover. Once the mapping is done, we can go back and take our time over the interesting bits." She picked up a fresh tank and slipped it on. "What are you waiting for? Let's do this. And I want the position of any more bodies noted carefully and photographed *in situ.*"

"Are you going to call the cops in on this?"

Lou frowned. "Most likely. Let's see what we find first." She reattached her face mask and mouthpiece, and slid backwards into the lake.

Slowly they made their way through the village. Each house had its own dark secret, whether it was pictures on the wall or the utter devastation caused by the fire.

AJ tugged open a cupboard and flailed backwards. Bubbles escaped from his mouthpiece. A body wearing a long dress floated towards him, arms outstretched, half of the skull caved in.

Lou pulled him to one side. She turned his face towards her, gaze searching his, asking him silently if he was all right.

He shook his head wildly.

Lou pointed upwards, tugging at his arm.

AJ kept still, then shook his head once more. He gave her a thumbs up and pointed to the body, indicating he should keep going.

Lou nodded, holding up five fingers. What disturbed her wasn't the bodies. She was used to skeletons in her line of work. What bothered her was the way the majority of them had been tied down. Had they accepted their fate and were determined to die in their homes? Or was it murder?

The really creepy thing was although some

110

of the bodies had evidently been burned, the majority hadn't. At least two showed signs of blunt force trauma, meaning they were dead before the fire began. And that added murder to the signs of arson.

12

Evan peered at AJ over the dinner table and tried not to sigh. This wasn't how he'd envisaged the evening going when he'd invited Lou to dinner at the manor the previous day. Of course, that was several hours before he'd asked her to move in. "How did you find our lake, Mr. Wilcox?"

"Colder than I expected," AJ commented with his mouth full. "But fascinating all the same. Did you know that the vast majority of Abernay is still intact down there?"

Evan somehow kept his face straight, despite his heart sinking to the soles of his polished shoes. "It's intact? I would have thought the flood waters would have destroyed the buildings. Other than the church, which we can still see."

"Nope, it's all still there. There's a cottage opposite the church with a plaque on it saying Dr. David Close. Is he a relative?"

"My great-grandfather." Surely Lou would

have informed her colleague of the connection between him and the dam?

Lou glanced at AJ, and then directed her attention to Evan as she spoke for the first time since the meal began. "You didn't tell me he was a doctor."

"You didn't ask."

"I assumed he was an engineer, as he was part of the team that built the dam. You confirmed that yesterday."

"He was part of the team, yes, but not in a building capacity. His main role here was as the village doctor."

Mrs Jefferson came into the room. "I'm sorry to interrupt, Mr. Close, but there's a telephone call for you. It's urgent."

"Excuse me." Evan stood with relief. He'd change the subject when he got back. He headed to the study and picked up the receiver. "Evan Close speaking."

"It's Varian. Have you seen her photographs?"

"Good evening to you, too, Varian. I assume by 'she' you mean Lou."

"How many other interfering women do you know?"

Evan sat and swung the chair to face the window. "That depends on how many you've sent up here to dive in the lake. And no, I haven't seen the photographs. Why

113

would she show me? More to the point, how have you seen them?"

"She uploaded them to her private server–"

Evan cut him off. "How did you get access to that?" He sucked in a deep breath, not wanting to be overheard. "They are called private servers for a reason!"

"I have my ways. She logged out of the company computer account and changed all her passwords first. Covered her track too well, who knows what damage the minx did. Anyway, back to the current problem. A lot of the village is relatively undamaged and still standing. Including your great-grandfather's house."

"They were telling me over dinner. Well, her colleague, AJ Wilcox, was. He's rather a chatterbox."

"You need to do something about it."

"I do?" He caught his breath in surprise. "Why me?"

"You're on site."

So are you. Evan shook his head. "News-flash, Varian. I don't work for you. I never have. In fact, I suggest you do your own dirty work. You proved more than capable of that last night."

"May I remind you that you stand to lose just as much as I do, if not more, should the truth come out? Undoubtedly it will happen with Lou working to uncover it. The woman is tenacious when it comes to her work." Varian's tone became decidedly snotty.

"So, I repeat. Why send her? Why not come up here yourself, pretend to investigate, or whatever you need to make all this go away?"

"I told you. I need to discredit her and her work. This is the only way to do that, because if she uncovers any evidence that points to me, it'll not look good on her when I fire her."

"And may I remind you, that both Lou and Mr. Wilcox are guests in my house," Evan snapped back. "And as such are under my protection."

"And what are you implying?"

Evan grinned. He could see the expression on Varian's face as clearly as if they were in the same room. He tapped his fingers on his thigh, pausing before what he was saying materialized into an actual threat. "I'm not implying anything. Merely stating a fact."

Varian muttered under his breath.

"Well, my dinner is getting cold," Evan said, swinging the chair back towards the desk. "So, if you don't mind, I'll be getting back to it. Good night." He dropped the receiver back onto the base, loving the old-fashioned phones that allowed him to hang up with a resounding thud. He rubbed his hands over his face and sighed.

"Problems?" Ira asked, as always seeming to appear from nowhere.

"I don't know. I hope not. Can you speak to your contact at the local police station and have them swing a patrol out past the dam two or three times a day while Dr. Fitzgerald is here? And check all the CCTV footage thoroughly."

Ira nodded. "What am I searching for?"

"Anything out of the ordinary." Evan stood. "I need to get back." He headed to the dining room and resumed his seat at the table. His food was, as expected, stone cold and he pushed the plate away. He glanced at Lou. "What are your plans for this evening?"

"I need to go over the data we gathered today. Is there somewhere we could work? I try not to work in the bedroom if I can avoid it."

"The drawing room should suit your purpose. It has ample table space and power points."

Her smile warmed his heart and lit the entire room. "Thank you."

"I must say I'm intrigued by the photos."

Her smile vanished like the sun going behind a cloud, leaving the room suddenly dark. "What photos? No one mentioned any photographs."

Evan looked at her. "No. Varian did. Apparently they weren't on the company server, so he hacked your private server and looked at them. It might be an idea to change all your passwords on there."

Lou muttered something in a foreign language. "Yeah, yeah, I'll do that, as soon as I get on my laptop. In fact I'll remove them from my server and put them on a flash drive. And they weren't on the company server for a reason." She exchanged a knowing look with AJ.

"Would it be possible to see the pictures of the village?" Evan asked. "Especially the ones of my great-grandfather's cottage."

"Once I've gone through them, I don't see why not. We found a few things that don't add up."

"Such as?" He picked up his glass.

"A body in the church for one thing," AJ said. "He and a few mates was sat there on the pews as if waiting for the sermon to end."

Evan's heart pounded and his fingers tightened on the glass. "A body?" he repeated, not sure he'd heard right.

"Well, skeleton, obviously. There was four of them, along with another one in your great-grandfather's house. We also found one in a cupboard in one of the other houses."

Evan dropped the glass, spilling red wine over the white tablecloth. The stain spread outwards. "I'm sorry?"

"And total spooky it was too. I opened the door and it floated out to give me a hug. I reckon they floated in from the graveyard, but Dr. F thinks otherwise."

"AJ, that's enough," Lou said sharply. "What we discuss privately about the dive stays between us, especially when it's just a theory. It's not up to you to tell anyone anything until we have proof."

Chilled, Evan glazed over, watching the wine spread further into the white table-cloth. One little mistake led to such a huge stain to remove. If it were possible.

"Do you have any of the original paper-work for the village, Evan?" Lou asked. "A map perhaps or photos of how it used to be before the flood came?"

"I'll go and see what I can find. Excuse me." He rose and left the room as fast as his unsteady legs would take him. He made it to the library and locked the door behind him.

He leaned against it and sucked in several deep breaths. This farce might unravel around him faster than he could fix it. The best thing he could do was give her what she wanted and hope it satisfied her before she decided to dig any deeper.

13

The first thing Lou did on reaching her laptop, was log onto her private server and remove all the photos she'd uploaded there — backing them up to a flash drive instead. Next she changed all the passwords, for something Varian would never guess in a million years. She used her favourite Bible verse, figuring even if he did work out it was Psalm 46:5, he'd never work out which letter was capitalised and which of the numbers she'd spelled out in letters. Or whether verse was a V or a v or a colon.

For the next couple of hours, she and AJ pored over the map Evan had found, comparing it to the photos she and AJ had taken earlier. Evan's map was surprisingly detailed, with little squares denoting each house. It made her job so much easier.

"And that's where we found the other body," AJ said. "That makes ten all together."

"OK, good. Have you got those housing records?"

"Yeah." AJ pulled over the laptop. "Easy when you know where to look. Ready?"

She grabbed a pen. "Yep." As AJ read, she scribbled the occupants' names onto the chart she'd made. She drew a large red cross onto the chart and tapped her finger on the map. "OK . . . Now, we know the main fire started here. The fires are in red. The bodies are in blue and were found in these locations, the majority in the church. Where were the bone fragments and other artefacts found?"

AJ picked up a green pen and marked the shoreline. "Along here."

"That's nowhere near the graveyard." She tapped the laptop screen. "There's no record of a fire. Nothing on the news or anywhere else. You'll need to check the local public records, newspapers, and so on. Maybe they haven't gotten around to adding them yet."

AJ huffed. "Sure. I'll add it to my incredibly long list."

"Thanks." She glanced up as the door opened.

Evan came in carrying a tray. "I thought you could do with some coffee."

She smiled. "Thank you. It's going to be a

very long night."

"Can I help?" He set the tray down and studied the chart. "What exactly are you doing?"

"Reconstructing the village. Building a picture of who lived where, what they did for a living and so on."

His eyebrow quirked upwards like the brows of her favourite TV character. "Fascinating." He even sounded like him.

She nodded. "It's what we do. Bring the past to life."

"And what have you learned?" Evan glanced up from the chart, his piercing gaze boring into her.

Lou touched the chart with her finger. "The main fire started here in the blacksmith's."

"Owned by Edward Smith, age forty-six," AJ added. "Supposedly that spread through the entire village."

"Fires spread," Evan said. "Take London in 1666 as an example. One small fire in a bakery in Pudding Lane destroyed half the city."

"Those were closely built timber houses," Lou said. "These are stone buildings. What makes this interesting isn't there wasn't only that one start point."

"So it jumped. Fires do that as well. Any

firefighter will tell you . . ."

"No." She cut him off, shaking her head. "So far, we have found four other incendiary points." She pointed to the red crosses on the map. "One fire could be accidental. Five most definitely aren't." She held Evan's gaze, noting he didn't seem surprised by that revelation. "I do this a lot, and my gut tells me that five fires only mean one thing, and I don't mean lots of candles being knocked over either."

"Someone set them," Evan said quietly. "You're saying this was deliberate arson."

"Probably to drive out those villagers who were refusing to sell up and leave. Did your great-grandfather leave any other papers about the village? Historical records, or a diary, that kind of thing."

"Why?" He stepped away from the table, visibly uneasy.

"It would be invaluable if he did. Evan, think about it. If he left a journal or anything we'd have an accurate record of the last days of Abernay."

"And you'd put all that in your paper, would you?"

She shook her head. "No. Just call it professional curiosity for a little human interest. A bit like that rich woman whose body was found with the gladiator in Pompeii. We can speculate as to why they were together, but no one really knows. Were they lovers and decided to die together? Was he escorting her out of the city and got caught up in the last volcanic blast? Or simply two strangers seeking shelter at the same time? Each explanation is perfectly plausible, but we'll never know."

Evan paced across to the window, gazing out at the deepening fog. "I could give you several reasons for those fires."

"So could I," AJ chimed in.

"You told me it was a bomb," Lou said. "Remember? One maybe, but unless you had a huge terrorist cell operating up here in the 1930s, that ain't gonna fly no more."

Evan's face worked madly as he backtracked. "Yes, he left a journal," he mumbled. "It's in the library. Along with other files and maps."

"May I see them?"

"I need time to find it all." He finally shifted to face her. "I'm not the best at keeping tabs on things."

She nodded. "Thank you. Anything pertaining to the dam you might find would be incredibly useful."

"Will tomorrow do?"

"Sure."

"But you'd prefer having the papers tonight."

Lou glanced at AJ. "It'd make things easier tomorrow when we dive again, but that's fine. We can spend tomorrow finishing the mapping of the village and then drop the sonar buoys on Friday."

Evan frowned. "Sonar? You didn't mention that before."

"It'll give us an accurate 3D image of the bottom of the lake. I also want to do a proper dive into the church crypt."

Something flickered in Evan's eyes. "In case there really were smugglers?"

"Yeah. Seriously, I want to check the foundations and wall integrity. Plus there might be something left there of historical value."

He sighed. "I shall let you get on. See if I can track down some of those files."

Lou watched him leave. He'd seemed eager to help at one point. Now the opposite was true. Her phone rang, and she grabbed it off her belt. "Hello."

"Lou, are you busy?"

She walked to the window and drew the heavy curtains across them. "Not for you, Varian. What can I do for you? Although I am surprised you're not here in person. I didn't think you trusted me to do anything."

"We're busy here," he stated. "I've seen your photos, at least the ones you saved to your servers. I was trying to see the rest but I can't get in."

She snarled. "Too right you can't get in — I changed all the passwords. My server, Varian. How dare you hack into it? Maybe you've forgotten what the word private means, but I sure haven't. That isn't all of the photos by a long chalk. Oh, and by the way, I won't be uploading anymore until my work here is completed. Only then will you get a written report. It's fascinating how much of the village is still relatively intact down there. We've made some interesting discoveries —"

"That isn't why I called." Varian cut her off sharply. "I wanted to discuss Llaremont."

She swivelled and waved at AJ, getting his attention, before miming the cutting of her throat. "What about Llaremont?"

"I want those files back."

Lou laid a finger to her lips and put the phone on speaker, laying it on the table beside her. "What files are those? The Dark Lake ones you gave me? Because right now, I'm using those."

"Don't be a smart-aleck," Varian barked. "It doesn't become you. You know darn well what files I mean. The Llaremont ones. All your files, photos, and notes have gone. No one has seen them since you left the dig."

Lou looked deadpan at the phone, not that he could see her. "I see. And that's my problem because?"

"The computer has been wiped. Around the time you logged onto the company server and changed your passwords. All the backups are missing. As is Monty's flash drive. I need those files."

"Well, *I* didn't take them," Lou told him. "I was angry you fired me from the Llaremont dig, yes. More than angry. I stormed out, leaving everything behind. Including my tools and personal belongings. AJ brought those up here for me. I changed my passwords because it was the third Thursday of the month. If you bother to check, I always change my password then. And I changed them just after midnight the day after I left Llaremont, if you bother to check the time. AJ told me the computers crashed, but he said it was much earlier in the evening."

Varian muttered an expletive.

"And there's no need to swear at me. Maybe Monty lost the files himself. He's good at that kind of thing."

"Monty hasn't seen them. Those files

belong to me."

Lou shook her head. "In point of fact, they don't. They're mine, but I promise you *I* did *not* bring them with me from Llaremont."

"It will take us months to re-catalogue everything. No one knows this dig like you do. It was your project."

"Exactly what I tried to tell you when you threw me off it," she snapped. Then she sucked in a deep breath. "But no more. Now it's your headache, not mine. Have fun attempting to reconstruct all my theories. You wanted me off the project; don't ask for my help now."

"If I find you've gone behind my back and published anything before Monty has a chance to . . ."

"You'll do what, Varian? Sack me? Discredit me?"

"It'll be the last thing you ever do." Varian's voice carried an unmistakable threat. "You will never work in archaeology again."

Lou sucked in a deep breath. "Well, it's been nice chatting with you. Now I must get back to work. Reports to write, photos to log, maps to draw. Good night, Varian." She hung up and leaned heavily on the desk.

AJ eyed her. "It's kind of funny that he can't find the files. What will you do?"

"Finish typing them up," she said, the decision made in a second. "I've just been told publishing Llaremont will be the last thing I ever do. So I'm going out with a bang, and he won't get a chance to fire me, either. How would you like second name on the paper?"

His eyes widened and his face lit up. "Seriously?"

Lou nodded. "Yep. You brought the notes up here for me. He'll probably fire you, too, when he finds out."

"Worth it. He's a sanctimonious old goat at times."

"Then let's go out in a blaze of glory," she challenged. "Dark Lake can wait until tomorrow. I want this paper prepped and ready to be published next week."

AJ straightened. "You can do that?"

"I have a contact at *History Today*. Let me give her a call." She hit the speed dial button on her phone. "Jackie, its Lou Fitzgerald. I have a last minute paper you might be interested in if you have a minute. You'd have world exclusivity on it."

Less than three minutes later, Lou beamed at AJ and gave a triumphant thumbs-up. "She'll publish it. As long as it's on her desk before midnight tomorrow, it'll make the next edition which comes out on Tuesday."

AJ grinned. "I'd love to see Varian's face when he finds out."

Lou cleared the table, carefully putting away all the Dark Lake maps and documents. "In all honesty, it'll probably be the last thing either of us see."

"Like you said, Dr. F. Out with a bang."

Having taken several moments to compose himself, Evan set about finding what paperwork he could pertaining to the construction of the dam. His great-grandfather had kept detailed records, and it didn't take him long to find everything that Lou would need.

Then he strode to the safe and pulled out his great-grandfather's journal. He opened it to the entry written on the day the village was flooded.

Sept 30th.

It's done. The fire that began three nights ago is finally out. Despite the ferocity of the blaze, many structures are still intact. There is no point in moving the bodies or attempting a mass burial now. By dawn everything will be buried under several fathoms of water anyway.

About now, the old dam fifty miles away is being blown. Water should reach us in just under an hour.

I wish none of this had been necessary. My job, my calling, is to save lives, not to be responsible for their loss, especially in such appalling circumstances. Maybe it's fitting I spend the rest of my life caring for the dam here. Caring for the lost, the damned, those I betrayed. The irony is not lost on me.

And I have chosen my words deliberately.

Mabel doesn't understand why I didn't fight this. Or why we will be moving back to the manor house. But I am the heir and, therefore, have to take my rightful place, even though it's the last thing I wish to do. I just hope someday, maybe in eternity, Father will forgive me this last act.

I have written more and sealed it in a watertight box and hidden it in the church crypt. Nowhere else is safe. The reach of CS knows no bounds.

Perhaps one day it will be found and the truth will be told.

Until that point, may God have mercy on my soul and on the souls of those innocents caught up in all this tragedy.

There go the warning sirens. The waters are coming. Just as the fog descends.

It's quite appropriate. Most of this work was carried out under the cover of the fog, and now the waters roll in the same way.

14

Unable to sleep, Lou got up at six and dressed. She made her way down to the kitchen, intending to make tea and toast to keep her going for the time being. Surprised to find Evan already sitting at the table reading the paper, she started to leave, rather than disturb him.

"Morning," he said. "You don't have to leave. There's a large pot of fresh tea on the table."

"Thank you. I had a hankering for tea and toast."

He grinned as the toaster popped. "So did I. I've made enough for two if you want to share. And before you say anything, you won't be depriving me. Mrs Jefferson will do her usual mammoth breakfast at eight thirty."

"OK, thank you." She sat next to him. "I really want to go around your maze. Does it have floodlights?"

He nodded. "I had the gardener clear the paths yesterday. I had a feeling you'd want to explore it."

"I love a good puzzle. I always have." She poured some tea, adding milk and sugar.

Evan brought the toast across and sat. "Help yourself."

"Thank you." She covered the toast with butter and marmalade.

Evan folded his paper to the crossword. "Was the bed not comfortable?"

"I'm sorry?" She frowned in confusion.

"For you to be up so early," he explained. "The guest rooms aren't used that often and the beds are quite old. I could put you somewhere else if the bed is too uncomfortable for you to sleep."

"Oh. No, the bed's fine. I get nights where I don't sleep. Either my mind is too active and won't switch off long enough, or I have nightmares, and I really don't want to go back to sleep."

"Which was it last night?"

"Bit of both. AJ and I worked quite late, so I was still mulling things over, thinking about today's dive, and then there's the fact it's September." She finished the toast.

"Do you have something against the month?"

"Yeah." She rubbed her hands on her

133

jeans. "So I figured I'd get up and maybe go around the maze. Fancy coming with me?"

He frowned. "I told you, I haven't been in it since I got lost."

"We won't get lost. And if I don't find the middle after fifteen minutes, we head back out."

"And how will you do that?"

She grinned. "I cheat. Come with me, and I'll show you."

He worried his bottom lip for a second and then agreed.

Evan stood at the entrance to the maze. *This must be the craziest thing I have done in a long time.* He tugged his coat collar around his neck. The autumn morning was decidedly chilly and still dark. The floodlit maze yawned before them. "Are you sure we won't get lost?"

Lou nodded and produced a large ball of brightly coloured wool from her jacket pocket. "As I said, I cheat." She tied the end of the wool to the sign at the maze entrance. "Ready?"

"As I'll ever be," he muttered. "And you are way too cheerful for oh-dark-thirty."

She grinned. "So I keep being told."

Evan shook his head, trying to push aside

the demons associated with the maze and walked beside her. The tall hedges towered over him, making him seem much smaller than his six-foot-two frame. He shivered.

Lou glanced at him. "Who built this maze?"

"It's been here as long as the house," he said. "Started life apparently as small box hedges and grew as they do. Small hedges would make it easier."

She shook her head, back tracking as they reached a dead end. "You'd have thought so, but no. They can be even more annoying, because you can see where you need to go, but still can't get there."

Evan turned right. He stood still as Lou headed left. "Where are you going?"

"Behind us is a dead end, right? If you go right, you can see the wool, so that's the way we came, therefore we go left."

He nodded slightly, whirling to face the other way.

"What's in the middle?"

"I have no idea."

She grinned. "We might never find out. I set the alarm on my phone, so we know when to head back."

"Or we might find out and regret it." He paused as they reached another junction. "Left."

Lou nodded and wrapped the wool around a branch. "Left it is. Regret it how?"

"It might be a bottomless pit. Or a madman with an axe."

She laughed. "He'd be a bit old by now. It could be buried treasure. Or a book to sign to say you've completed it. I've done several like that. Do you have any aerial photos of it?"

"No. Why?"

"Because then you'd have an accurate map of it. You wouldn't need the string and would never get lost."

He smiled. "That is a very good idea. I shall organize one for this afternoon."

She tilted her head. "You can do it that quickly?"

"I have my own plane."

"Oh, how the other half lives," she chuckled. "I own my car, but that's it." Her alarm rang. "Time's up."

Evan gazed at her. Never mind being lost in the maze. He was lost in her eyes and would quite happily stay there. "Leave the wool. We could continue at another point if you wish."

Lou smiled. "I'd like that."

15

Having spent the entire day diving and mapping the lake, Lou ate dinner quickly then vanished into the drawing room. She wrote up her notes and then focused her attention to finalizing the Llaremont paper. After all the work she and AJ had put into it the previous night, plus what she'd done in the wee small hours, it was almost ready to be sent. One last read through to check for typos should do it.

AJ cleared his throat from where he sat planning the next day's dive. "About this dive tomorrow . . ."

Lou glanced up. "What about it?"

"We need a third person out there."

"Not happening. I can't trust a bloke from the pub with a bit of diving experience to do this properly. And Varian won't send anyone else. It was hard enough convincing him to send you."

"Look, Dr. F. You and I both know you

137

can't dive alone. It flouts a dozen safety laws, never mind anything else. That's not taking your past into consideration."

Lou narrowed her eyes, her hackles rising. "What has that got to do with anything?"

"What if you have another panic attack out there, inside one of those buildings this time? If I'm not there you'll be stuffed."

"We managed perfectly well the past two days."

He tapped the table. "Besides, a one-legged archaeologist has no place in the field. You need to get in a lecture room or behind a desk where you belong."

Anger flared, and she slammed her fist into the table. "How dare you?" she yelled. "You know I actually believed you were on my side in all this for a second. Did Varian send you up here to sabotage this?"

"No." AJ scowled. "Would I have brought those files up if he had? He wanted you out of the way so his son could take the credit for your discovery. He still does. He doesn't want you publishing first."

"Good luck with that," Lou hissed. "This will be sent in the next couple of hours or so. And you're fired."

AJ glanced heavenward. "Not again."

"I mean it this time. You don't want to work with, and I quote, 'a one-legged archaeologist,' then get out. Now. Go on. Get out. Don't come back." She returned her attention to the file in front of her, ignoring him.

After a second, the door slammed shut.

Lou buried her head in her hands. All she'd ever wanted was to be an archaeologist or a swimmer. Her stepfather, Jack, had assured her both professions were possible after the docs on the airbase in Guam took her leg. She'd believed him, along with a lot of other stuff he'd said. Over time, those things, along with part of her faith, had been eroded. Perhaps this wasn't true either. Maybe she'd been right in her assertions that she was a waste of space.

She glanced up as the door to the drawing room opened. She somehow managed a faint smile as Evan came into the room. At least her heart no longer did that wow-he-is-so-handsome-and-he-is-talking-to-me-I-think-I-might-pass-out-from-joy thing that it did the first few times she saw him.

His dark gaze swallowed her whole. "Am I disturbing you?"

She shook her head, hit save, and closed the document. "Not at all. I was about to take a break anyway."

He sat beside her. "When I promised you dinner at the manor the day we met, this wasn't what I had in mind."

"No?"

His hand covered hers. "I was thinking more you and me, a few candles, a small intimate dinner, you know." He glanced around. "Where's AJ?"

"He's up in his room. Sulking, most likely."

"Sulking or skulking?"

Lou sighed. "Sulking. I fired him. For the third time in as many days."

Evan raised an eyebrow. "You can do that?"

"He's on my team, so yes, I can hire and fire whomever I please. However, he isn't convinced I mean it, as he's still here."

"May I ask what he did?"

"You may not. And he's probably right. He's too valuable to fire. And I'd rather not talk about AJ or work, if you don't mind."

"Not at all." Evan stood and moved over to the sideboard. "Can I get you a drink? It sounds as if you could do with one. I have brandy, whisky, and scotch. There is also wine if you'd prefer, or several mixers."

Lou glanced over at the bottles. She didn't want to start drinking because with the mood she was in, she'd end up drunk, and in an even worse temper than she already was. Never mind the fact that a hangover on a dive wasn't a good idea. "Is that bitter lemon?"

He nodded. "You'd like that?"

"Love it."

He poured her a glass, and then poured himself a glass of one of the amber liquids.

Lou never had been able to tell brandy and whisky apart. She closed the laptop and took the glass he offered her. "Thank you. You should try mixing this with grapefruit juice. It's amazing."

He scrunched his nose. "I don't like grapefruit." He sipped his drink. "You were supposed to tell me about yourself over dinner. As we never got around to having that conversation, perhaps you could do so now."

Lou eased back in her chair. "I have a much younger brother and sister from Mum's second marriage. They live in the States with Mum and my stepfather."

"And your leg?"

"A swimming accident." She frowned at the drink in her hand. "It still gives me nightmares now. Especially this time of year."

His hand brushed hers again, sending sparks flying along every nerve. "What happened?"

"It's a long story. Jim, Staci, and I left on his boat to find their parents. They'd been caught up in a tsunami following the Philippines earthquake several years ago, and no one was searching for them. So we decided to conduct the search ourselves." She broke off. "And the short story is a shark."

Evan's eyes widened and he paled. "A shark?"

"Yeah," she said quietly. "Shark. We were miles from anywhere. Jim did his best, but by the time we were rescued, I was almost dead. My stepfather found us. Well, technically he kept finding us, and he wasn't my stepfather then as he was only dating Mum at the time. Not that I knew that, and I wasn't impressed when I found out either. Sorry, I digress. He rescued us, and the medical team on the air base he worked at saved my life. They couldn't save my leg though."

"Who's Jim?"

"My best friend. The bloke I really liked that I told you about. He and Staci lived with us sometimes when their parents were on the mission field."

Evan nodded. "Ah, right."

"Anyway. He married Ailsa, whom we also picked up on our jaunt across the world. They now have one and a half kids." She drained the drink and put the glass down on the table beside the laptop. "Even Staci is dating now. Her boyfriend's in the army."

"What about you?"

"Kids aren't on the agenda. Nor are boyfriends. I'm too old now."

He scoffed. "Thirty-two isn't old." He tilted his head. "I got your age from the Internet."

"Remind me to delete my birthday from every social media page I have," she muttered. "Besides, I'm married to my career. No time for boyfriends or kids or a life. It would have been nice. I always said my first son would be called Benson after my dad. Keep the family surname going somehow. But it won't ever happen."

"Never say never." Evan nodded to the laptop. "May I see some of the photos of the lake?"

Lou opened the laptop. "Sure. It needs a few seconds to boot up again." As the pictures loaded, she pointed things out. "Here's the church, here's the steeple . . ."

"Open the doors and here's all the people," Evan quipped. He did the accompanying movements with his hands. "Here's the parson going upstairs and here's the parson saying his prayers."

Lou smiled, saying the last phrase with him, her hands mimicking his. "Haven't heard that one in years. Do you know the knives and forks one?"

Evan shook his head. "Never heard that one."

"This is mother's knives and forks . . ." Lou showed him how that rhyme went then pointed back at the screen. "It must have been some fire," she said, indicating the scorched stone above the waterline. "As you can see the damage is even more intense here and here." She clicked through the photos. "The flames reached part way in to the interior of the church, which is remarkably well-preserved despite the water and fire. My guess is the flooding of the village extinguished the remaining fire."

"Fascinating," Evan managed. He was unable to hide the expression of wonder and something she couldn't quite pin down. It could be shock or concern, but something definitely disturbed him about the photos. His eyes widened and his finger touched the screen. "What is that? It looks like . . ."

"That is a body."

"Just sitting there?" Horror affected both his gaze and his voice, and he shifted uncomfortably on the chair.

She nodded. "I took some close ups." She angled the screen to give him a better view.

Evan shuddered, seemingly unable to tear his gaze away despite his obvious need to

144

do so. "How did he get there?"

"Like AJ said at dinner last night, his theory is he floated in from the graveyard, but my photos and preliminary examination of the graves show none have been disturbed. His placement there in the church is too precise. See here and here?" She pointed. "Remains of ropes. My guess is he was tied to the pew before the waters came."

Evan blanched. "He was murdered?"

She nodded. "He could hardly have committed suicide, could he? And he wasn't the only one. Some of the bodies show clear signs of head injuries that couldn't have been caused by the fire or the flood. Either way, I want to bring the bodies to the surface tomorrow or the day after. Get a coroner to examine them."

"It's a little late for that. Any physical evidence of murder, aside from the obvious, would have been washed away years ago." He cleared his throat. "Do you have photos of my great-grandparents' house?"

She clicked a few more times. "Right here, along with the rest of the village." She showed him some of the exterior shots and then closed the folder. "You don't want to see the rest."

"Yes, I do. I'd like to see the interior shots."

"Trust me. You don't. It's only stones, piles of old furniture, plaques on walls, and so on. There really isn't much left inside at all. The church gives you a false idea of what you'll find anywhere else."

Evan reached out to open the folder. "I insist."

Lou grabbed his hand, desperate to stop him. The last thing he needed was to see a body there as well. "Evan, I —"

His gaze met hers, his eyes widening. Did he feel it, too?

That almost electrical charge that shot from her hand straight through her, tingling every nerve ending she had, plus a few she didn't know about?

Evan drew her towards him, his lips almost crushing hers with a passion that apparently consumed them both. His firm body pressed against hers. His hands moved through her hair, down her arms, fuelling the fire that raged within her.

Her phone rang, jerking her out of the kiss. She moved back. "I have to take this." Her chest rose and fell as she glanced at the screen. "Hi, Jim. Why aren't you working?"

"Lunch break. We do get them you know. Are you OK? You sound out of breath. Have you been running?"

"I'm fine, and you know I don't run

anywhere unless I absolutely have to." She wasn't about to tell him she'd just been kissed senseless and breathless. She leaned back in the chair. "What's up?"

"I'm really worried about you and this whole work situation."

"Don't be. This new case is rather intriguing. I have all my notes from Wales, and I'll finish proofreading the paper tonight and have it on my publisher's desk before midnight. That's at least a week sooner than anyone else can. Though if what I've heard is accurate, it'll be months before they piece things together again over there."

Evan paced across the room, obviously trying not to listen to the conversation.

"Is that legal?" Jim asked, dragging her attention away from Evan.

She sighed. "At this point, I really don't care. It's my work. I'm not taking this lying down."

"You need to tread carefully, Lou. Or you may end up getting fired."

"Not if I quit first, which I intend to do as soon as possible. Varian crossed a line today and that is the last straw." She paused. "No, that doesn't make me a camel before you suggest it. And yes I know I have the hump with him. I have a couple of things in the proverbial pipeline. Changing the subject, have you heard from Mum recently?"

"No. Why?"

"You told me to call her, so I have been. She isn't answering her phone, that's all. I wanted to ask her something, nothing important, mind, but it's not like her to ignore messages."

Jim's chair squeaked in the background and he spoke to someone in the background, his tone muffled by what Lou assumed was a hand over the phone. "Sorry about that. Perils of being in command of the squadron. No matter where I hide with my lunch, they find me."

Lou laughed. "So, don't hide in your office."

Jim chuckled. "That obvious, huh? I wouldn't worry about your Mum. Jack's probably taken her somewhere nice as it's their wedding anniversary soon. Alisa and I are heading up there this weekend, to tell the honorary grandparents the baby news. It's a shame you can't join us."

"Work," she said quietly, secretly loving the fact that Jim loved her parents as much as he loved his own, treating them like the in-laws he didn't have. "Never mind that Vegas is a long way from here and not do-able in a weekend. I should let you get on. Give Mum and Dad my love when you see

148

them." She hung up and pocketed the phone. "Sorry. Where were we?"

Evan came over to her and lifted her to her feet. His finger ran over her lips. "Just about here."

His second kiss was as mind blowing as the first. Lou found herself floating several feet off the ground, transported by the sensations he was producing in her.

Finally, he broke off and pressed his lips to her forehead.

"Wow," she whispered.

Evan smiled. "Anyone would think you'd never been kissed before."

"I haven't." Her cheeks burned. "Well, not until you kissed me a few seconds ago."

His gaze held hers, his knuckles grazing her cheek. "Really?"

She nodded. "Never." Her breath caught as his face lowered to hers, and he kissed her again. Part of her wanted to run; afraid of where this would lead, but the other part of her didn't care.

A faint rumbling resonated in the air and the ground under her feet shifted. "What was that?"

"The earth moving," he quipped, kissing her again.

A loud crack and an explosion rocked the building sending them both to the floor.

Evan landed beside her. The ground shifted violently. Pictures tumbled from the walls, one narrowly missing them. Evan jerked her closer, rolling them both under the table, shielding her with his body.

The rumbling and shaking increased and the lights went out.

16

Lou held onto Evan for dear life as the ground shook and something heavy hit the table above them. "Is it an earthquake?" she asked.

"I don't know."

The shaking stopped.

Evan glanced down at her. "Are you hurt?"

"No, I'm fine." Lou pulled out her phone. "No signal." She flipped up the torch app.

Evan checked his handset. "Nor here." He also flipped on his torch before crawling out from under the table and standing. He helped Lou to her feet. He shone his phone light around the room and stepped over things on the floor as he headed to the sideboard. He picked up the landline phone and listened. "Got a line here."

"How, if there's no power?"

"Old-fashioned rotary phone. It gets its power from the line itself. I kept it for this very reason." He dialled quickly.

Lou gingerly crossed over to the window and stared. An orange glow lit the horizon, plumes of thick, black smoke rising from it. Wherever the fire was, it was huge.

Evan replaced the receiver. "The power plant blew."

"That explains the fire then."

He nodded. "I'm afraid this will put paid to your report writing. I have a generator out the back. I'll get it up and running in the morning."

"The battery on my laptop is wonderful. Besides I'm almost done, just got half a page to spell check." Lou was relieved to see the computer unharmed and working, still on the table and not tossed to the floor and broken. "But I'll call it a night anyway."

"Do you need a light to get upstairs?"

She gathered her things. "No, the torch on my phone will do. Thank you though."

"OK." He paused. "Lou?"

She pivoted on her heel. "Yeah?"

"What report are you going to publish?"

She hesitated. So he had been listening, but what harm could it do if he knew? "Something I've been working on for a while."

"Wales?" Evan frowned.

"Yes, Wales. I am not taking being thrown off my dig lying down. I put too many years into this discovery to have someone else take all the credit. Plus, the worm has finally turned. This has happened at the end of every single dig I've worked on for the past six years or so. Well, no more."

"I can't say I blame you for feeling that way."

She wanted to do nothing more but stand here and kiss him again. And again. But she knew that would only be inviting trouble. "I'll see you in the morning. Good night."

Lou left the room quickly, and headed for the stairs. She made her way upstairs to find AJ standing outside her bedroom door. "Can I help you?"

"Are you all right? That was some shaker."

"I'm fine. The local power plant blew. Evan says he'll have a generator running for power here in the morning."

AJ nodded. "Dr. F., I'm sorry. I screwed up, I know that. I should never have said what I did. But you need me out there."

"No, I don't."

He didn't move. "Yeah, you do. You can't dive and drop sonar buoys on your own. Not in the amount of daylight we'll have tomorrow." He lowered his voice. "Besides, I wouldn't trust anyone from around here to help. Mr. Close gives me the creeps and his bodyguard, security bloke, whatever you want to call him, even more so. I found him outside your room when I came up. He might have been trying to get in or coming out."

"And he might not have been." Lou sighed. She didn't want a debate on this, but AJ did have a point about not being able to do this alone. "OK, but I want to be on site at eight."

"Sounds good. We'll leave at half seven and grab something to eat on the way."

"Might be an idea. Well. Good night." She let herself into her room and lit the lamp with the matches next to it. She settled on the bed and finished proof reading the paper. With the battery on the laptop down to its last twenty per cent, she was satisfied, and amazed, that she could find a Wi-Fi signal. She e-mailed the document to the publisher along with a copy to herself. She also e-mailed it to Jim for safekeeping.

Next she changed every single password she had on line, making sure each one was different this time.

More rumbling came from outside and the room shook. Nowhere near as much as before, but she gripped the bedside table anyway. As the shaking died away, she let out a deep breath.

Footsteps ran down the corridor outside

her room. A scream echoed from some-where. Lou grabbed the lamp and carried it to the door. Maybe someone was hurt. She opened the door and headed down the hallway. She rounded a corner to find Evan standing there with a powerful torch in his hand.

"Everything's fine," he reassured her.

"Someone screamed. I thought . . ."

"It was most likely Mrs Jefferson thinking the suit of armour on the landing was a ghost again. In candlelight, things are never what they appear. I've arranged breakfast at seven for you. AJ said you wanted to get an early start."

She nodded, going with the abrupt change of subject. She ought to be used to the strange noises around this village after dark. "Thank you. Good night, again."

"Good night." Evan stood and watched her head back to her room. He only moved when her door shut. He glanced down the hallway and walked swiftly to the end where Ira stood before what he now hoped was a locked door. "Well?"

"Everything is secure."

"It should have been secure in the first place. How did Lilly get out?"

"I don't know, sir."

Evan huffed. "Well, see it stays secure from now on. I'm beginning to think that Varian is right, and we should burn everything before people find out the truth. Was it just the power plant?" He took the offered tablet and headed down the back stairs, Ira beside him.

"No, sir. There were several explosions at the dam as well."

"What?" Evan stopped walking and studied the tablet.

"All timed to go off at the same time as the one at the power plant."

"That can't be a coincidence." Evan sighed. Was it all happening over again? "I need to get down there."

Ira shook his head. "Probably safer not to go over there tonight. The dam engineers are checking the integrity of the walls."

"OK. I'll call Varian, find out what he's playing at."

"You think he was behind this?"

"I'd bet the house on it. He was behind the assault on Dr. Fitzgerald. In fact, perhaps we should let the authorities know who let Bart Manchester out of Tanmoor. An anonymous call to the local police station should suffice."

Ira tilted his head. "Very good, sir. I'll see one is made."

"Thank you. Good night." Evan made his way to the library and closed the door. He picked up the phone and dialled. Again, he was thankful for the fact he'd kept the old-fashioned phones and had recently installed additional lines.

Varian answered after two rings. "Sparrow speaking."

"It's Evan."

"A little late for a social call, isn't it?"

"What in the blazes are you playing at?" Evan struggled not to yell down the phone.

"Right now it's poker at the club. Why?"

"You know full well what I mean."

Varian coughed. "No. I'm afraid I don't."

"There was a series of explosions at the dam and reservoir. The power station also blew."

"You have a generator, don't you?"

"That isn't the point. Any explosion close to the dam is asking for trouble. Are you trying to destroy it?"

"Are you accusing me of something here? Because if you are, you need to think twice about it."

Evan scowled at the wall and changed the subject. "I overheard Lou on the phone earlier. She said something about publishing a report in the next day or two."

"What?" Varian's anger-filled voice

screamed down the phone at him.

"Don't shoot the messenger," Evan snapped back. "And you need to stop blowing things up around here. Someone will get hurt if you don't."

"I intend to do whatever it takes to keep things quiet. The past has to stay dead, Evan. You know that as well as I do."

Evan straightened. Once again the man hadn't denied the accusations. "Then you shouldn't have sent her up here to work on the lake!" He sucked in a deep breath. "If you want this matter closed, then sack her and publish your report stating there is nothing to tell up here." He slammed the receiver down onto the base and closed his eyes.

He didn't want Lou here, uncovering the secrets of the past, exposing the lie he'd helped cover his whole life, but he didn't want her to leave either. Didn't want this fledgling spark between them to be extinguished before he'd had a chance to find out how brightly it would burn and whether it would turn out to be an eternal flame.

17

Lou leaned backwards off the edge of the boat and entered the murky waters of Dark Lake. Cloudier than the previous few days, alarm bells sounded in her mind. There had been an abundance of activity going on at the dam since first light. Trucks, marked police cars, and equipment lined the road leading to it, stopping her from parking where she normally did. In a way, it had worked in their favour. They'd been able to park right next to where they moored their boat. This, in turn, meant she could leave her prosthesis in the car and use crutches to get to and from the boat.

Small chunks of debris floated in the water. Debris that hadn't been there on any previous dives. AJ tapped her on the shoulder and pointed to it. She nodded in response, wishing the diving budget had extended to full facial masks that would give them proper communication with each other.

Kicking hard, she swam down the side of the church, heading towards the main door. A pile of bricks lay in front of it. She frowned and did a slow three-sixty.

The cottage behind her had gone. She exchanged a horrified glance with AJ. They swam slowly along Main Street. All the houses had been destroyed, leaving piles of rubble in their stead. Her mind whirled, and her temper rose. She desperately tried to tamp it down. She needed a clear head. Needed to be able to think, to process this unexpected development.

But this was more than she could do underwater. She needed to breathe.

Lou pointed upwards, kicking hard until she and AJ surfaced. She tugged off her mask. "What on earth is going on here?"

"Must have been those explosions last night. The power plant blowing must have been the cover blast for this lot. No wonder there was an earthquake."

She nodded slowly. "Obviously, someone is hiding something big." *And I would give my eye teeth to know what.*

"The question is who. Evan Close, perhaps?"

"I was with him when the first blast happened."

"Doesn't mean he couldn't have arranged it and used you as an alibi."

She shook her head. "The other question is what are they hiding, and more importantly, why? Why go to the bother of flattening everything? Are we that close to finding something? Let's go check out the crypt. Assuming the door on the far side of the church isn't blocked as well."

It wasn't, but it took their combined strengths to open the door. Lou swam the length of the nave and found the crypt door open. She entered slowly, shining the torch around. The water was clearer down here. AJ swam in front of her and headed to the left. She swam to the right.

A pile of chests stood on the far wall. As she touched one, it disintegrated, spilling its contents onto the floor. A plume of miasma enveloped her, and she twisted away, waving a hand in front of her face to clear the water. A smaller box lay tucked in the corner. She swam over to it and picked it up. The box had to have been constructed from waterproof material as it appeared to be intact.

The alarm went off on her tank, and she tapped AJ on the shoulder, pointing upwards. He nodded, and together, they exited the church and surfaced.

"What've you found?" he asked.

"Not sure. It was tucked away in a corner, and this stuff is waterproof. I imagine it was intentionally hidden. I want to get it in the car and safe for now."

"Then let's break for lunch," he suggested. "We can change the tanks and eat while you stash that somewhere for safe keeping."

"Yeah." She hefted it into the boat then heaved herself over the side. "We're being watched."

"You mean the men on the dam?" AJ glanced over his shoulder. "They've been there all morning and seem too busy to be bothered by us."

"No. On the shoreline. There's a glint of binoculars every so often. Which will stop me from checking out the rest of the lake bed this afternoon."

AJ shook his head. "We're dropping sonar buoys, right? I drop them while you swim across and check the positioning is right. You can survey the lake bed at the same time."

She frowned. "I thought you said no diving alone for one-legged people . . ."

"I was mad, OK? You're more than capable. 'Sides, I'll be right up top." He tilted his head, starting the boat and heading to the shore. "And I was wrong."

"I'm sorry. I thought you said you were wrong." Lou laughed. "Can I have that in writing?"

"Don't push your luck, boss."

Fifty minutes later they were heading back out, a boat load of sonar buoys and spare tanks with them. Lou glanced over at AJ. "Start at the church and go across in a zigzag pattern. Make sure you drop one by the foot of the dam."

"You reckon they have a problem up there?"

"I don't know. But those engineers are still there. Maybe they're being thorough, but then again, maybe they really do have something to be concerned about."

AJ shook his head. "If that thing goes . . ."

"Tell me about it. Let's just get this done. Then tomorrow we can pick up the images from the boat." She surveyed the lake. "Not that there is much left. We might be able to pack up and go home by Tuesday at the latest."

"You working Sunday, Dr. F.?"

Lou raised an eyebrow. "You know I don't work on a Sunday. Ever."

"Just checking."

"OK. See you on the other side." She slipped on her mask then rolled over the side of the boat. Now that she was alone, the water seemed darker, but it was nothing more than her imagination. She swam slowly, following the buoys, making sure they landed in the right place. At the far end of the village, a single house stood untouched by the devastation around it.

Her interest piqued, Lou swam to the door and pushed it. It gave way, and she swam inside. She caught her breath, not having expected the sight that greeted her. The whole house was wired with explosives. She took photos, wondering why it hadn't been blown along with the rest of the village the previous evening. But at least she now had proof the destruction was deliberate.

She swam into another room, to find a body floating. Unlike the others they had found, this one was fully dressed and not a skeleton. Hair floated around his head, his eyes wide, mouth open, a gunshot wound to the side of his face.

Shocked into stillness, she gripped the doorframe for support. Her heart raced, and she swallowed bile.

Forcing herself into work mode, Lou took several photos. Perhaps the police would be able to ID him. As soon as she surfaced, she'd arrange for him to be brought ashore.

As she left the building, a massive concussion ripped through the water, sending her tumbling head over heels, wind-milling in the current. Her ears rang, and once she regained her equilibrium, she headed for the surface. Ripples and waves crashed around her. Had the dam burst? She shook her head. No. She'd be dead if that were the case.

Lou ripped off her mask. "AJ?" she yelled. She twirled, using her arms to keep afloat. Her heart stopped, and her breath caught in her throat.

The boat was gone.

In its place lay burning debris.

"AJ!"

She swam over to the wreckage, heart pounding, terror gripping her. Floating, burning debris hindered her, and she pushed it out of the way. AJ lay across a large piece of wreckage.

"AJ?" She flipped him over and gasped, tears stung her eyes and a huge lump obstructed her throat. "No, AJ . . ."

18

Evan's car swung into the last remaining parking space. He leapt from the backseat before the driver had switched off the engine and raced over to Lou in several long strides. The small jetty was a hive of activity. People talking, cars, noise, emergency services, but she sat small and quiet on a bench by the wall, with a blanket around her shoulders, seemingly unaware of it all. Tears tracked her cheeks. At that instant, he wanted nothing more than to wrap his arms around her and take her away from all this.

"Lou?"

She raised her head slowly. Her eyes were red, face white. She wrung her hands against her lap. Her bottom lip trembled. "He's dead . . . AJ's dead."

Evan sank down beside her and took her hand. He noticed that she had her prosthesis on and although that puzzled him as he knew she swam without it, now wasn't the time to ask. "I'm sorry. What happened?"

"He was dropping sonar buoys. I was following underwater to check their positioning. There was another explosion. When I surfaced, the boat was gone and AJ was . . . was . . ." She broke off, struggling for control. "I should call Varian."

"I already have. He's on his way. Have you spoken to the police?"

Lou nodded slowly, the fingers on her free hand worrying the edge of the blanket. "Yeah, they took a statement. I gave them copies of the photos I've taken below the water today. Along with all the photos I had originally of the artefacts and burned bones. They are coming by the manor this afternoon to collect the originals, along with the actual pieces themselves."

"Why weren't you in the boat as well? Your unbreakable rule . . ."

She shrugged. "I broke it. It's my fault. I wanted to check the remains of Abernay. We were being watched from the shoreline, so he said he'd stay with the boat and drop the buoys. I swam supposedly to check their position."

"None of this is your fault." Even as he spoke, Evan's mind whirled. This was the second attempt on her life in three days. She should have been in that boat right alongside AJ.

"Abernay is gone," she said quietly. "Blown up last night. The power plant was a cover. There is one house down there they missed. It's wired ready to go."

Evan swallowed, his burning stomach sending bile upwards. "You have proof?" he asked.

Lou nodded. "I took photos. Like I said, the police have copies of them now. And there's a body there. A recent one. It's possible that's where the explosion came from, but that wouldn't have taken out the boat. Not like this." She glanced up as a camera crew arrived and began filming. "I should give the press a statement."

He shook his head. "Wait. You need to tell AJ's family first."

"He doesn't have any. He lost his parents last year." She sniffled, more tears falling. "It should have been me. I fired him, I don't know how many times this week. He was way too stubborn to accept it."

The reporter came over. "Dr. Fitzgerald, do you have a moment to answer some questions?"

Lou nodded. She pushed to her feet.

Evan stood and moved out of camera shot. He glanced to his right as a black sedan drew up, and Varian exited the back.

"Didn't take you long to get here. I assumed you hadn't left town."

"You know full well I haven't," Varian replied. "What happened?"

"The boat exploded. Too early to tell why. AJ's dead."

Varian nodded to Lou. "But she isn't."

"You don't sound happy about that." Evan paused. "You don't even sound remorseful about AJ."

Varian scowled. "I'm calling this dig off. The church is dangerous in that condition. There's a demolition team coming in tomorrow to take it down."

"She won't like that."

"I don't care. I'm also terminating her contract with immediate effect."

"That's heartless, even for you." Evan studied him. "Does she scare you that much?"

"I'm protecting our interests," Varian began.

"Don't you draw me into your mess," Evan hissed. "*Your* interests, not mine." He paused as the recovery crew unloaded a body bag onto a waiting gurney. Even from here, he could tell the body in the bag was much shorter than it should be. That just gave added weight to Lou's comment that the house couldn't have caused this. Another crew unloaded the remains of the boat onto the jetty.

Varian cleared his throat. "She's responsible for the hiring of the boat and for AJ's death. If she'd done her job properly . . ."

"She'd have been on the boat and also be dead." Evan rounded on Varian. "Or is that what you wanted? You couldn't scare her off, so you tried killing her. And now that's failed, you're going to sack her?"

"Not immediately. There will be an investigation."

"Witch hunt more like." Evan shoved his hands into his pockets, curling them into fists. He noted that Varian didn't attempt to deny trying to kill Lou. He spun around; his attention caught by the reporters interviewing Lou a few feet further down the jetty.

Not wanting to be anywhere near Varian, Evan edged closer to Lou. One of the reporters had shoved a microphone in Lou's face.

"Dr. Fitzgerald, Dark Lake has a history of death, never mind the rumours and troubles that surround it. Would you attribute the death of AJ Wilcox to this or was it, as has been insinuated, mismanagement of the diving expedition?"

Evan shook his head and strode swiftly to

Lou's side. He tugged the microphone towards him in an effort to deflect the question. "Mr. Wilcox's death was, as far as we know, a tragic accident. The police will conduct a detailed investigation into the cause of the explosion, and you will be informed of the outcome in due time. Meanwhile Dr. Fitzgerald has lost a valued colleague and friend. Now if you'll excuse us, the interview is over."

He wrapped an arm around Lou and led her back over to the waiting ambulance.

"Thank you."

"You're welcome. Let's get you checked over."

"I'm fine."

"Humour me, please. I'll meet you at the hospital."

She quaked in his arms as AJ's body was wheeled past them. Tears swam in her eyes, and she choked back a sob.

Evan drew her closer. "Don't hold back," he said gently. He held her as she sobbed. A desire to protect her overwhelmed him, along with an insane desire to go back to Varian and knock his block off for attempting to kill her. Because he knew that was what had happened. No matter what the police report would finally indicate, this was too much of a coincidence to be anything else.

Lou lifted her head from his soaked jacket. "Sorry," she sniffled.

Evan retrieved a clean hanky from his pocket and pressed it into her hand. "It's fine."

Varian appeared, the perpetual scowl seared into his brow. "Lou, we need to talk."

"It can wait," Evan told him. "Lou needs to get to the hospital."

Varian's scowl deepened. "No, it can't. Lou, what happened?"

"The boat blew up," she said. "AJ died."

"I need a report."

She glared at him. "The boat blew up. AJ died," she repeated. "Want it a third time? Let me borrow a phone, and I'll text it to you."

"And you'll get your report," Evan interrupted. "For crying out loud, Varian, leave the woman alone. Right now she needs to be checked over at the hospital." Evan helped her into the ambulance. "I'll meet you there, Lou." As the paramedics shut the door, his gaze raked over Varian, and he lowered his voice. "You get a grip."

"I lost a good man out there. If she did anything . . ." Varian hissed.

"Oh, please! Pot, kettle, black." Evan

stepped to one side as the ambulance drove away. "If I find you have anything to do with this . . ."

"Are you threatening me?"

"Oh, I don't make threats. You know that. I make promises. I need to go."

Varian smirked. "Then by all means go. I'll handle the press."

Evan turned his back on him and stomped over to the car. His gaze flicked to Ira. "Take me to the hospital." He paused. "I'd like you to do a complete background check on Varian Sparrow. I want to know everything there is to know about him. And try to get ahold of his financial records as well, if you can. Also the health and safety records. I want to know how many on site accidents there have been and their causes."

"You think this was deliberate?"

He climbed into the car. "I know it was. I just can't prove it. Yet."

19

Back at the manor Lou spent a couple of hours being interviewed by the police and giving them all the original photos from the Dark Lake files. Relieved that was over, she went in search of Evan, finding him in a small, cosy living room. She flopped next to him and glanced at the TV. The local news was full of the accident at Dark Lake. She stilled Evan's hand as he grabbed the remote. "Don't change the channel. I want to watch it."

Varian's face filled the screen. "The remains of the church are in danger of collapsing and as such will be demolished, for safety reasons, first thing in the morning, with the permission of the police. AJ Wilcox lost his life here, it's only fitting that no one else does. Destroying the church will ensure no one else dives here."

"What about Dr. Fitzgerald?" the reporter asked.

"This whole area is a crime scene, so she won't be diving again. However, she did hire both the boat and equipment. The police are conducting an official investigation into last night's explosions and today's tragic events."

Lou leaned back in shock. "He's trying to blame me? And destroy the church? That building is sound. I've been in it myself."

Evan grasped her hand, rubbing the back of it with his thumb. "It's called passing the buck."

"He can't blame me. I should have been on that boat with AJ or dropping the buoys instead of him. He told me I had no place in the water. He was right."

"— worked with Dr. Fitzgerald?" the reporter continued.

"She's been with me ten years now and has an impeccable record. She's one of the best in her field. That's all I have time for now. Any further statements will come from the police or from my press officer."

Evan hit the off button on the remote. "Are you all right?"

"Fine." She paused. In all the fuss, she'd forgotten about the box she'd retrieved from the crypt. "My car is still at the lake. Can you give me a lift over there? I have a meeting at seven o'clock this evening, and I left some important documents in the car."

"Cancel it," he said. "You're in no fit state to do anything."

"I can't." She wasn't about to put Professor Cunningham off again. Otherwise, she might never get this job at the university.

"OK. Then I'll take you."

"That's very kind, but I can't ask that of you. Besides, I need those papers from my car anyway."

"Then I'll drive you to the car myself."

"Thanks. I'll grab my bag and coat." She paused. "I need to be at the lake at first light."

"You heard what he said. The whole area is a crime scene. The dive here is finished."

She tilted her head. "I know Varian's hiding something. That village was destroyed deliberately last night. Besides the church, all that is left now is a pile of rubble. I have proof. The only house that remained intact was wired with explosives that, for some reason, didn't go off. I owe it to AJ to find out what's going on."

"Hey." He caught hold of her and wrapped his arms around her. "Please take it easy. It's been a very long, rough day."

"I'm not hysterical."

"I never said you were." He brushed his lips against hers. "It wasn't your fault, so

176

don't blame yourself."

Lou looked up and once again drowned in his intense blue gaze. "OK. Can't make any promises."

He smiled and pressed his lips against her forehead. "I know. Let's go and get your car."

When they arrived at the dam, Lou frowned. Crime scene tape fluttered around where she'd parked. A police car along with a couple of white vans remained in the car park. Flood lights lit up the area along the edge of the water. Several white suited SOCO's worked quietly. Varian's car was parked in front of the office. "What's he doing here?"

"I'll go find out. You get to your meeting. You don't want to be late."

She nodded. On impulse she leaned over and kissed his cheek. "See you later." She got out of the car and hurried over to hers. She unlocked it, making sure the box was still in the boot. She closed the boot and climbed into the front. AJ's jacket was still tossed on the passenger seat where he'd left it. Tears burned and slowly tracked down her cheeks.

Lou closed her eyes. Her phone rang. She dragged it from her pocket and didn't bother reading the screen as she answered.

"D-Dr. F-Fitz-g-g-gerald." Her voice wobbled, but she didn't care.

"Lou?" Her stepfather's voice was uncharacteristically concerned. "Dark Lake is all over the news here. They said an archaeologist died. Are you all right?"

"No," she answered honestly, her voice still wavering. Jack was the one person she never hid her emotions from. He'd seen her at her worst several years ago, so hiding anything from him was pointless. She'd called him Dad since she was a teenager, but her head still referred to him as Jack. "AJ's dead. It should have been me out there, not him."

"I'm coming over on the next flight I can make." His tone left no room for argument. Lou had learnt long ago that arguing with him was a waste of breath.

"Is Mum coming, too?"

"She wants to, but Emily has a ballet recital this weekend, and one of us ought to be here for it. I imagine Jim will be fighting tooth and nail to come with me, so I'll leave first."

Lou shook her head. "There's no need . . ." She rubbed her eyes. "Emily needs you both there." As much as she wanted her mother, her younger siblings ought to take priority. She'd always tried to take a backseat as far as that went, and most of the time it had worked.

This time, however, she desperately hoped they'd see through it.

"There is every need," he said. "I'll be there in two days. Sooner if I can hop on an Air Force flight." He hung up before she could object.

Lou stared at the phone. It'd be good to see him, but how did she explain all this? And more to the point, how did she explain Evan? Somehow in less than a week, he'd gone from someone in her way, to an acquaintance, to the bloke putting her up in his house after saving her life to . . . what?

She wasn't sure he fitted into the boyfriend category — yet. But she'd kissed him. More than once. And she had feelings for him.

How would she explain that one to her stepfather?

She sucked in a deep breath and tucked her phone into her bag. Time to go meet this professor and try to get herself a new job. That way she could resign without fear of unemployment before Varian fired her in the morning. Failing that, she'd just resign. Anything had to be better than this.

20

Evan parked as close to the office on the dam as he could. As he got out of the car, a man in a suit and long overcoat approached him.

"Mr. Close?"

Evan nodded. He flipped up his collar against the rising fog. "Yes. Can I help you?"

The officer held up a warrant card. "DI James. I understand you own the lake and the dam?"

"Yes. I've already spoken at length to one of your officers and gave them permission to dive to corroborate Dr. Fitzgerald's story."

DI James nodded. "I thought you'd like to know that our dive confirmed the presence of explosives. It might be an idea to get some engineers to check the integrity of the dam itself."

Evan nodded. "Thank you. I'll arrange for one of my diving teams to come in at first light. I'm in charge of the company who has the contract for care of the dam. Assuming you don't mind me doing that? I appreciate it's a crime scene."

"That's fine. What's the name of your company?"

"Xenon — our contracts include the Thames Barrier. The man you really need to speak to about the dive is Varian Sparrow. He's ultimately responsible for anything archaeological that happens here."

"I'll do that. Good night."

"Good night." Evan spun and headed inside. Varian and Jasper paused what was evidently a heated argument. "Is this really a good idea?" Evan asked, skipping the niceties of hello.

Jasper rolled his eyes and headed to the door. "I'll leave you blokes to it. I have work to do."

"The explosives need setting, and I have to oversee it," Varian said, his voice about as testy as Evan had ever heard it.

"That is not what I meant, and you know it. The police are investigating AJ's death. This is a crime scene, or had the tape and officers out there escaped your notice?"

"He was on the lake, not in it. And that church is dangerous."

"That church is in the lake! Therefore part

181

of said crime scene. Another few days won't make much difference. Besides, they'd been diving earlier this morning. Lou says —"

Varian cut him off. "Lou says what?" His eyes narrowed and his posture stiffened.

"She says the village was in ruins down there. Only the church and one other building remained intact. And that one was wired to explode. Meaning that those houses down there were intentionally destroyed."

Varian remained straight faced. Either this wasn't news to him, or he was a better actor than Evan gave him credit for. "She does, does she?" His voice was cold, his words deliberate. "Does she have proof?"

Evan hesitated. For some reason he couldn't fathom, telling Varian the truth would be inherently dangerous for Lou. In a split second, he decided to deliberately keep his comments vague. "How would I know? I'm not exactly her confidant or work colleague. If she has, I imagine she'd have handed it to the police by now. The point is, she's planning on diving again at first light. Any more blasting down there, and she'll know something is going on."

"I ended the dive. She knows that. If she dives, it'll be against a direct order. Not to mention breaking a police cordon."

"She doesn't care," Evan shot back. He

wasn't going to mention he'd got permission for his own team to dive. "You told her to do a job, and she'll keep going until she's completed it."

"She can't dive alone. I'll bring someone in to assist. Someone I can trust." Varian slid his hands into his pockets.

Someone who will write the report the way you want it, more like. Evan had more sense than to voice the thought. "You should have left things alone. They were just fine until you decided to interfere and dig up the past. I was arranging for extra water to be diverted here. The church would have been covered again by the end of next week. Now you've stirred up a hornets' nest."

"You need to make sure your great-grandfather's records don't contain anything they shouldn't. And keep your girlfriend on a tight leash."

"My what?" he spluttered. "I'll have you know there is nothing going on between Dr. Fitzgerald and myself."

Varian scoffed. "And yet you knew exactly to whom I was referring."

The door flung open. "Evan, I need a word." Jasper's pale face, along with the edge in his voice, set all Evan's nerves ablaze with concern.

"Sure. What's up?" Evan gave Jasper his

full attention, grateful for the distraction.

Jasper looked from Evan to Varian and back. "We got problems. Big problems."

"That doesn't sound good." Varian peered at him.

"It isn't." Jasper gave Varian a sideways glance, before dumping the plans he carried on the table. "If you'll excuse us, this is dam business."

Varian jerked his head. "That's my cue to leave. I need to brief my team. We'll be back in the morning to lay the charges. Tell Lou she'll have a new partner at lunchtime and to stay out of the lake until then."

"Tell her yourself," Evan sighed. "I'm not on your payroll. And you'll need permission from the police before you enter that lake." He waited until Varian had gone before turning his full attention to Jasper. "What's up?"

Jasper kept his voice low. "I don't suppose he's out there listening, but just in case . . ." He spread the blueprint over the desk. "This is the diagram for the internal walls of the dam. We have an integrity issue. Those explosions in the lake last night caused damage here and here." His finger stabbed the papers as he spoke.

"Can you repair it?"

"We can patch and reinforce the inside.

The problem is, we don't know what damage was done on the outer walls. We'll have to drain the lake by six to eight feet to ease the pressure on the entire dam. If we don't, then the whole dam could fail."

Evan's heart pounded and his mouth dried. "When?"

Jasper shrugged. "You tell me. You're in charge of the contract for the dam's upkeep."

"You're the engineer onsite. I mean it, when? Are you talking next week, or in the next few hours? Or are you simply scaremongering? If she does fail, what damage is there likely to be?"

"Total."

Evan's whole body went cold, and he shivered. "I'm sorry?"

"If the dam goes, it will flood the entire valley. The village, manor, school, everything will go. Any loose debris down there will go with it. People will die. And if I find out who ordered the blasting down there —" Jasper let the threat hang.

"He isn't too far away," Evan muttered. "He wants to bring the church down."

"And I've told him no, not that he's listening."

Evan tapped the plans. "Did the explosions in the lake cause this?"

"Possibly, but I suspect it was caused deliberately. At least the internal damage. I was going to ask Dr. Fitzgerald to dive down and check the outside walls but didn't like to after all that happened today. I would send my usual diver, but he's vanished. He's not at home, and he isn't answering his phone. I've reported him missing. They're saying another body was found down there . . . a recent one."

"Talk to the police about that. I've already got permission to dive to check the dam. I know Dr. Fitzgerald was planning on diving first thing anyway, so I'll go with her — find out what we're facing. I'll call head office when I get home and get the team on standby. I can have the whole shooting match here in a matter of hours."

Jasper jerked his head. "Thanks. Tell Varian not to blast anything until the dam's been checked completely."

"Sure. When are you opening the overspill gates?"

"In around ten minutes, to coincide with the tide. A controlled release won't cause any flooding downstream. You'll need to sign off on it."

Evan held out his hand for the paperwork and scrawled his signature on the bottom. "There you go. If the dam does go, how much warning will we get?"

Jasper shrugged. "Depends what we find down there. I just pray she'll last until morning."

"You and me both."

"Thanks, boss. I'm testing the dam alarm system at ten, but I'll put a warning out before then."

Evan nodded. "Keep me posted. G'night."

He headed outside and back to the car. "Home." He looked at Ira. "There are several calls I need to make." He paused. "It might be an idea to call your mum as well. Suggest she go to her sister's in London for a few days. And that she leaves tonight." Ira frowned. "Why?"

"We have problems with the dam. If it fails, there might not be much warning."

"I'll call her as soon as we get back. Thank you."

Evan climbed into the front of the car. "Welcome." He did up his seatbelt and tugged out his phone, hitting the message screen, followed by Ralph's name. Ralph was his second in command at Xenon and the one man he trusted the most, other than Ira. "Ralph, it's Evan. Get the whole team on standby to go to Dark Lake. Possibly big problems at the Aberfinay Dam."

21

Lou headed into the pub, her stomach twisting. She hadn't had a proper job interview in years. She had no idea what this Professor Cunningham looked like, and she'd never been interviewed in a pub before.

A tall, blond man by the bar stood as she entered. His suit was partly covered by a long dark overcoat. He crossed the crowded pub towards her. "Dr. Fitzgerald?"

She tilted her head. "Are you Professor Cunningham?"

He nodded and held out a hand. "It's a pleasure to finally meet you. Although I'm surprised you didn't cancel after all that happened today." His voice softened. "I'm sorry to hear about the death of your colleague."

"Thanks," she said quietly. She blinked hard. She wouldn't cry again. Not in front of the bloke she was trying to impress.

"Shall we get a table?"

"Sure." She followed him across the pub to a relatively quiet corner. She sat and sighed. "Sorry, Professor Cunningham. It's been a very long day."

He handed her a menu. "I understand. And please, call me Tobias."

"Only if you call me Lou," she replied.

"What happened out there on the lake if you don't mind me asking?"

"Probably exactly what the news said." Lou opened the menu. "The boat exploded. I'm not sure why, but I can hazard a guess."

"Sounds intriguing."

"Far from it. I've been here less than a week. In that time, there has been at least one attempt on my life. Today would make it two. It should have been me on that boat and AJ under the water." She studied the menu. "Someone doesn't want me here."

Tobias glanced up for a second then turned his attention back to the menu. "You really think the boat being destroyed was deliberate? Do you have any idea who would want to hurt you?"

"I can think of someone, yeah." She took a deep breath and closed her eyes. "It should have been me. Oh, AJ, I'm so sorry."

Tobias's hand touched hers for an instant. "I'm sure he doesn't blame you. So, what do you fancy eating? Unless you'd rather reschedule."

She shook her head. "No. I'm fine." Glancing at the menu, she picked the first thing she saw. "Shepherd's pie, chips, and whatever veg they have."

"Sounds good. And to drink?"

"Whatever you're having."

Tobias rose and carried his menu with him. "Be right back."

Lou shoved her menu back into the holder on the table and leaned back in her seat. She picked up the beer mat, twisting it over and over in her hand. Around her the hum of conversation continued unabated. Life carried on as normal. But she was, once again, broken.

Tobias came back and set a pint glass in front of her. "Food will be around fifteen minutes. Bitter, OK?"

She rubbed her hand over her eyes. "That's fine, thank you."

He sat. "So, why change your mind about the job? When I originally wrote to you, offering you the place sight unseen, you turned me down flat. Most people your age would give their eye teeth to get a professorship so young."

"My work situation changed. Things have become, shall we say, increasingly difficult.

No, to be totally honest with you, difficult doesn't even begin to cover it. My situation is fast becoming untenable and I don't mean only because someone wants me dead. Projects I work on get taken away from me just as they get interesting and my theory becomes reality. Someone else gets given first name on my papers. Or I don't get to write them at all." She paused. "Sindlesham is one example of that."

His eyebrows winged up. "That was your work? The paper said Monty Sparrow. His was the other name put about by the board for this position."

"Case in point." She sighed. If Monty was also up for this job, then she may as well leave now. "Monty is my boss's son. He took over at Llaremont." She picked up her glass and sipped the cold beer. "I spent three years on that project, trying to convince people I wasn't insane, trying to relate that site to Stonehenge. Then the day we prove my theories correct, I get yanked off the dig for no reason whatsoever, and Monty was given the project instead. I get told to hand over all my notes, files, photos, and then I'm sent up here. And my boss tells me if I publish anything I'm sacked. However, AJ decided that wasn't fair. He brought all my notes when he arrived and gave them to me.

So I finished the paper and sent it off. It comes out Tuesday at least a month before Monty can publish anything."

Tobias raised an eyebrow. "So basically, you're sitting here talking to me because you'll be jobless by the middle of next week."

She shook her head. "I'd planned on quitting before he fires me. I intend to do that as soon as I get back to my room tonight. I'm tired of having work I've done be credited to someone else. Tired of being told I'm too disabled to dive, to dig. Maybe it's time I acted my age and tried to enthuse the next generation of archaeologists. Or I go back to my parents' place in the States and do something totally different."

"Would you be happy doing something else? From what I've read and discovered, you're one of the best archaeologists in the country, if not the world. You could have any position you wanted."

She snorted. "Not once my boss has finished smearing me through the mud. Don't get me wrong. I love field work. It's just been pointed out to me over and over again that there's no place in the field for someone like me. People wait for me to make mistakes. To slip up — literally."

The food arrived, and she inhaled the rising steam. It smelled wonderful.

Tobias smiled at the barmaid. "Thank you." He turned his attention back to Lou. "I assume by your disability, you mean your leg?"

She unwrapped her knife and fork. "Yeah. I lost it when I was sixteen in a boating accident."

"However, you're incredibly good at your job. You hold the world record in swimming. Your leg hasn't hindered you in any way. Why let it now?"

"You sound like my stepfather." She shoved the fork into the potato. "He'd say the same thing."

"He must be right then."

Lou glanced up at Tobias. "Maybe it's time for a change. I'd rather go straight into another job, somewhere I'm valued, needed, and my contributions mean something rather than to be given to someone else. However, if that's not possible, I'll join the ranks of the unemployed until something else crops up. I'm not a glory hunter, I merely believe in reaping what I sow and rewarding someone for all the hard work they put in. Whether that's in the field, or in an essay, or a research project."

He held her gaze, something flickering in his eyes. "The academic term starts on

October third. You'd spend term time lecturing, holidays in the field or running summer classes. There is the chance of doing field trips with the students in their final year. Four weeks paid vacation outside of term time. Some lab work. You'd be expected to file and publish at least one paper a year."

Her heart leapt. "I can do that."

"How much notice do you need to give?"

She shrugged. "None if he fires me, which he probably will. Or none if I quit first." She sucked in a deep breath. "Forgive me. Rule number one, never slag your current boss off to a prospective one."

A slight smile crossed Tobias's lips as he studied her over his fork. "Tell me about Llaremont."

Between mouthfuls, Lou told him about her theory connecting that site and Stonehenge and the way it had panned out.

"Interesting."

"That's one word for it. And I'm literally proving it when I get sent here to the back of beyond to investigate something the police are now handling and probably should have been from the start." She paused. "Sorry. No offense meant for calling this place the back of beyond."

"None taken. I can see why you're upset."

"Thing is, none of this current project here adds up."

"Which bit exactly?"

Lou swallowed her mouthful and picked up her glass. "There are bodies under Dark Lake, in the houses, the church. Or there were. Last night everything was destroyed. Bar one house, which contained a shed load of wires and explosives which hadn't detonated, along with a fresh body. Today, while I'm out there gathering evidence to prove all this, AJ dies. Someone is desperately trying to cover something up. And yes, I have given all I have to the police."

The waitress came over and picked up their empty plates. "Can I get you any dessert?"

Tobias nodded. "Apple pie and custard, please. Lou?"

"The same."

Lou leaned back in her seat and set her empty glass on the table.

"Can I get you another?"

She shook her head. "No, but I'd love a coffee, please."

Tobias smiled. "Sure. Be back in a minute."

Left to herself, Lou withdrew her phone from her bag and checked her messages. There was one from Jim, demanding she call him as soon as possible. One from her parents saying virtually the same thing word for word. And one from Varian. That one she deleted without reading. She didn't want his condescending platitudes which would turn, as always, into an ultimatum.

Gazing across the pub, she came to a decision. No matter what the outcome of tonight's meeting, she was resigning as soon as she returned to the manor. Whatever secrets lay beneath the surface of Dark Lake would remain with her and the police. No one else needed to know. The report wouldn't be published. Her findings would vanish, nothing put to record. It was simply another village drowned to make way for a reservoir. The investigation had cost too much.

Anything else she found out was for her benefit only. To satisfy personal curiosity.

Tobias sat opposite her and slid a mug of coffee across the table to her.

"Thanks." She watched him sip his second pint.

"You've heard the history of the place?" he asked.

"Only a little. Most of the records have been buried, destroyed in the flood, or are impossible to find. Those we did track down are incomplete and don't match my findings."

"The whole area was owned by the Close family for generations. Have you met the current owner, Evan Close?"

Lou nodded, choosing to keep how well she knew him to herself. "Yes, our paths have crossed a few times."

"His great-grandfather was the Abernay doctor back when the village was flooded. His great-great-grandfather was the local squire."

"Evan mentioned that."

Tobias raised an eyebrow as the puddings arrived. "Evan? You two are on first name terms?"

Lou's cheeks heated. "He saved my life, so yeah, we are. It seemed kind of silly to keep calling each other Dr. Fitzgerald and Mr. Close after that."

"Then maybe it's my turn to bite my tongue," he said, picking up his spoon. "How did you put it, never complain about one friend to another."

Lou shook her head. "No, please, carry on. If my boss is serious about blowing up the church and closing my investigation down, then I want to at least satisfy my own curiosity about the true history of this dam."

"OK. Both rumour and legend have it that

the villagers didn't want to leave."

"The news reports told me that much." She stabbed her pie with her spoon. "They protested in Downing Street."

"But did the news reports tell you that the people never left?"

"Huh?" Her mind flashed back to the bodies she'd found, tied to pews and chairs or stuck in inner rooms and cupboards under the stairs.

"A huge fire swept through Abernay, lasting three days. No one saw the villagers afterwards. For several weeks before that, they had cut themselves off behind barricades."

The fire wasn't news to her, however the fact the village was barricaded off was. "How did the fire start?"

"Under the cover of the fog. There were only a few people who survived it. The Closes for one. Your boss's family for another and a few others. Maybe fifteen in total."

"What?" She choked on the pie. She coughed hard and swallowed several mouthfuls of coffee.

"Didn't he tell you that? Chester Sparrow was Varian's grandfather. He was the chief architect and stood to benefit the most from the construction of the dam. He also had a large stake in the hydroelectric company the dam feeds."

Lou inhaled sharply. That explained a lot. Her mind whirled. "So why send me to dig all this up? He must have known all along. Surely . . ." She paused as she pondered. "No. Not even Varian would stoop that low, would he?"

"What are you thinking?"

"He sends me here, let's me dig all this up, then he can sack me legitimately. Because if I publish this, it'll seem like I have an axe to grind." She sighed. "Damned if I do and damned if I don't."

Tobias nodded. "You need a new job."

"A new life would be better. One far, far away from the Sparrow Foundation."

"Or maybe he wants you to disprove the rumours and clear his name."

Lou tilted her head. "Elaborate on these rumours."

"That all the villagers were murdered. Either burned or buried alive. Or drowned when the waters came. All under the cover of the fog. The Sparrows made their fortune from this dam. Money is a great incentive for murder."

"What about the Closes?"

"They had to know. They were the only other survivors."

The back of Lou's neck prickled. She glanced up to find Evan standing right behind Tobias. A dark scowl covered his face, his blue eyes glinted like ice. Before she could say anything, he spun on his heel and strode from the pub.

Had he known all along?

What kind of a man was she involved with?

Maybe Varian wasn't behind the attack on her life. She shivered.

"You OK?" Tobias asked.

She nodded, draining the rest of her now cold coffee. "I'm fine."

"Good, let me get you some more coffee, and we can talk more about the position at the university."

22

Lou drove back to the manor, hoping against hope that Evan would already be in bed and asleep. She really didn't want to face him tonight. Not with her mind so conflicted and so many unanswered questions about him and Varian tumbling in her brain. She needed to sort through her feelings before she did or said anything she would regret.

Resigning being the exception to that.

Fog swept in off the mountains as she drove, and she shivered, remembering what Tobias had said about the murders and the cover of the fog.

She parked her car and removed the box from the boot. She wrapped it in her coat before locking the car and heading up the steps to the front door. It opened as she got there and closed behind her almost as soon as she stepped into the hall.

Evan kept his face impassive. "How was

your meeting?"

"It was interesting," she said. "How was your evening?"

He scowled. "Fine. Who was he? You said you were going to a meeting."

"And I did exactly that." Lou hefted the box in her arms. "I met with Professor Tobias Cunningham from Cumbria University. We were discussing a potential job offer, not that it's any concern of yours."

"That isn't what is sounded like from where I was standing." He paused. "A job interview. In a pub? Do you really think I came down in the last shower?"

She gritted her teeth. "No, I don't. And yes, a job offer. There's a position going in the university here. He wanted to talk to me and he suggested dinner in the pub. We arranged it on Tuesday. Were you spying on me?"

"Why would I waste my time doing that? I fancied a quiet drink in the local pub. Did you get this job?"

"He'll let me know. But either way I will be out of your hair and your house by Tuesday at the latest." She shifted the box again. The longer she held it, the heavier it appeared to get.

He tilted his head. "What's in your coat?"

"Nothing much. Just some stuff from the car."

"It looks heavy."

"It is. Well, it's been a very long, very rough day, so I'll call it a night." She moved to the foot of the stairs. "Did you ever find your great-grandfather's journal?"

"I . . ." He visibly hesitated. "Yes. But it won't be much help I'm afraid. The ink is rather faded."

"I'd still like to see it."

"OK." Was that reluctance in his voice? Would it prove his family's involvement in the deaths of all those people? If the rumours were, in fact, true. "I'll bring it up to your room for you."

"Thank you." She headed up the stairs and down the hallway, managing to balance the box long enough to open the door and flick on the light. She closed the door with her hip and set the coat wrapped box on her bed then unwrapped it and grabbed the camera, photographing it from several angles. Next she examined the box. There was a key hole, which indicated it was locked as well as rusted shut.

So involved in her work, the knock at the door made her jump. "One minute," she called. She shoved the box under her bed and draped her coat over the back of the chair. Then she opened the door.

Evan held out the book. "The journal."

"Thank you." She reached for it, but he didn't let go.

"Some things are best left buried in the past, Dr. Fitzgerald."

A spear shot through her. They were back to titles were they? How much of the conversation with Tobias had he overheard? "Is that so, Mr. Close?"

"Yes." He let go of the journal. "The coroner called. She'll have the autopsy report tomorrow."

"That's awfully fast. And you know this how?"

"She called out of common courtesy. It's my land, AJ was your friend, and you're staying here."

Lou bit her lip, the all too familiar grief welling up inside her again at the mention of AJ's name. Sirens wailed outside. "I'll never get used to that fog warning. Don't see why you need it when we're nowhere near the coast."

"That's not the fog warning, it's the dam evacuation warning. They're testing it. Which reminds me. Jasper asked if you could dive the dam in the morning. He's worried about the integrity of the walls, and his diver has gone AWOL. They're running six to eight feet of water off tonight, but he'd feel happier if someone could check the outer walls. It's a crime scene still, but I have permission from the police to check the dam integrity. The last thing we need is a major disaster on our hands."

"I'm not a builder or a structural engineer, but sure, I can dive and take photos."

Evan nodded. "Thanks." He turned to go then paused. "Oh, and Varian said to tell you that Monty will be here around lunch-time. He'll be your new partner."

Lou growled, anger consuming her. *I knew it!* "Great. That's just what I wanted to hear." She didn't bother to hide the sarcasm.

Evan nodded. "Well, good night."

She shut the door with slightly more force than absolutely necessary. Monty's coming out could only mean one thing. Varian was planning on sweeping all this under the carpet. Discrediting her completely. Or he was covering something up.

Or knowing Varian, all of the above.

Either way, perhaps this journal held the answers.

However first there was something she needed to do. She flipped open the laptop and e-mailed Varian, copying it to head office, Evan, and herself.

Dear Varian,

Please accept my resignation from the Sparrow Foundation with immediate effect. I have several weeks leave accumulated and that will serve as my period of notice.
Dr. L.W.B. Fitzgerald.

Feeling better than she had in a long time, Lou hit send and closed down the laptop. She curled up on the bed, wrapped herself in the duvet, and began to read.

23

June 24

No one likes the idea of having to move. Frank Philips called a village meeting in the church tonight. He's talking about going to London and handing in a petition to Downing Street. Father, of course, is dead set against the idea. He can only see the profit and good that will come from the dam. But then he and CS are making far too much money from this venture to want it stopped.

The weather is more than a little unusual for June. Thick fog sweeps off the mountains each evening, blanketing the village all night, clearing only with dawn's first light.

Despite our misgivings and objections, work continues on the dam, day and night. Some are calling it Close's Folly. Many a true word spoken in jest.

We are settled into our cottage opposite the church. I use the rooms to the side as a surgery. It has its own door and waiting area.

It isn't perfect, but it will do for now. Both of us are enjoying being away from the manor with all the stresses and strains that brings with it.

Mabel's morning sickness has now eased, and she's adapting to being 'a lady of leisure' although I get the impression she would rather be doing work of some sort. Perhaps I'll let her help out with the receptionist's duties in the surgery.

July 3

Another accident at the dam site. Once again in the fog. That's the tenth in as many days. A fatality this time — John Perkins, a young lad of only nineteen — crush injuries. There was nothing I could do other than suggest to the foreman he ceases work under the cover of darkness and fog, but he will not listen to a "mere doctor who stands against progress and construction."

He seems to forget who will be squire after my father's passing.

My beloved Mabel, bless her, wants us to leave this cursed place and take a position somewhere miles from here. She says the babe within her is uneasy. Leaving is exactly what Father wants of me.

He will never forgive me for marrying Mabel. He often tells me that I married beneath me and am, thus, not fit to be his heir.

If I could find a position elsewhere, leave all this behind, I would do so. But with Frederick perishing on the Titanic and William's death in a car accident, I am the one remaining son. I have no choice but to stay.

July 10

The march in London accomplished nothing. The flooding of Abernay and Finlay will go ahead on the completion of the dam in September. The resulting conflagration will be the Aberfinay Dam and Reservoir. Father is talking about adding the necessary modifications to make it one of the new hydroelectric power stations. This would make him even more money.

The foggy nights continue. No one can remember weather like this before. On my way home from delivering the Fletcher baby, a girl they called Melissa, I found the body of Frank Phillips. There was no doubt he'd been murdered as the back of his head had been caved in with a sharp object. I alerted the local constabulary, but they do not think they will find the person responsible. Sgt. Johns thinks it was a vagrant, a robbery as Frank's wallet was missing.

How many vagrants carry hammers? A simple mugging would have resulted in Frank's wallet being taken. There is no doubt in my mind this was deliberate, as with the investigation into Frank's death, the protest against the dam will likely fold.

Lou glanced up. Rising, she padded across the room and gazed across the foggy courtyard. Lights glowed from the wing opposite. Who could be over there? That part of the manor was usually in darkness. She closed the curtains and reached to grab her sweater from the chair. She tugged it over her head and threaded her arms through the sleeves as she walked back to the bed.

She climbed in and snagged the covers over her.

Despite the journal's many missing pages and sections too faded to read clearly, the account was chilling.

August 13

Plague. I had hoped, prayed, I was wrong. Tommy Philips, Frank's boy, died just before ten o'clock this morning. More cases come by the hour. I am unprepared for such great numbers.

Food supplies are being left beyond a barrier half a mile away. We have no contact with the outside world at all. Strangely there is no mention of our plight on the wireless. Perhaps they do not wish to alarm anyone. I fear something more sinister is afoot.

August 20
I have quarantined all those infected in a building on one side of town. But numbers are rising, and I fear it may be too little too late. I am treating the patients myself, along with Nurse Mount. Not that there is much I can do. I lack the proper medication or facilities. It has been a week since the first case, and the deaths are increasing to a point where the dead outnumber the living. I am dog tired and long to see Mabel but cannot risk infecting her.

The next few entries were in a different hand, each signed R.M., so Lou surmised they must have been written by Nurse Mount. Each consisted of a list of names and ages, presumably those who had succumbed to the disease.

Tears tracked down Lou's cheeks unattended.

Whole families wiped out, so many children taken by so cruel a disease. It certainly explained the barrier that Professor Cunningham had mentioned.

Lou made out the words Dr. Close and sick, so he too had succumbed to the plague.

Strange that Evan never mentioned it. She

knew he didn't die, as Evan had said he remained in Dark Lake and lived in the manor after the village was flooded.

September 1

Finally I am well enough to write. It is thanks to Nurse Mount that I am recovering, albeit weaker than I have been for some time. Mabel has also been helping out, though I now fear for her. She looks pale and tired. Over half the village is now sick. CS says it is fortuitous as only those who oppose the construction of the dam and flooding of the villages are sick. He took my illness as proof that I also am opposed, but as the person treating the afflicted, I am at most risk of infection.

September 5.

Mother is sick. I have moved her from the manor. Father wanted her to remain there with him, but it is best she does not stay there and infect any more of the servants. Her lady's maid, two of the parlour maids, and a cook are already sick. One of the gardeners is showing symptoms, so I have moved him to the outer cottage here. That way, if he does turn out to be infected, he will not be putting the lives of his family at risk also.

September 7

My father is numbered amongst the sick as are all the servants who remained. The manor lies empty. The servants I was caring for here are dead.

My mother died early this morning. Father is unaware of this, and I shall not tell him. So much wasted time. So much I wish I could tell her, that now I never can.

Mabel is yet untouched. I pray she will remain so. I cannot lose her, too.

September 10

Father died this morning. This means I now own the house and land and the burden of the dam. I do not want it. If I could revoke the planning permission I would do so, but I fear it would be too late if not impossible. CS is impossible to work with and becoming more and more demanding. He wants access to the manor for some papers of Father's, but the whole village is sealed, and I will not allow him to enter the building until I have a chance to go through Father's papers myself. I am no longer sure of what CS is capable of doing. The dam is complete. All that remains is for the flooding to take place once the epidemic is over and the bodies burned, the ashes buried deep in a concrete vault underground.

September 20

Finally, it looks as if the plague is over. There are around twenty of us left alive from the original 200 that lived in Abernay. We are exhausted, our eyes sore from shedding tears, faces reddened with grief. I should have been able to save them, but I failed in my duty as a doctor, in my calling, and as a result the village is lost.

The old rhyme never spoke a truer word. It says for the want of a nail the shoe was lost, the horse was lost, the battle was lost, the kingdom was lost. So for the want of a decent doctor the village was lost.

September 27

A fire began almost simultaneously in five parts of the village shortly after seven o'clock tonight. At almost the same time, fog rolled in off the dam and off the mountains, shrouding Abernay and Finlay. With so few of us left, there is little we can do to fight so many fires. It is spreading quickly.

Mabel thought she heard explosives, but I did not. We are safe here in the manor. We have with us the remaining survivors. As I write this, it is just past midnight. There are only ten of us. The others, we hope, escaped by other means, rather than being caught in the flames. We will not know until morning or until the fires die down.

Sept 30th
It's done.

24

As she finished the last entry, a knock at the door made Lou jump. "One minute." She flung the covers back and padded across to the door. She was stiff and cold and wondered who would want her at this unearthly hour.

Evan smiled. "Morning."

She did a double take, staring at him in confusion. "It is?"

He nodded. "Half past seven on the dot. You wanted to be at the lake by eight. And when you weren't at breakfast, I thought I'd come knock you up." He paused. "I apologize for the wholly inappropriate choice of words there."

She grinned. "It's fine, I know what you mean." Had she really been reading all night?

He moved past her into the room and opened the thick, heavy drapes. Sunlight filled the room, the dust shining in the rays.

"See, its daylight. You look dreadful."
Concern shone in his blue eyes. "Have you slept at all?"

"No. I was reading and didn't realise the time. Have you read the journal at all?"

"Bits of it. Enough to know my great-grandfather was part of what happened here."

She frowned. "I don't think he was."

Evan picked up the journal from the bed and read from the last entry. " *'My job, my calling, is to save lives, not be responsible for their loss, especially in such appalling circumstances. Maybe it's fitting I spend the rest of my life caring for the dam here. Caring for the lost, the damned, those I betrayed. The irony is not lost on me.'* And a bit farther on. *'I just hope someday, maybe in eternity, Father will forgive me this last act. Until that point may God have mercy on my soul and on the souls of those innocents caught up in all this.'* "

He rubbed the back of his neck, his spirit in obvious torment over this whole affair. "Over and over he refers to what he did, why he did it." He put the book down. "All of this," he indicated the room, the gardens beyond the window, "paid for with blood money."

"You should read all of it," Lou said. As

Evan shook his head, she raised an eyebrow. "There are pages missing, and parts too faded to read, but there is enough there to know the truth. He didn't kill anyone. There was a plague epidemic. He couldn't save them, Evan. They died because there weren't medications or the hospital services like there are now. He was a doctor, and he couldn't save them. That's why he blamed himself."

She studied her hands. She ought to tell him. She had avoided it last night because she wasn't sure he wasn't involved somehow. But now, what did she have to lose? "He mentioned hiding a box in the church crypt, didn't he?"

Evan nodded, reading the text again. " *'I have written more and sealed it in a watertight box and hidden it in the church crypt. Nowhere else is safe. The reach of CS knows no bounds.'* I'm not sure who CS is."

"My guess would be Chester Sparrow," Lou muttered. "I discovered last night that Varian's grandfather was the chief man responsible for the building of the dam. He also had a large stake in the hydroelectric company the dam feeds. I'm guessing Varian still does."

Evan didn't seem surprised. "Why did you ask about the box?"

218

"We found it yesterday morning." She dragged it out from under her bed. "It needs a key to open it, besides being rusty."

Evan picked it up. "Heavy. Is this what you tried to sneak in under your coat last night?"

"I wasn't sneaking it in, but yeah, it was wrapped in my coat. We found it in the church crypt. There is a crest of some kind on one side."

Evan set the box on the bed and traced it with his fingertip. "The crest belongs to my family. Did you try opening it?"

"Even without the key, which I don't have, it's rusted shut. I have the tools to force it open, but didn't want to damage it."

"Where would he have put the key?" Evan wondered aloud.

"I can think of two places. In the crypt with the box or the cottage they lived in. But that is now in ruins."

"There is one other place." Evan glanced up at her. "When I was a kid, before he died, Grandad told me about a cave that meant a lot to his parents. We drove up there once, but a rock fall had sealed it."

"Can you take me up there and show me? Perhaps there's a way in or the rocks might have shifted as a result of all the tremors."

Evan nodded. "Sure. Once you've checked

the base of the dam."

Lou smiled. "I hadn't forgotten. I also want to go over the inside of the crypt one last time before Varian makes good on this threat to blow up the church."

"I'll put this in the safe."

Lou took the box from him. "It stays here."

"It belongs to me."

"Right now it's part of the dig," she pressed. "Therefore it's mine. Once we've opened it, documented its contents, and photographed it both inside and out . . ."

". . . then Varian will know what it says," Evan interrupted. Fear roughened his voice, clouding his gaze. "That isn't a good idea. He still owns the company that runs the dam. Chances are, he's behind all of this, as well as the attempt on your —"

He spun around, shutting his mouth firmly. "Forget I said that."

She moved in front of him. "Don't leave it there. Finish what you were saying."

"Varian was behind the attempt on your life in the hotel —"

"What?" Lou interrupted him, anger bursting from her. As Jim once said, Mount Lou was in full scale eruption. "He did what? How do you know? Are you in on it?"

"That is the most ridiculous idea I have

ever heard." Evan's gaze pierced her. "If I wanted you dead, woman, I'd hardly do this, would I?" He pulled her against his firm body and fastened his lips over hers.

The kiss was sudden, passionate, and breathtaking. It siphoned all the anger from her, leaving her dizzy.

Not moving from his arms, she gazed up at him. "OK, but that doesn't answer how you know."

"He didn't deny it when I accused him of it. And he was responsible for the boat blowing up yesterday."

"He killed AJ?" Her voice was no more than a whisper, her heart aching, her stomach twisting within her. "I should have been on that boat."

"That's what he was banking on," Evan said. He guided her back to the bed, sitting her down, and resting beside her. "He wants this lake business covered up and if killing you is the way to do it . . ."

"Then why did he send me up here in the first place?" Lou said. She sank into him and buried her face in her hands. "I don't get it."

"He told me it's so he can control what gets reported and made public."

"What do I do?"

"Finish what you came for," Evan

said. He held her close, rubbing her arm gently. "Find out the rest of the truth of Dark Lake. Publish it. Show him that you'll not be scared away."

"But what happens to your name and your reputation if I publish?" She raised her head, her eyes glistening. "You may well lose everything."

He shook his head. His finger reached out and wiped away the tears that slid down her cheeks. "The truth is what matters. Varian killed once to prevent it getting out. He won't hesitate to do it again. I have to know what other secrets the lake is hiding. And in return, I'll be totally honest with you as to what I know. But first we need to go and check the dam."

The clock chimed. "Give me a minute to change and grab my stuff."

Evan nodded. "I'll see you downstairs. You should eat first."

"No time. I'll eat later. I shouldn't dive on a full stomach anyway." She shut the door behind him and glanced around the room.

Where would be the best place to hide the box? Not under the bed, obviously. Wrapping it in a plastic bag, she shoved it in the black sack containing her dirty laundry. Then she shoved that in her suitcase and hefted it on top of the wardrobe.

Dressing in her wet suit, she strapped her leg over the top and finished the outfit with tracksuit and trainers.

Every nerve ending tingled. She was close to finding answers. This was why she did what she did. There was nothing quite like the thrill of it.

25

Evan waited for Lou in the hallway. Rather than bother the staff, he swiped the keys from the cupboard and drove the car himself. He wound down the windows, letting the breeze ruffle his hair. "Not too cold are you?"

She shook her head. "No."

"Good. I don't get to drive very often. Or sit in the front. It makes a nice change."

A wry smile turned up her lips. "I don't get to be driven very often." She pushed back in the seat. "It's nice to let someone else do it for once."

He drove in silence for a minute then cleared his throat. "About last night."

"If you mean Professor Cunningham, there is nothing going on between us. There is no reason for you to be jealous whatsoever, because it isn't as though you and I are going out or anything. A couple of kisses doesn't commit either of us to anything."

Evan glanced sideways at her. A rosy hue covered her high cheek bones, and the intensity of her gaze gave him pause. Somehow the lady was protesting too much. "Hold that thought. That wasn't what I meant."

She widened her eyes. "It wasn't?"

He swerved into the side of the road and pulled up the handbrake. The indicator ticked as he twisted in his seat to gaze at her. "No." He swallowed, somehow tearing his gaze from those perfectly, kissable lips to her eyes and found himself drowning once again.

Lou studied at him. "Then what?"

"You've been up all night. You've had no sleep, and you haven't even begun to grieve or process what happened yesterday. Not to mention skipping breakfast."

Her eyes glittered. "Don't you presume to tell me what I feel or don't feel. And as for skipping breakfast, you're the one who rushed me out the door. Plus I won't dive on a full stomach as it's asking for trouble." She sucked in a deep breath, fingers digging into her palms. "AJ's dead. Nothing will change that. I want to know why. The answer is in that lake. And I won't rest until I find it."

Evan nodded. "OK. By the way, I got your

e-mail. Good on you for quitting." He checked over his shoulder and swung back onto the road.

"The worm turned," she said dryly. "What time is Monty getting here?"

"Varian said lunchtime."

"That doesn't give me long. They'll cover all this up. The bodies, explosions, AJ." She paused. "Can you find out if there is anyone missing from the village?"

"Why?" He veered off the main road, taking the road to the dam.

"There was a fresh body down there yesterday. And before you ask, he wore modern clothing and there was no decomposition."

He clicked his fingers. "Jasper is missing one of his divers. Did you get pictures?"

"Yes. I gave copies to the police, but I still have the originals."

Evan swung into a parking space and switched off the engine. "Show me."

Lou pulled up the screen on the camera. "Here."

Evan scrolled through the shots, his stomach turning, threatening to eject the coffee he'd downed before leaving. "That's Daniel Davies. He used to own a demolition company before the recession." He handed back the camera, eyes burning. "He was a friend."

Her hand rested on his arm. "I'm sorry." She peered out at the lake. "You can see the entire spire now."

Evan rubbed his hand over his eyes. Now wasn't the time for sentiment. He glanced out of the windscreen across the lake, and his gaze narrowed. There was a huge hole in the side of the church spire. "It appears as if it's leaning to one side."

"And it wasn't yesterday." Lou heaved a sigh. "It's possible it was being supported by the weight of the water, but I doubt that, given everything else that's happening. I need to get down there and fast."

"You're not going alone. I'm diving with you."

Surprise crossed her face, making her look cute. "You dive? I thought you said . . ."

"No, I said I left my wetsuit at home. I assume your suit has a universal helmet lock?"

"Yes, but —"

He cut her off again. "Good. I have a wet suit and dive gear in the boot. It goes with me whenever I travel, which is usually on business when I need it. My master's degree is in civil engineering. I know dams and buildings. You know diving and history. We should make a good team."

"Wow." She let out a slow whistle. "And

there I was thinking you were just a pretty face."

He chuckled. "Not even that. And I'm far from the lord of the manor who sits on his backside all day drinking coffee." He laughed as a rosy hue spread over her cheeks again. "Sorry to disappoint you. I run my own company in London, called Xenon. It's an engineering firm. One of our contracts is the Thames Barrier. Another is the Aberfinay Dam. So yes, I know what I'm doing. I already have police permission to dive what is essentially still a crime scene."

"Impressive." She tilted her head. "Then you should dive the rest of the lake with me. See for yourself what's down there, or rather what's left of it. Help me search for this key or anything else that might help the investigation."

Evan nodded. "I'd like that. We'll use my helmets. They have radios fitted." He got out of the car and opened the boot. "Give me a sec to put the wetsuit on, and I need to check in with the office. Then we'll dive the dam."

She nodded as she climbed out of the car and shut the door. Then as he stripped off his jumper and unbuttoned his shirt, she pirouetted, facing out over the water.

He grinned. "Is the prospect of me undressing that frightening?"

"You flatter yourself," she said. "I'm just not ready to see you scantily clad this early in the morning."

"Probably wise. No doubt I'm not a sight for sore eyes." He tossed his clothes into the boot and tugged on the wetsuit. Then he slid his feet into sneakers. "Come on then."

"I'll give the boat a thorough inspection and get the gear checked. Especially the air tanks," she said. "After yesterday, I'm leaving nothing to chance. We've also been running out of air much sooner than we anticipated."

"Then I'll leave the boot open for you." He tossed her the keys and headed up towards the office.

Jasper came out to greet him, a scowl on his face instead of the customary smile. "Morning."

Did he ask, or just assume the worst? "How is it?"

"Not good, boss. We drained off seven foot overnight, but the pressure is still too high."

Evan wrinkled his nose, his mind whirling. "I want to go down and check the inside myself before we dive."

"I wouldn't. Wait until you come back." Evan shook his head. "It'll take me five minutes tops to get down there and check the gauges and come back. Dr. Fitzgerald will need that long at least to check the tanks and get the equipment ready for the dive." He paused. "I suggest you call the Environment Agency and get the panel inspectors out ASAP."

"Varian said he'd already called them. They're sending someone out today."

Not believing that for a second, Evan grabbed the clipboard, resolving to call the Environment Agency himself once he got back up from the tunnels. "Back in a few."

26

Evan headed outside and took the lift down to the concrete service tunnel which ran the length of the dam. His footsteps echoed as he exited the lift. He studied the chart in his hand and checked the places Jasper had marked. The walls were damper than he'd have expected, but nothing unusual.

The pressure gauges, on the other hand, set alarm bells ringing in his mind. He spun to leave the control room, his trained eye catching a glimpse of something in the far corner. He crossed to check. A tiny hairline crack snaked down the wall from ceiling almost to the floor.

He trotted back to the lift, punching the call button. Once on the surface, he ran to the office. "Jasper, I don't want anyone going down there until I'm back."

Jasper raised an eyebrow. "Not even the panel inspectors?"

"No. I don't trust Varian not to send his

own men in their stead. I have a contact over at the Environment Agency, and I'll call them myself. Pull strings if need be."

"You're the boss." Jasper turned back to the dials. "I'll give you a shout if anything changes up here."

"Thanks." Evan headed outside into the chill morning.

Fog drifted down off the mountains as he crossed over to where Lou hefted several tanks of air into the boat.

"Lovely weather for ducks," Lou said, barely glancing up as he approached.

Evan grimaced. "Oh, yeah." He drew his phone from the glove box. "I need to make a couple of quick calls before we go." He dialled quickly. "Yes, this is Evan Close from Xenon. I need to speak to Wallace Teague."

He leaned against the car and filled his friend in quickly. "So what I need to know is who's coming out and what time."

Typing came over the phone. "No one is coming."

Evan closed his eyes in dismay. "Figured as much. Someone is sabotaging things up here. I need panel inspectors here today. We have a situation at the Aberfinay Dam — right now it's a yellow. There is a strong possibility it'll become a red. I've checked the service tunnel, and I'm now about to dive and check the outer wall. The run off isn't enough to reduce the pressure."

"I'll send a team out now. As a courtesy to you, I'll tell you who. Even though it's not normal procedure." More typing clicked. "OK, Cliff Barnes and Pat Stewart will be with you by three at the latest."

"Thank you. I'll speak to you later." He hung up and gave Lou a thumbs-up. "Let's go."

"Do we have a problem?"

He locked the car, tossing his keys and phone into the boat. "Quite possibly. There's a crack in the internal service tunnel. I need to check the outer walls and see if there are any corresponding marks. So, get in the boat and let's go." He helped her in. "You got everything?" As she nodded, he cast off and headed across to the dam. "And, for the record, I'm not jealous. Well, maybe a little."

She frowned. "Huh? Jealous of who? Varian or the Environment Agency?"

"Neither. Of Professor Cunningham. I've gone back to that train of thought I told you to hold in the car on the way here." He glanced at her. Oh, she was beautiful when she was confused or angry or passionate about something. In truth, she was beautiful all the time.

He grinned. "I like being with you. I shouldn't. I admit I came to this point from being ready to hate you, or at least distrust you. I was afraid you'd unearth my deepest, darkest secrets and tell the world."

She tucked her hair behind her ears. "You're really that bothered by your great grandfather's involvement in all this?"

"Yeah, I am. I was afraid I'd lose everything because of this."

"Like what? I don't understand how, because you weren't even born when all of this happened. So you can't be held responsible for his actions."

"He may have murdered or had a hand in the murder of half the village. If he profited from any of those deaths, then my company, this land, everything I own is built with blood money. The manor was renovated with that money. I know that, and I still live there, own the land, the dam . . ." He broke off, staring out over the water, trying to rein in his emotions and control the embarrassing wobble in his voice.

Her hand touched his cheek. "Evan, look at me."

He blinked hard, before doing as she asked.

"He didn't kill them. Not unless he unleashed a plague virus. And if all this 'blood money' as you called it bothers you that much, then sell it. Give the money to the church or a charity. If you work in London, you must have a flat or something there."

He nodded. "Yeah."

"There you go then."

He sighed. Maybe he should. "I guess it depends on what's in that box you found, if we ever get it open."

The boat stopped by the dam and Lou tied the rope to a ring on the side of the concrete structure. "First, let's see how much of a problem we have here."

Shouts came from above them. Lou shifted on the seat. "Great, we got trouble."

Evan winked at her. "I reckon that's trouble with a capital *V.*"

Lou giggled.

Evan glanced upwards. "Morning," he yelled, waving at the figure glowering over the edge of the dam.

Something rectangular and black fell from the top of the dam. Evan caught it and rolled his eyes at Lou. "Radio." He turned it on. "Morning, Varian. Can we help you?"

"What are you doing?"

"Checking the dam. Care to join me?"

"The explosives are set to go. It's not safe."

"I've notified the environment agency about the potential threat to life this dam currently holds. I'm diving the dam in an official capacity as head of Xenon. There will be no more blasting until they, or I, deem it safe to do so. In any event, the police will not give you permission to destroy any more of this crime scene."

Varian's scowl was evident from here. "Lou, I told you the dig was off. There's no reason for you to be diving again."

She snatched the radio from Evan and hit the button. "That's why you're sending Monty up here, right? To take over, hide things. The way you're so good at doing. And you need to check your e-mail once in a while."

"You dive off that boat, and you're fired."

Lou tugged up the hood of her wetsuit. "Sorry, I can't hear you." She seized her helmet and fitted it securely. Then she unstrapped her leg and rolled backwards off the side of the boat.

Evan laughed.

"Tell her she's fired," Varian yelled.

"Actually, she's on Xenon's time this morning, not yours. You need to check your e-mail from last night. You can't fire someone who's already resigned. Don't wait up. We may be some time." He dropped the radio into the bottom of the boat and waved at the figure leaning over the dam. He fitted

236

his helmet and eased back over the side of the boat. He turned on his helmet light and hit the mic. "Radio check."

"Right behind you." Lou swam over to him, the concrete wall of the dam looming through the dark water behind her. "I like being able to talk to the person I'm diving with. Varian would never buy these."

He grinned. "Perks of being the boss. I choose the equipment. By the way, Varian says you're fired. And please don't make any dam jokes."

"Really? Because I've got several I could come up with."

Evan shook his head. "Anyway, I told him you're working for me this morning. We're diving the dam in an official capacity as part of the Xenon contract." He began to swim downwards.

Lou followed him. "I am, am I?"

"Will that be a problem?"

"So long as your orders are sensible ones, nope." She tapped him on the shoulder. "That crack isn't good, is it?"

Evan grimaced, his fears confirmed. His headlight illuminated the walls of the dam. Even given the lower lake level, he still wasn't happy. The slight hairline fracture on the outside walls, combined with the pressure, could escalate quickly into a full scale collapse. He was ready to recommend draining the lake completely, but a controlled release of that much water would take weeks. They didn't have weeks.

Lou swam back and forth, taking photographs every foot or so, while Evan carried out a detailed check of the walls. She made her way over to him. Even with the mask on, concern etched his handsome face and chiselled jaw.

"What do you think, Evan?"

"I don't like it. We can't swim the rest of the village yet. I need to get this information top side, and call my team in." He headed upwards, breaking the water. He glanced around, treading water. Lou was nowhere to be seen. "OK, where are you?" he asked.

Her voice came over the comm. "Evan, get down here. You need to see this."

He headed back down, following her light to find her. "What — ?" The word died in his throat as horror struck him with the force of a mallet.

The light illuminated a decided crack on the dam wall.

27

Evan strode past Varian, ignoring him, and into the office. "Jasper, a word."

Varian followed him. "What's going on?"

"This doesn't concern you," Evan didn't bother to hide his irritation with the man. "I don't care if you own the hydroelectric company and think you have a right to poke your nose into dam business. But this is my dam, my land, and I'll thank you to leave my office now."

"And if I don't."

"I'll call the police and have you escorted off. I don't have time to deal with you at this precise moment."

Someone knocked on the door.

Evan groaned. "Come in."

Two uniformed officers entered. "We're looking for Mr. Sparrow."

Timing, Evan decided, was everything. He pointed. "Right there. Please take him. He's trespassing on private property." He turned his back and stared at Jasper. "We have a serious problem here."

"How can I help you officers?" Varian asked.

"Your office said we'd find you here. We need to ask you some questions down at the station about Bart Manchester, the bombing of the power station, and the death of AJ Wilcox."

"Are you arresting me?" Varian raised an eyebrow, and Evan envied his ability to remain so calm.

"Not yet. If you could come with us."

Varian glared at Evan. "This isn't over."

Evan shook his head. "Don't threaten me in front of the police, Varian. That's not clever or wise under the circumstances." He waited until Varian left with the officers then turned to Jasper. "You need to see this." He showed him the photos on the camera and pointed to the blueprints.

Jasper shuddered. "It's worse than we thought."

"I'm going to wait here for the panel inspectors. Make sure they're the ones the Environment Agency are sending. We need to continue the run off and see if we can increase it."

"Do you want an alert put out?"

"I don't want to start a panic." Evan

tapped his fingers on the desk. "We issue a red, people will assume the dam will fail. It could simply be a surface crack caused by the blast or normal stress. Get someone down to the control room to monitor the pumps and gauges. I'll get a team from Xenon up to go over the dam completely."

"Sure. So, the warning?"

"Yellow. That's normal with a run off anyway. I'll draft a press release in a bit."

Jasper moved to the window. "What is Dr. Fitzgerald doing out there?"

Evan glanced up in time to see the boat tied to the remains of the steeple and Lou vanish over the side. "For Pete's sake! I'm taking your boat. She can't dive alone. There's too much debris out there. The inspectors are Cliff Barnes and Pat Stewart. Due around three. Don't let anyone else near the dam unless it's the team from Xenon."

He ran from the office, calling on his mobile. "Ralph, it's Evan. I need the whole shooting match up at Dark Lake ASAP."

"Big problems, boss? You did say . . ."

"Yes. We could be looking at a total dam failure. How soon can you get the whole team up here?"

"We can be ready to leave as soon as everyone gets into the base — twenty minutes or so. After your phone call last night, I put them all on standby."

He reached the boat. "That's great. I'll send the jet for you. I need you all here no later than two o'clock." He jumped into the boat and started the engine. "Be ready." He ended the call and dialled Ira. "It's me. Send the jet to London to pick up the team from Xenon. I need them at the dam by two. I also need a press release. There are three in a file marked alerts on the computer in my study at the manor — red, amber and yellow. Make sure you change the dates for today."

He guided the boat to the church spire. "Before you ask, we have huge problems at the dam. For now issue a standard yellow alert, stating the run off is due to damage from the explosion at the power plant. Let me see it before it goes out. The amber and red are just in case. I also need you to contact Judge Derbyshire and get an injunction against Varian to prevent any further blasting here. The cops took him in, but knowing the scoundrel he'll be out before long. I got to go."

Evan tied the boat next to Lou's. Fitting his helmet and tank, he dropped his phone into the boat and dived. "Lou, you'd better answer me, right now. You are not the only one who has rules about diving alone. And right now you're breaking an unbreakable one."

"I'm fine, Evan."

Light came from inside the church. He swam inside and found Lou by the crypt door. He grabbed her arm. "What are you doing? We have to go up. Now."

"No way. I have to finish here."

"Humour me. I need to talk to you. Preferably not over the radio."

"Fine." She kicked for the surface and broke the water, glaring at him. She yanked off her helmet. She tossed it inside the boat and pulled herself in after it. "OK. The helmet is off. What's so important you drag me back up here?"

Evan heaved himself inside the boat and sat as close as he could get. "What are you playing at?"

"Diving while I still can. I want to check the crypt before it gets blown up, too." The radio in the bottom of the boat crackled. Lou grabbed it. "What now?"

"There's a Monty Sparrow here for you, Dr. Fitzgerald. He says you're expecting him."

Lou muttered something under her breath in what sounded like a foreign language. "Tell him to wait in his car. I'll be a while yet. No, better idea, tell him to go home. He's not needed here. This dive is over."

"I can't do that, Lou." Monty had obviously taken over the radio as his voice came over the airwaves. "Dad sent me to help."

"Your father was the person who shut this dive down. And I no longer work for your father. So, no, I don't need your help. Besides aren't you busy in Llaremont?"

"Not since you stole all the files and wiped the computers."

"That wasn't me," she snapped. "But I don't intend to debate this with you. I am not being pushed around anymore. As I just said, your father stopped this dig last night and this whole area is a crime scene following AJ's murder. If you don't believe me, ask him yourself."

"I would if I could find him. And if the dig is over, what are you doing out there?"

Evan held out a hand. "May I?"

She tossed him the radio. "Be my guest."

Evan grinned. "Mr. Sparrow, my name is Evan Close. I own all the land around here along the dam and lake. As of this morning, Dr. Fitzgerald is working for me." He ignored the expression of sheer amazement on Lou's face. "We need to check out the structural integrity of the dam and surrounding lake bed following the explosions."

"What explosions?"

"The ones your father set, when he blew up the power station and the remains of Abernay. I suggest you call him a lawyer and go to the local police station to find him. Out." He turned off the radio and smirked. "That was fun."

"Are you serious?" Lou still had that I-can't-believe-what-I'm-hearing look on her face.

"About what? It being fun baiting Monty or Varian being down at the local cop shop, because, yes, I meant them both."

"No, me working for you."

He nodded. "You want to dive and find answers. So do I. You also need a job as Varian fired you. Therefore, I'll give you thirty quid an hour until we finish unearthing all the secrets Dark Lake has to offer."

"Thank you, but there's no need . . ." Her face changed. "Wait a sec. Did you say thirty quid an hour?"

"Isn't that enough?" He checked the gauges on her tank and his. "I can go to forty, but don't tell the other lads that when they arrive."

"Thirty is more than enough, thank you. It's double what Varian was paying me."

"Then what's the problem?"

"No problem." She smiled.

Evan grinned and put his helmet on. "Then Dr. Fitzgerald, I suggest we dive."

"Wasn't there something you wanted to discuss? Not over the radio."

He held her gaze. "I wanted to remind you of my unbreakable rule. No diving alone. And since you're working for me, I expect you to keep it. At all times. Or there will be consequences."

Lou smirked and fired off a mock salute. "Yes, sir, Mr. Close, sir. When did you want to go to that cave you mentioned?"

"My priority right now is this dam. So maybe tomorrow." He nodded and dived below the surface of the water, trusting her to follow him.

As much as she hated it, Lou had to admit Varian was right about the church. The tilt of the spire was becoming more pronounced every time she saw it. And as she laid a hand on the stone walls, she was aware of a vibration that hadn't been there before. She glanced over at Evan.

His face was downcast as he surveyed the piles of rubble. "Should have come earlier. I would have liked to have seen the house before it was destroyed."

"You weren't to know," she said.

He swam over to where something glinted

in the light from their helmet. He picked it up, wiping his glove over the metal surface. "It's a plaque from my great grandfather's house," he said.

"The crypt is this way." She didn't get an answer. "Evan." Still no answer, so she swam over and touched his arm. "Hey, are you all right?"

"Yeah." He held out the plaque. "Can we take this?"

"Sure. Tie it to the descent rope, and we'll get it on the way back." She watched as he did so. "This way." She led the way over to the door to the crypt. "That's strange."

"What's that?"

"I left this door open."

He glanced from the door to her and back again. "It's closed now. What could have caused that?"

"I don't know." She pushed against it, but to no avail. "It won't budge."

"Allow me." Evan shouldered the door and opened it enough for them to squeeze through.

"The box was over here." Lou swam to show him. She began to search on the ground for a key or anything else that might prove valuable.

She touched the wall. The vibrations had increased. A wave of apprehension swept over her. "Evan, we need to get out of here. Right now."

"Why?"

She captured his hand and placed it on the wall. "That's why."

He frowned, worry tingeing his gaze. "OK." He headed to the door.

A huge disturbance in the water knocked Lou off balance as she followed him. Debris cascaded slowly around her, twisting her around. "Whoa!"

"Lou?" Evan asked.

"I don't —" Something hit her, forcing her to the ground. More debris fell, blocking her view of Evan. She raised her hands to protect her face and head as the falling rocks buried her.

28

Lou opened her eyes. *Am I dead?* She tried taking a deep breath and closed her eyes.

Nope, not dead. It hurts too much to be dead.

Panic began to frazzle around the edges. It was dark, pitch black and she couldn't move. Soft movement around her meant she was trapped under water. She reached up with her free hand and flicked the helmet light on. Blinding light filled the small space. An eye gazed at her, then swam away. She screamed.

A voice in her ear cut through the scream. "Lou, are you all right?"

"E— Evan?"

"Yes, I'm here. Are you hurt?"

"I can't see you. I'm trapped."

"Just keep still for me. I'll get to you."

She tried sucking in a deep breath, but there wasn't much air. "What happened?"

"I'm guessing the spire collapsed." His

calm voice resonated through the helmet speakers. "Where are you? Flash your light for me so I can pinpoint your location."

Lou switched the light on and off a few times.

"Got you. There's lots of debris in the way. I need you to hang on."

"W— what to?"

"Your sanity," he shot back as he grunted.

"That went years ago."

"Oh, well, worth asking. Can you see my light?"

"No. Too much debris." She struggled, trying to free herself. She couldn't stay here. It wasn't safe. Why on earth had she agreed to such a stupid assignment in the first place? Her life wasn't worth thirty quid an hour. Nothing was. "Please, you have to get me out . . ."

"Don't move. I can see your light moving. I need you to keep still so nothing else shifts and traps you further." There was a pause and several grunts. "It's no good, Lou. I need to go and get help."

She twisted her head to the left, crying out in pain. "No, I can see your light."

"Good. I'll be a few minutes, but I'll be back."

"Don't leave me." Lou's stomach clenched. She didn't want to be alone.

"I can't lift this without help. I'll be right back. I promise."

His light vanished.

The darkness pressed in on her, and she struggled, desperate to free herself. Something brushed against her trapped arm and she screamed. Struggling harder, she hit something, bringing a pile of debris crashing around her. Something hit her helmet and the light went out.

Evan surfaced and removed off his helmet. He leaned over the side of the boat and grabbed the radio. "Jasper, is my team here yet?"

"Nope, but they're on their way. Ralph called from the airport, said they'd be here by one or thereabouts. You should look behind you. Where's Dr. Fitzgerald?"

Evan turned and gasped at the sight of the spire. Most of it was gone. "She's under that lot. How's the dam?"

"Holding for now."

As he watched the remaining piece of the spire fell, sending shockwaves through the lake. A scream echoed through his helmet, cut off before it reached its peak. "I need help down here. Lou is trapped in the crypt." He threw the radio down and seized his phone, dialling 9-9-9. He explained

251

quickly to the operator that he needed the underwater search and rescue team — a combination of both police and fire brigade divers. He quickly gave all the details he could, including telling them to use the boat as a marker.

Then he hung up and reattached his helmet. "Lou, can you hear me?" Not getting an answer, he immediately dived under the water. The murk prevented him from seeing clearly. The entrance he'd left by was completely blocked. He began to lift the stones, grunting with effort. It was slow, laborious work, and he began to despair that he'd not reach her in time.

He knew how afraid she must be. Trying over and over to communicate with her, he could only conclude her radio had gone down. The other possibility was one he'd rather not let cross his mind. That she was pinned down hurt, unconscious, or worse.

Shadowy figures appeared beside him. Help had arrived. But instead of relief his anxiety increased.

One of the officers held up a board which read *channel three if you have comms, but you need to surface.*

Evan shook his head, flipping his radio over to channel three. "I'm not leaving her down here. She's in the crypt. To get to that you have to move this lot. You'll never find her without me. She's on channel two."

He flipped his radio back. "Lou, answer me. Please, let me know you're OK."

"Ev-an?" Her voice was faint and saturated with pain and fear.

Relief engulfed him. "See, told you I'd come back. I have the underwater search and rescue service here. We're working on getting you out."

"Hurry . . . my ear is beeping."

He frowned. "Beeping? What does your tank say?"

"Can't see it. So tired."

Evan shifted a rock and slid through a gap, several divers following him. "Don't you go to sleep. Keep taking to me."

"Sorry . . ."

"Lou." There was no answer. "Come on, sweetheart, talk to me."

"Don't call me that unless you mean it," came the breathless response.

"Then talk to me." He swam over to where he'd left her. "She's under that lot. Where's your light, Lou?"

"Broke."

"OK. We're almost there now." He watched helpless as the divers began shifting the debris. As much as he wanted to help, he'd only hinder. "Where are you trapped, Lou? Arm, leg?"

"Chest and arm. I can't breathe . . . no air."

"The tank is probably damaged." Evan noted the change in her voice. The higher pitch and hysterical tone indicated how scared she was.

She cried out. "There's something in here with me."

"We need you to calm down, Lou."

"Get away!" she screamed. "Noooooo."

"Lou?" Evan could see her now.

She screamed again, moving frantically. "Sh . . . hark . . ."

Fear speared him. She was hallucinating. That wasn't a good sign. "Lou, we're nearly there. I can see you. There's nothing in there with you."

"There is."

"There isn't. I promise. Keep still, honey, another minute and we'll be there." Something golden glinted in the light from his helmet. He reached and scooped up a key. He shoved it into his belt.

Lou stopped thrashing and her head slumped.

"Lou, wake up." Evan pushed his way past the diver and into the small gap. Somehow he managed to shove a piece of debris out of the way, enabling them to reach her. He clutched her hand. "Lou? Wake up."

Her eyes fluttered.

"We're here. We'll have you out in a few more minutes." He checked her tank. "She'll need a new one, unless you can get her out of here in three minutes."

The divers began working on shifting the huge slab lying on top of Lou. Evan squeezed her hand. "Just hold on."

"Tell Jim . . . he was right . . ."

"Jim's your best mate, right?"

"Yeah." Her eyes slid shut.

He shook her hard. "Don't you give up on me, you hear?"

The lead diver tapped him on the shoulder. "We need you to surface, sir."

"I'm not leaving her."

"I have to insist. We'll be right behind you with her. This building is coming down."

He squeezed her shoulder. "See you top side." Reluctantly, he circled and swam out of the crypt. Vibrations and water movement increased around him as he headed to the surface. Stones fell to the bedrock, sending clouds of sand into the water as the structure collapsed around him.

29

Evan sat in the hospital ED waiting room. His hands clenched and unclenched in his lap. It had been hours, and all he'd done was wait. Waited on the surface for the rescue divers to surface with Lou's battered and apparently lifeless body. Waited while they worked on her. Waited for the air ambulance when they deemed she was too time critical to be transported by road.

He'd tried praying; something he hadn't done in years. He wasn't entirely sure that his mumbled, 'don't let her die' even counted as praying. He knew enough not to bargain with God. That simply didn't work. He'd tried it when his sister got hit by a car on her way home from school when he was sixteen. He'd told God that if Rosie lived, he'd be a good boy and do everything he was told. When Rosie died, he assumed God wasn't listening and stopped praying and going to church.

Evan glanced at his watch and shook his wrist. Maybe the battery had died, but the clock on the wall said the same time. His phone vibrated in his pocket and he tugged it out. "Hello."

"Boss, it's me. You were right. We got a problem." Ralph didn't bother with the niceties.

Evan's stomach clenched even tighter. "How bad?"

"Urgent repairs. The lake needs to be drained completely. And quickly."

"Just do whatever you need. Call anyone you need and tell them you're acting on my authority. And raise the alert level to amber."

"Will do. Is there any news on your friend yet?"

"No." Evan's eyes flicked up as two people came into the room, a nurse and a tall grey-haired gentleman. "I have to go. I'll be there as soon as I can. Keep in touch."

The nurse pointed to a chair. "Have a seat. The doctor will be here as soon as he can."

The man shook his head as the nurse left. "I don't want to sit," he said, his clipped American accent resonating in the small space. "Why won't they tell me how she is?"

"I know how that goes," Evan said. "I've

been waiting hours. Or so it seems."

The American slumped into the chair next to him. "Relative?"

"Friend. She was injured during a dive at the dam." He paused as the American's eyes narrowed. "What?" Evan asked.

"Are you Evan Close?"

Evan swallowed. "Yes, but how did you know?"

The American held out a hand. "Jack Fitzgerald. Lou's stepfather. She's mentioned you on the phone."

Evan shook his hand. "She's mentioned you as well, sir."

"Just Jack. I get called 'sir' enough at work. What happened out there?"

"We were diving the dam and ruins when the church collapsed."

"She knows better than to go into unsafe structures." Jack frowned.

"We didn't know it would collapse. I wouldn't have let her go in if I'd thought there was any danger. She's done it many times in the past week with no problems." He paused. "Well, kind of."

"I know about AJ. That's why I'm here, to reassure her mom that Lou's fine. Only she isn't, is she?"

Evan sucked in a deep breath. This was so not the first conversation with Lou's father that he'd wanted to have.

The door opened and a man in burgundy scrubs stood there. "Lou Fitzgerald?"

Both men stood. Then Evan stepped aside. Jack was her next of kin. Not him.

"I'm her stepfather," Jack said. "How is she?"

"She'll be all right. She has a nasty bump to the head, lots of cuts and bruises. She'll need to stay in overnight until we're sure there are no after effects from the concussion. We'll move her up to a ward as soon as a bed becomes available. She was lucky." He paused. "Although she insists she doesn't do luck."

Jack smiled. "That sounds like her. Can we see her?"

"Sure. But one at a time for now."

Evan glanced at Jack. "I need to get back to the dam."

Jack frowned. "Don't you want to see her?"

Evan was torn. He did desperately want to see her, but she had family here now. "I'll say hi on my way out." They followed the doctor down the hallway to a cubicle.

"I'll go in when you come out," Jack said.

Evan nodded and slid behind the curtain. "Lou?"

The all too pale and bruised figure blinked

a couple of times and tilted her head. "Yup. Still Lou."

"I'm glad about that." He stood beside the bed, feeling awkward. "I can't stop long; I need to get to the dam. But I wanted to see how you were first."

She shrugged. "They say I have a bump on the head, a few bruises. What happened?"

"Don't you remember?"

Lou shook her head. "We were diving and then I was here. I don't remember anything that happened in between."

He perched on the edge of the bed. "OK. The church spire collapsed, trapping you inside the crypt. I called the underwater search and rescue blokes and they got you out. I brought your leg and clothes with me in the car." He paused. "Your leg is by your locker, and I guess your clothes are inside. So when you need to get up, you can. Let me know when they let you out, and I'll either come and get you or I'll send the car." He stood to leave.

"Thanks." She caught his hand, stopping him. "What's wrong? Why have you suddenly gone all formal on me? Don't I get a good-bye kiss?"

"Your stepfather's here."

"Really?"

"He's right outside the curtain. They'd only let one of us in at a time."

Lou looked past him, saw Jack through the gap in the curtain, and waved. Then she glanced back at Evan. "So you're ashamed to be seen with me now."

He shook his head. "Far from it. It's just . . . I said I was your friend, and if I kiss you now, then the cat is out of the proverbial bag."

Her face fell. " 'K."

"Is that a 'K or a 'K dot?" he asked. He had enough people in the office who texted each other to know the difference between the two. K meant fine. K dot meant whatever.

She shrugged and pushed back into the pillows.

Evan's throat burned. He'd upset her. He grasped her hand and gently kissed it. "I'll be back later."

30

Loss sliced through Lou like a knife through butter as each step took Evan further away from her.

Jack came in, tugged the curtain around the bed and enveloped her in one of his bear hugs. She felt safe and loved. His chest rumbled as he spoke over her head. "Not the kind of welcome I was anticipating, kiddo."

"I'm fine, honestly." She leaned back on the pillows and held his gaze. How old would she have to be before he stopped calling her kiddo? " 'Tis a bit familiar, however. Me in a hospital bed, you visiting with that concerned look in your eyes. I half expect Jim or Staci to jump around the curtain in a minute or Mum to appear in tears."

Jack sat on the bed beside her. "I thought you said you were fine. And this certainly wasn't what I was expecting to find when I got off the plane earlier today and powered up my phone."

"Does Mum know?"

"She does. And I promised her proof of how you were. She'll be driving to ballet or something now, so I'll send a video message." He pulled out his phone. "Can I use this in here?"

Lou leaned back on the pillows. "Other people have been. I think it's only in ITU and resus where they have all the monitors that they don't like it."

Jack activated the camera. "Hi, Nicky. I'm with Lou now." He swivelled the phone to face her. "Tell your mom how you are. She won't take it from me."

Lou waved at the screen. "I'm fine, Mum, honestly. They won't let me out until they're convinced my head is all right, so I'll be home in ten years or so."

Jack groaned and turned the phone back towards him. "See, hon, nothing changes. Call you later. Love you." He sent the message and slid the phone back into his pocket. He sat on the chair beside the bed. "So, tell me about Evan Close."

"He's a friend."

"And I'm an orang-utan's uncle."

Lou poked her tongue out. "I'm not an orang-utan, Uncle Jack." She repressed a grin as she got the reaction she loved.

Jack raised his eyes heavenwards. "I've told you I don't know how many times, kiddo. Enough —"

"— of the uncle," she chorused.

He laughed. "I don't think there's much wrong with your head. So, do I need to track down Mr. Close and ask him what his intentions are towards my daughter?"

"Not yet." She sighed. "Things got intense for a while, but he's backed right off. We're friends, but it didn't start out that way."

Jack leaned back in the chair. "Really? Do tell."

"Yes, but I can't talk about it here. Everything got all mixed up with the case I'm working or was working, and it's complicated. More than complicated." She rubbed her temples and bit her lip. "I was meant to be on that boat yesterday, not AJ. Add that to the fact that someone tried to kill me on my first night here."

Jack's face changed, flames smouldering in his eyes. "Back up, young lady. You've been here less than a week, and you've almost been killed three times? What kind of a town is this?"

"Really, Dark Lake is a village." Lou sighed, knowing what he would say. "And yeah, three times. I know who it was, well, the first time anyway, and the cops are handling it."

A voice drifted from the other side of the curtains. "I'm sorry, sir, you can't go in there. Dr. Fitzgerald is only allowed one visitor at a time."

"I'm her boss." Varian spoke over her. "I just want to make sure she's all right."

"Is that him?" Jack asked. "The jerk of a boss who has been undermining you all these years?"

Lou nodded. "Yes. Only he's not my boss anymore. I quit last night, about eight hours before he fired me, and he knows it."

She reached for him as Jack leapt to his feet. "Dad, please don't make a scene."

He pivoted and held up a hand. "I'll not make anything, kiddo. I'm assuming you don't want to see him."

Lou shook her head.

"Then let me deal with him." He stepped to the curtain, tugging it aside a little. "You must be Varian Sparrow."

"I am." Another hand reached around and the curtain was yanked back completely. Varian snarled, running a dismissive gaze over Jack. "Who are you?"

"Lou's father. She doesn't want to see you."

"I'm her boss. I have every right to see her."

Lou shook her head. "No, you're not my boss. I quit last night, or have you forgotten that?"

"There you go, then," Jack defended. "You have no reason to be here."

"She was hurt on my dive," Varian said.

Lou sighed. "How many times? I was working for Evan today. He told you that himself."

Varian shoved Jack out of the way and strode two steps towards the bed.

Jack moved fast, grabbing Varian's arm, twisting it behind him and shoving him against the wall. "The lady asked you to leave," he hissed. "I suggest you do so, or I'll call the cops myself."

Varian glared at Lou. "This isn't over. You'll pay for this."

"Is that a threat?" she asked.

"Too right it is."

Running footsteps crossed the ward and two cops in uniform appeared by the curtain. "Is there a problem here?"

"This man threatened my daughter," Jack said. "I want him arrested."

"Again, Mr. Sparrow?" one of them asked, tugging Varian's hands behind his back. "Varian Sparrow, I'm arresting you for . . ."

Lou tuned them out and looked at Jack. "Thanks."

He ruffled her hair. "Any time, kiddo."

She twisted her head away, smiling. "I'm not sixteen anymore."

"Just as well. I know what you did when you were sixteen. Let me go have a word with the cops, and I'll be back." He headed across the ward after them.

Lou grabbed her phone from beside the bed and dialled quickly.

The call answered on the fourth ring. "Evan Close."

"Hi, it's me."

"Hey, Lou. How you doing?"

"Varian was here. He made a scene, threatened me. The cops took him away." She paused. "I'm discharging myself. I'm not safe here."

"No, you're not." Banging and thudding echoed down the line. "You have a head injury. You stay in hospital for twenty-four hours observation. No debate."

"Are you saying this as my friend or as my boss?" She wouldn't add boyfriend to the list. That hope seemed to have dissipated with Jack's arrival. Or maybe it was the stress of the situation that had thrown them together and made a mountain out of the proverbial molehill and something out of nothing.

"Both. I care too much to let anything

happen to you. Leave it with me. Tell your stepfather he can stay at the manor while he's here."

Jack came back in and sat beside the bed.

"Evan says you can stay at his place rather than a hotel, Dad."

"Thank him for me. My flight back is Tuesday. I need to rent a car from somewhere."

"I heard that." Evan's voice echoed in her ear. "Tell him that Ira will collect him when he wants. Send me a text me from your phone. I have to go. Be good, and I'll see you later."

Lou hung up. "He said to text him from my phone when you want to leave. His bodyguard, Mr. Miles, will come and pick you up."

"He has a bodyguard?"

"Well, more like a jack-of-all-trades, you know. Mr. Miles is a mixture of bodyguard, manservant, secretary, personal assistant, whatever. He's also an excellent shot. Not to mention a good bloke to have around in a crisis. You'd like him."

The nurse came over. "We're moving you up to a ward now."

"OK."

Jack raised an eyebrow. "Really? You're not arguing?"

"Evan said I had to stay in for twenty-four hours. So I'm staying."

Obviously flabbergasted, Jack shook his head. "I'm sorry. Say that again?"

Lou didn't remember the last time he'd been at a loss for words and tried not to smirk. "I said, Evan told me to stay so I'm staying."

Jack let out a long, low whistle as the porters began to move the bed. "Now I know I need to have a long conversation with this Evan of yours."

31

It was almost eight in the evening before Evan got back home. He'd left his team from Xenon at the dam. They'd be working around the clock in shifts to oversee the run off and start repair work. His phone would stay on all night, and he could drive to the dam whenever they needed him.

Ira met him in the hallway. "General Fitzgerald is in the lounge. I've put his bags in the room next to his daughter. I've also arranged for an armed guard outside her ward at the hospital."

"Thank you." Evan paused. "Ward? I thought I asked for a private room."

"Four beds, only two of which are occupied, including hers. The west wing here is secure. Did you want a guard posted there as well?"

Evan shook his head. "There's no need. The staff knows to keep away from there."

Ira nodded. "And Dr. Carter said he'll be

back this evening to check on Lilly."

Evan hung up his coat, really hoping the vet would bring good news this time. The dog had been struggling to stand since being caught in a trap a few days ago. "OK. Let me know when he arrives."

"Of course, sir. Mrs. Jefferson kept a plate of dinner for you and General Fitzgerald in the kitchen. She said to ring for her when you're ready to eat."

"Thank you. I'll get it in a few, no need to bother her further. Likewise with you. We'll be fine. If I'm needed over at the dam tonight, I'll drive myself." He headed to the lounge and glanced over to where Jack sat behind the paper. "Evening."

Jack stood. "Evening."

Evan smiled, unsure why he was so nervous all of a sudden. This was awkward, although it shouldn't have been. A kind of meet-the-parents, but without a proper dating history and without his significant other by his side to help him out. "Have you eaten?"

Jack shook his head. "I ate on the plane, but that was several hours ago."

"Then we should do that. My housekeeper left dinner for both of us in the kitchen."

"Do you have many servants?" Jack followed him into the hallway.

Evan shook his head. "No. Mrs Jefferson is the housekeeper and cook. Ira oversees security. I have a gardener who comes over once a week or so. Living in London as I do, I don't have time to tend to the grounds here as much as I'd like. Even if I didn't, there's no need for a huge staff. I'm not adverse to a little dusting or hoovering."

"What do you do?"

"Civil engineering. Dams mostly, including the Thames Barrier and the one here at Dark Lake. What about yourself?"

"Paper pushing normally, but I was a pilot."

"I've always wanted to do that. I have my own jet but never found the time for lessons." He named the model and a few of the specs, grinning as Jack's eyes lit up. "I'll take you up in it before you leave."

"I'd like that. Thank you."

Evan pushed open the kitchen door and signalled his housekeeper. Somehow, he knew she wouldn't have listened to Ira and left. "Mrs Jefferson, go home. I can manage tonight. It's about time you had the evening off."

"It's no bother, sir —"

He cut her off. "I happen to know your daughter is leaving for university in the morning. Go home and be with her." He paused. He needed her safe and that meant nowhere near here. Same went for the rest of the staff. "Why don't you take the next few days off and spend time with her properly. Drive her down to Winchester and settle her in."

Mrs Jefferson's face was a picture of delight. "Thank you. I wanted to ask but didn't like to presume."

"It isn't presuming at all. Have a lovely few days and see you in a week." He winked. "So get outta my kitchen . . ."

Mrs Jefferson laughed. "Yes, sir. How's Dr. Fitzgerald doing?"

"As far as I know, she's OK. Jack?"

"She was almost asleep when I left her. But she's fine. She should be out of the hospital tomorrow."

"That's good. She's a nice girl." Mrs Jefferson undid her apron. "I'll be off then. The plates are in the warming oven. Good night."

" 'Night." Evan grabbed the oven gloves and tugged open the door to the warming oven. "You don't mind eating down here?" He set the plates onto the thick oak table. "Just saves carrying the stuff upstairs, only to bring it down again."

"Not at all."

He found cutlery and a couple of cans of

soda from the fridge. He held them up. "Or I have beer. I picked up the US habit of drinking it cold on a trip a few years ago. Something Lou and I discovered we have in common early on."

"Beer's fine."

Evan put the soda back and took out two bottles of beer. "Can you grab the bottle opener from the third drawer, please?" He took the bottles to the table and straddled the bench. "I used to love eating here when I was a kid. Much less informal than the stuffy dining room upstairs."

Jack nodded, sitting opposite him. "Do you mind if I say grace?"

Evan shook his head. He was surprised, but he wouldn't argue. "Sure."

Once Jack finished praying, he picked up his knife and fork. "Lou speaks very highly of you."

"Does she?" Evan swallowed. "Is this a 'what are your intentions towards my daughter' conversation?"

Jack held his gaze. "Does it need to be? I mean, Lou normally argues every single doctor's decision. She hates hospitals, yet here she is, staying in overnight because, and I quote, 'Evan told me to.' You obviously have some hold over my daughter that no one else has. Including her mother and I."

Evan cut his meat and chewed slowly, formulating the answer in his mind before voicing it. "I like her — a lot. More than like her. We've only known each other a few days, but, yeah."

"She's staying in your house rather than a hotel?"

"Under my protection. I'm not sure how much she's told you, but her hotel room got broken into her first night in the village. Someone tried to —" Evan broke off. "Let's just say I got there in time to save her from the demise he had planned for her."

"Say that again."

"The bloke had her pinned down with a knife to her throat. He was a convicted rapist. The cops have him now; I can assure you of that."

Jack glowered at him, his knife and fork hitting the sides of his plate with a clunk. "And you just happened to be passing her hotel room, although you have a perfectly good house here? And then invited her to stay at your place rather than finding her another room?"

Evan swallowed and backtracked fast. "She was going out alone in the fog to find somewhere to eat. I stopped her. We spoke for a while, then she went up to her room. I was standing outside, with Ira, my body-guard, and saw Lou in the window. She waved, I waved back. There was a man wearing a balaclava behind her. We ran upstairs and stopped the attack. She's safer here. I have CCTV everywhere."

His phone rang. "Excuse me. Evan Close."

"Evan, it's me." Ralph spoke quickly. "I've finished the checks on the dive gear you used earlier. I'm assuming it wasn't ours."

"The helmets were. The rest were what Dr. Fitzgerald said Varian Sparrow provided. The wetsuits were our own. Why?"

"The tanks had been tampered with. That's why she ran out of air. You both would have if you'd been trapped down there. And that's another thing . . ."

Evan interrupted him. "Wait a sec, let me put you on speaker." He eyed Jack. "You need to hear this." He hit the speaker button and put the phone on the table. "Say that again, Ralph."

"Both of the tanks had been tampered with. Had you been trapped when the spire fell into the church you'd have run out of air, right along with Dr. Fitzgerald."

"Are we talking a faulty valve here or what?"

"The regulator had been damaged yes, but

the tanks didn't contain only air. They contained the mixture of gases used for longer and deeper dives. I'm assuming she checked them?"

"I watched her do it. She wouldn't have dived if she'd known." Evan closed his eyes. "So they were deliberately mislabelled?"

"That's my bet, yes. Aside from the fact there's no way those regulators were certified for use."

Evan looked at Jack and took a deep breath. "OK. I want you to take photos of the gear. Send a copy of those, plus the report, to the police. Make sure it goes to Sergeant Drake and no one else. From now on, no one dives unless they are wearing our gear and you or I have checked it. How's the dam faring?"

"Not great. The overspill and run off isn't fast enough for my liking."

"How's the pressure on the gauges?"

"Still rising." The tension in Ralph's voice set Evan's teeth on edge. "Did you want to raise the alert status from amber to red?"

The short answer was yes he did. But that would cause a panic, and he didn't want that on his conscience. "Not yet. Call the emergency services and warn them of a possibility of a red. I'll be up there at first light. I'll make a decision then."

"Sure, boss. I'll call if anything changes overnight."

"Thanks." Evan hung up. "I had wondered about the tanks when her air ran out too soon. She mentioned that also happened the other day."

"She shouldn't be here," Jack said firmly. "That's three attempts on her life now — the hotel, the boat, the tanks. What is someone trying to hide? And who is it?"

"That is a long story and one Lou needs to hear. As I'd rather only tell it once, do you mind if it waits until morning? I have an armed guard keeping watch on Lou. She'll be perfectly safe tonight."

"That's fine." Jack stifled a yawn. "I'm calling it a night. It's been a really long day, not including the jetlag."

"Of course. I'll show you to your room. It's right next door to the one that Lou is using."

32

Lou watched the world go by from the hospital window. The sooner someone came and picked her up, the better she'd feel. If she'd had her purse with her, she'd have caught a taxi ages ago. At least Evan had the foresight to bring her leg in, so she wasn't stuck in a chair.

A bald man wearing a suit and overcoat came in and held out a warrant card. "Dr. Fitzgerald, I'm DCI Haniwell, Cumbrian CID."

"How can I help you?" she asked. Perhaps they were finally investigating the accidents and attempts on her life and wanted a more detailed statement.

"I wanted to talk to you about a theft. If you could accompany me down to the station, please. I have a car waiting outside."

Lou sat still, shock running through her. "Theft? Someone's accusing me of theft? Do I need a lawyer?"

"Not yet."

"I haven't been discharged yet," she said. "I can't go anywhere." She glanced up as two men entered the ward. "Dad, Evan, this is DCI . . ."

Evan nodded curtly. "Peter and I know each other. About time you got here. This is the third attempt on her life in less than a week."

DCI Haniwell frowned. "I don't know anything about that. This is pertaining to the theft of documents and photographs from a dig site in Wales."

"And not in your jurisdiction." Evan's tone matched that of the police officer. "You know it and I know it. Can I have a word?"

Lou twisted the sheet in her hands as Evan and the police officer headed into the corridor. "I didn't take them. This is another ploy by Varian to discredit me. AJ brought the files up with him, but he's dead."

"Your notes, I assume."

Lou lowered her voice. "Varian is putting the kibosh on me again. If he can't kill me, then he'll ruin me another way." She broke off at the confusion on Jack's face. It wasn't often now she caught him out with an unfamiliar phrase. "Kibosh . . . wreck, destroy, wreak havoc, ruin," she explained. "It's always the same. I do all the work and

Monty comes in and gets all the glory. Well, I'm sick of it. You know the *zitahisji* is here, don't you? Varian dragged me off both digs and gave them to him. Or tried too."

"Mind your language," Jack interrupted.

She sighed, forgetting he'd picked up a little Agrihan from her over the years. The fact she'd only called him a weasel was beside the point. "Sorry. No, I most definitely am not sorry. I'm tired of being trodden on the whole time. That's why I already published the Llaremont findings. That's why I quit my job with Varian. Coming here was a mistake."

"All of it?"

"Yes, Dad, all of it."

Evan coughed from the end of the bed. "So, I'm a mistake, am I?"

Lou's cheeks heated as her gaze travelled up slowly. "Not you. You are the one blessing this place has. Can I leave now, or am I under arrest?" She glanced past Evan for the police officer, but he was nowhere in sight.

"I spoke to him, explained the situation. He's looking into the attempts on your life and will be by the house tomorrow for a statement." He paused. "I told him the only things you brought here with you from Llaremont were your personal belongings, clothes, and so on. That was right?"

She nodded slowly. "AJ brought the rest down with him. All of *my* files from *my* folder on the computer at the dig site."

"Don't worry about that now. The regulators on the tanks, and the tanks themselves had been tampered with."

She swallowed hard. "What? Varian provided those."

Evan nodded. "That's what I told the police. We need to get you out of here. I'll talk to you back at the house."

Lou slowly pushed off the bed.

"Do you need a hand?" Jack asked.

She shook her head. "I'm fine." She sucked in a deep breath. "Let's go. Sorry yesterday was a total waste of a dive."

"It wasn't. Evan stayed by her side as they began walking from the ward. "I found a key in the crypt. I haven't tried it yet as the box is still in your room."

"When we get back," she said. "I want to know what's in it."

"Me, too. However, I don't want you diving again."

Lou glared at him. "Excuse me?"

He held up a hand. "Don't take that tone of voice with me. Let me finish . . ."

"You are not my father. He is." She pointed at Jack. "And for your information,

I don't do what he tells me either."

Jack rolled his eyes as he held the main exit door open. "Will you shut up and let the man speak?"

She mimed zipping her mouth closed and tossing the key over her shoulder.

"Thank you." Jack grinned at Evan. "Miracles will never cease. She stopped speaking."

Evan shook his head. "I don't want you diving alone and in non-Xenon gear. That includes tanks, valves, regulators, the whole shebang. I want Frank to check your wetsuit."

"Good luck with that," she muttered. "It got cut off me. It was a bespoke one and cost a fortune. There is no way I can afford a replacement. Anyone would think you don't trust anyone."

"I don't, at least not with the important stuff that counts."

"Does that include me?" She caught her breath. Did she want to know the answer to that question? What if she didn't count as something that mattered?

"Of course that includes you, Lou." Evan's hand brushed against hers, the slight touch thrilling her very core.

If Jack hadn't been right there, she'd have grabbed hold of it. She glanced over at the car. Two men stood beside it and she stopped walking. One man she recognized, the other she didn't.

Evan tugged her sleeve gently. "You're OK. You know Ira. The other man is your bodyguard."

"My what? Why do I need a bodyguard?"

"Because I say so. Lou, this is Zach Roma, one of my security team. He'll be guarding you from now on."

Lou eyed up the stocky, tall, bald man, wearing the trademark black suit, white shirt and black tie. Maybe she'd design a new outfit for bodyguards, something a little more casual that didn't shout security. Something that would let the secret service blend in for once. She turned to Evan and pouted. "Why do I even need one?"

"There have been three, if not four, attempts on your life in as many days. Varian made a direct threat against you. I'm not losing you."

Lou glanced at Jack. "Daaaad, Evan's being mean to me. I don't need a watch dog or a bodyguard."

"Don't bother trying, kiddo. Evan and I discussed this over breakfast, and I'm in agreement with him. It's either this guy or I get a detachment from the local air base to protect you." He quirked an eyebrow. "Remember what happened the last time I did that? This time it would be ten heavily armed soldiers. Or one man. It's up to you."

"So I'm not getting a choice." She glanced at the bald security officer. "No offence, Mr. Roma."

"None taken, Dr. Fitzgerald."

Lou frowned. "That's a mouthful. How about you call me Dr. F., and I call you Mr. R.?"

"Sounds good to me." He paused. "Actually, why don't you call me Zach? Most people do. I'll stick to Dr. F. for you though."

"OK."

"And before you ask, yes, he dives." Evan told her. "Not that anyone is diving the lake today."

She crossed her arms. "How is it? The dam, that is."

"Not great. I just left it, having been there since first light."

"That makes breakfast rather early." She looked from Evan to Jack and back again.

Jack shrugged. "Jet lag."

"Ah." She climbed into the car as Evan held the door open. "Evan, are you raising the alert status?"

"It was escalated to amber last night. A low level evacuation order was issued at nine o'clock this morning. That's for care homes, schools, hospitals, and so on."

She frowned. "You're that worried the dam will fail?"

Evan didn't say anything. He didn't need to. The expression on his face alone gave away his answer.

33

Evan laid a clean white cloth over the table in the study and stood back as Lou set the box on top. He fingered the gold key in his pocket. Impatience tingled every nerve ending. It was like being a kid at Christmas, longing to open the presents and see what Father Christmas had brought him. He hoped desperately he wouldn't feel the keen sense of disappointment which usually followed when what he got was nothing he wanted or even needed.

Lou reached for the key, her gloved hands almost taunting him. "You don't need to be here for this, Evan."

The way she spoke his name thrilled him, even though she was potentially throwing him out of his own study and away from something that concerned him. "Yes, I do." He held the key out of reach and raised an eyebrow at her camera. "Is that really necessary?"

"Yes. I need to log every part of this. The chain of evidence, so to speak, has to be clear and undisputable." She switched on the camera and her tape recorder. "The box was found in the crypt of Abernay Parish Church by Lou Fitzgerald and AJ Wilcox." She rattled off both date and time. "Present now, are Lou Fitzgerald, Evan Close, and General Jack Fitzgerald of the United States Air Force."

She glanced up. "Lurking in the corner of the room are security personnel, Ira Miles and Zach Roma. The key was found in the crypt by Evan Close." She nicked the key from Evan and held it up to the camera. "As you can see it's a small, gold key, rusted from prolonged contact with the water."

She picked up a bottle and sprayed the key, wiping it carefully to remove the rust.

Evan stuck out his hand again. "May I open the box?"

She held his gaze and then nodded. "Sure. You'll need to put gloves on first." She waited until he'd complied before she gave up the key. "Try not to break it in the lock."

The gloves made things more difficult than he anticipated. Could the others hear his heart beating? The pounding was so loud in his ears, he could barely hear anything else in the room. Above him the clock ticked

288

and then chimed. Was it really only ten? They'd picked Lou up just after nine, and she'd wanted to do this as soon as they stepped over the manor's threshold.

Slowly, very slowly, Evan inserted the key into the lock. It fit like a glove.

Lou spoke into the camera, detailing everything he was doing.

He exhaled sharply. "I'd wondered if it wouldn't work after all that. That this was some random key lying on the crypt floor." His stomach tied in knots as he slowly turned the key. The Christmas morning feeling within him grew, and his heart leapt into his throat. With an audible click the lock opened. He tried lifting the lid, but it wouldn't budge. He tried both hands, but nothing.

"Let me."

"No." The word came out sharper than he wanted, so he inhaled and tried again. "No. I have some stuff to clean brass in the desk drawer. Let me try that first."

Lou hesitated before answering. "OK, but be careful."

He tugged off the gloves and binned them. Crossing the den to the desk took ten long seconds. He was aware of the clock ticking and everyone in the room watching him.

He needed to calm his nerves. The answers

he sought might be in that box, and they also might not be. He shouldn't get his hopes up. Whatever was in the box, he couldn't keep any of it. Not yet. Perhaps when all this was over, Lou would let him at least keep one item. Evan rummaged in the drawer and produced a spray can. He liberally applied it to the hinges of the box and then grabbed a cloth.

"Gloves," Lou said.

He scrunched up his nose. "I'm not touching the box," he snapped. He rubbed gently to remove some of the rust. "Now I'll put the wretched gloves back on."

Lou tossed him a clean pair.

He pulled them on and slowly attempted to lift the lid. This time it opened like a charm. He reached for the contents, amazed they seemed dry. Whatever the box was made of had done a great job at protecting its treasure.

Lou stayed his hands. "I need to document it *in situ,* first." She picked up her camera and began taking several photographs.

After what seemed like hours, but in reality was probably no more than a minute, if that, she glanced at him. "OK. Take the contents out one item at a time. I'll need photos of all angles before you lay them onto the clean cloth."

Evan sighed. "Do you open your presents like this, too? Peel the tape off a millimetre at a time, before you then fold and reuse the paper?"

"Yeah." She glanced at him sideways, her face straight as a dice. "Doesn't everyone?"

"No." Evan shook his head in despair. "Remind me never to use tape on anything I give you. String is faster."

Jack laughed as Lou pretended to sulk, crossing her arms in front of her, but being careful not to touch anything with the gloves.

"Come on then. Let's do this." Evan lifted a pen from the box, holding it so Lou could catalogue it. "It's engraved with Great-grandad's name."

"It's possibly what he wrote the diary with."

"It's amazing none of this is ruined." He placed the pen down and picked up a leather notebook. The craftsmanship on it was amazing. Fine tool work made it easily the best journal he'd ever come across, and far surpassed anything in his library. "May I?"

"Sure." Lou's camera clicked constantly.

Evan's excitement built as he opened the book. Was this the promised journal containing the answers? There was nothing on the first page.

He flicked through the remaining pages. Every single one was the same.

Blank.

Hollow disappointment replaced every other emotion in him. "It's empty." He put the book on the cloth. *Just like Christmas. Never lives up to your expectations.* He pulled out the rest of the contents. A few photos of the village, a few pictures of people, which he assumed were ancestors of his. There was a seal, a dried up ink pad, and sealing wax.

"Is that it?"

"Yeah." He picked up the box, twisting and turning it in his hands. His fingers ran over the inside and outside.

Lou frowned. "What are you looking for?"

"It's still heavy." He shook it and nodded when it rattled. "There's still something inside, but I can't find a way to get to it." His frustration got the better of him, and he slammed it down on the table.

"Hey!" Lou glared at him. "You'll break it. Let me."

Evan shoved it across the table at her. "Have at it."

"Sulking like a baby." She grinned.

"Am not." He picked up the notebook

again. "Why hide a blank notebook? Why even mention a hidden journal if there's nothing to hide?"

"Maybe he was afraid someone would do exactly what we've done. Dive down into the crypt and retrieve it." Lou pressed the box all over, pushing and sliding her fingers expertly. "Maybe whatever was there was removed years ago. The box simply replaced with the blank notebook in it."

Evan rubbed the pages in desperation, not really sure he expected words to appear. "Perhaps I wave a stick at it or . . ."

Lou shook her head. "No such things as magic wands. Not in the real world."

Click.

Evan dropped the book in the sunlight, the open pages face up. "What was that?"

"The bottom of the box opened. Here, hold it for me," Lou held it toward him.

Evan took the box, trying to turn it to face him.

"Will you wait a second, Mr. Impatient?" Lou grabbed the camera. She rapidly snapped several pictures. "OK." She reached into the space and pulled out the small file, crammed full of papers. She held it out to Evan. "Here."

He set the box down and eagerly made a grab for the file. He went through the papers and drawings one at a time, holding each one for Lou to photograph. "There's nothing pertaining to the village or dam." He laid the last one down on the table. "Just old family stuff."

"You're a strange one." Lou scribbled on her clipboard. "Most people would be jumping and leaping for joy at finding old family stuff. But you? You'd rather have blueprints or financial records that prove your theory."

"I'd rather have them disproved," he muttered. "I want answers. Can't you, of all people, understand that?"

"Maybe there aren't any." She glanced at the notebook and raised an eyebrow. "What did you do to it?"

"Nothing. Why?"

Lou grabbed it and rotated it to face him. "You said it was blank, the photos show it was blank. Look."

Faint words now covered the two open pages.

"What?" Astonishment ran through him. "I didn't do anything. Simply opened it in the sunlight."

Lou laid it down. "This is incredible. The ink is darkening as we watch." She began taking more photographs. Excitement rippled in her voice. "The ink must have been activated by sunlight, perhaps in the same way lemon juice ink is."

"I thought that was just in spy movies," Zach said.

"No, it's very real." Lou studied the book.

"Let me see." Evan reached for the book, ignoring the phone as it rang.

Ira picked up the handset. "Evan Close's phone."

Evan flipped through the book. "The rest of it is still blank."

"Give it time," Lou said. "Each page will have to be exposed separately and then photographed several times in case the ink fades again."

"Sir," Ira held the phone out to him. "You have to take this."

"I'm busy."

"It's the dam. You *need* to take this call."

Evan's stomach pitted, and he lifted the phone. "Close."

"You need to get down here, boss." Words tumbled rapidly from the normally unflappable Ralph. "Bring Dr. Fitzgerald. There's something you need to see." He paused and then swore. "However, I would suggest that you first turn on the BBC News. Then get here as fast as you can."

The line went dead.

Swallowing the rising bile, Evan strode to

the wide screen TV on the wall and switched it on. He flicked to channel 503.

"— and as you can see the remains of the villages of Abernay and Finlay are clearly visible," the reporters voice spoke over the images of the lake. "As is the huge crack in the side of the dam. So far there has been no comment from local landowner, Evan Close, although a team from his engineering company, Xenon, are working on the dam as I speak. An amber warning has been issued and a low level evacuation of the surrounding area is underway."

A dozen swear words filled Evan's mind, but he managed not to let them spill from his lips. "I'd better go."

"I'm coming with you," Lou said firmly. "I need to get all this on film for the records."

"Not alone," Jack told her. "I promised your mom I wouldn't let you out of my sight."

"I don't care who comes, but we need to go now." Evan stretched out a hand, his fingers pausing as the reporter spoke again.

"I'm joined now by archaeologist in charge of the dig here, Monty Sparrow, VC of the Sparrow Foundation. Mr. Sparrow, can you tell us what happened here?"

"It's quite simple. The explosions both at

the power plant and here were due to the negligence, and deliberate acts of sabotage, by my former colleague, Dr. Louisa Fitzgerald. Another colleague, AJ Wilcox died as a direct result of that negligence." He pointed behind him at the dam. "As you can see, the potential flooding of the valley and deaths of everyone downstream will also be a result of her actions."

Evan clicked off the TV and stared at Lou. He was tempted to offer to punch out Monty's lights but had the feeling her father would want first dibs on that one.

She jumped to her feet, hand over her mouth, no colour in her face whatsoever.

"Lou, we all know who was at fault here."

Her hand dropped to her side, and she swallowed hard. "Yeah. Me."

34

Lou didn't speak on the way to the dam. If she did, she'd throw up. Her stomach was in knots. Her eyes stung, and she wanted to run. Run so far away that no one would ever find her. Although she knew from bitter experience that running away didn't help, it only succeeded in making the situation so much worse; she didn't care. She didn't want to be here. Didn't want to face what she knew would greet her at the dam.

Varian had succeeded in his threat. He'd discredited her in a very vile, public way and ensured she'd never work as an archaeologist again. The phone in her pocket chirped. She ignored it and when the caller finally rang off, she chucked the handset under the seat in front of her.

Jack's phone rang. "Fitzgerald . . . Yeah, Jim, she's here." He held out the phone. "It's for you."

Lou shook her head, the lump in her

throat and ache in her heart growing. She didn't want Jim's sympathy. Just the sound of his voice would cause the flood of tears she was barely containing, to fall.

"Sorry, mate, she doesn't want to talk right now. Sure, I will." He tucked the phone away.

As they turned off the main road, she shifted her gaze to the window, staring out at the scenery. It was crazy. She'd called Jack Dad for years, but he'd always be Jack in every other way bar name. Closing her eyes, she could see him the day they'd first met in Cornwall and again on the beach on Agrihan where he'd saved her life.

Maybe he should have let her die.

Jack pinched her arm, and she glared at him. "I know that look, kiddo," he said in that tone she hated. The one that meant she was in for a lecture.

"Can't I even have one second of self-pity?"

"No. It isn't good for you."

She folded her arms tightly across her chest. "Fine, but it's my innermost thoughts, and right now the whole world thinks I'm a cold, calculating, murdering cow."

"That's not true," Evan said. "There's an Indian tribe on the African subcontinent that doesn't."

"An Indian in Africa?" she repeated. "They don't even have TV in some places."

"They read it on the Internet," he retorted quickly. "This tribe doesn't think you're a cow. They're convinced you're a cat. And don't laugh. You're not allowed to laugh because you're cross and sulking." He paused. "Don't smile either."

Lou tried to keep her face straight and failed. "Jim does that, and I hate it."

He nodded.

"Varian won." A low whistle escaped her lips. "My career is over just as he promised. I can kiss that university job good bye as well."

"The one that combines field and class work?" Jack asked.

"Yeah, that one. I spoke to him the other day, told him how interested I was. He said he'd get back to me and now there is no chance."

"Hey. You don't know that, kiddo." Jack rubbed her arm.

"Yeah, I do." Her phone rang. She toed it further under the seat in front of her. "That's probably him now."

"Answer it."

She shook her head. "No."

Evan leaned down and grabbed the phone.

"Dr. Fitzgerald's phone. Evan Close speaking." He paused. "I'm sorry; Dr. Fitzgerald isn't available right now. She's gone to ground because of the news coverage and subsequent defamation of her character, while she watches her career dissipation light blinking and going into overdrive."

"Give it here. You two are as bad as each other." Lou groaned and snatched the phone. "I'm here, please ignore him."

"Dr. Fitzgerald, it's Professor Cunningham at Cumbria University."

Lou covered the mouthpiece. "I hate you."

"Hate isn't a very nice word," Jack chided.

She wagged her head and spoke into the phone as the car pulled into the road leading to the dam. "I planned to call you this morning."

"Really? May I ask why?"

"I'm sure you've seen the news reports. I don't want to tarnish the reputation of either your department or the university. That's what would happen once the media found out I worked there."

"I've also read the article you had published in this month's *History Today*. I receive an advance copy, and your paper really is excellent work. Your theories panned out beautifully, and you backed up every single one with evidence of proof.

Answer me one question. Are the news reports true?"

"Of course not." She shifted on her seat, aware of the fact everyone was listening even if they pretended not to do so. "I didn't kill AJ. In fact there have been . . ."

She broke off. She was digging herself a bigger hole and needed to stop. "No, no, they're not."

"After the conversation with you the other day, I didn't think they would be. I was actually phoning to offer you the position, but if you'd rather not take it . . ."

"Hold on. You were?" She could scarcely believe her ears. Her heart pounded and a faint spark of hope began to burn. Perhaps it wasn't just Evan and Jack who believed in her.

"I still am. Take a couple of days to think it over. Let the media circus die down, and let me know by say, Thursday."

"OK, I'll call you back on Thursday. Thank you. Bye." She hung up and stared at the phone. "I don't believe it."

"What did he want?" Evan asked.

"He offered me the job." Even saying the words out loud didn't make them any more real.

Evan grinned. "See. Congratulations."

"He's given me until Thursday to think it over."

"You should take it," Jack said. "You just said you always wanted a job like that. Something that combines field work and teaching."

Lou shrugged. "There's a job to finish here." She inhaled sharply as the car swung into the car park overlooking the dam. "Good grief. Look at it!"

A huge crack ran the height of the dam. From this angle it appeared to be a couple of feet wide. Huge piles of rubble were visible on the lake floor. A slight vibration under the car coincided with chunks of concrete falling from the side of the dam, splashing into the water below.

"Evan, how long has it got?" Lou rubbed clammy hands against her legs.

Evan seemed as pale and shocked as she felt. "It's impossible to say. I need to get down there and check for myself. But looking at it, barring a miracle, it doesn't have more than two days at the most."

Jack nodded to the swarm of journalists and TV cameras standing at the side of the car park. "We have to get through that first."

"That's easy." Evan's lips thinned. "It's what I pay these blokes for. Ira, park as close as you can to the portacabin without going onto the dam itself." He pulled out his phone and dialled. "Ralph, it's me. Where are you?"

Lou couldn't tear her gaze away from the dam as the car edged closer, the sight both mesmerizing and terrifying.

"OK, give me a few minutes. We're pulling up in the car now."

Lou regarded the media swarm with trepidation, unable to keep from shuddering. "I don't want to go out there."

Evan put his phone away. "So don't. Stay in the car and hide. Or you go out there, face them, and tell them that this is a criminal investigation, which it is. Therefore you can't answer any of their questions."

She sucked in a deep breath. "OK."

Evan touched her hand. "Just stay between me and your dad. You'll be fine." He glanced towards the front of the car. "You blokes get to earn your keep for a change."

Both security men laughed. Then they got out of the car and moved swiftly around to open the door.

Lou stepped out of the car. The journalists circled, shoving mics and cameras in her face.

Ira and Zach stepped closer, as the others got out of the car.

"Dr. Fitzgerald, do you have anything to

say about the allegations Monty Sparrow made against you?" a reporter shouted.

"Are you responsible for the death of AJ Wilcox?"

Evan stood on one side of her, Jack on the other.

Inwardly quaking, Lou almost lost her balance as the ground beneath her feet moved, sending another torrent of small chunks sliding down the dam into the water. They didn't have time for this. *OK, here goes nothing.* "I'm not answering questions, but I do have a short statement."

Silence fell over the reporters.

"AJ was a friend. I am, in no way, responsible for his death. All the events of the past week here at the lake, including the four attempts on my own life, are the subject of an on-going police investigation. As I'm sure you're aware, that means that I can't discuss any of them with you. I have confidence in the ability of the police to find whoever is responsible and bring them to justice. I understand they have made an arrest and suggest you speak to them for any further details they may be able to provide. Now, if you'll excuse me, I have a job to do here."

Evan glanced at Ira. "OK, let's go."

Flanked by Evan and Jack, Lou let the security officers lead her through the journalists. She ignored their shouts. Varian wouldn't like that statement one bit, but she hadn't named him. Unlike him, she had some principles, and mudslinging to the media wasn't one of them. She glanced at Evan. "Now what?"

"Pray we can stop that dam from falling," he replied quietly. "But that will take a miracle."

Jack grimaced. "We'll be fine. I know Someone in the miracle business."

35

Evan gazed at the pressure gauges in the control room. Dismay and worry ramped up each and every one of his already taut nerves. The ominous figures on the clipboard in his left hand didn't help. He tapped the gauge in front of him, and groaned as the needle jumped up a notch. He scribbled the new numbers down, and then focused on the panel behind him.

The radio on his belt crackled. "Boss?"

He snatched it. "What is it, Ralph?"

"We're getting intermittent vibrations up here."

Evan frowned. "I don't feel anything down here." He rested a hand on the wall in front of him. "No, nothing."

The radio went dead. Shrugging, he put it back on his belt and carried on checking the gauges. Clanging came from the metal staircase in the corridor. "What? Don't you believe me?" he called.

There was no answer, despite the fact he could hear footsteps.

Evan moved swiftly to the door and flung it open. There was no one there, instead a thick, yellow fog consumed the tunnel.

He raised his radio. "Ralph, are you there?" Static hissed. "Ralph?"

The sound of a muffled conversation drifted around him, carried in by the fog. He strained to listen. He could just make out two, maybe three voices, all men.

"Hello? Who's down here? This area is off limits."

Shaking his head, Evan grabbed the flashlight from the wall and flicked it on. A powerful white beam pierced the fog only a half foot, but it was better than nothing. Barely. He set off into the fog to search for the voices.

He couldn't hear his footsteps as he walked, but he could hear the voices. The fog thickened. Cold tendrils wrapped around his body, his face, inside him as he breathed. The voices were always in front of him, but he could never catch them. The flashlight illuminated the steel locking ring of a metal door. Spinning the ring one handed, he opened the door, clambered through and pulled it shut behind him.

The fog hadn't permeated this side of the

door, and he wanted to keep it that way. Five feet further down the corridor the tunnel ended in a metal spiral staircase. Evan climbed it, reaching a hatch at the top. He popped it open and climbed out into bright sunlight.

He spun around. He was in the forest one hundred feet above the level of the dam. Below him lay the lake, car park, and . . .

He did a double take. The dam was completely shrouded in fog. Thick, yellow fog that touched nothing except the dam.

Evan tried the radio again, but still only heard static. Pulling out his mobile phone, he rang Lou. Dead air. The call didn't even try to connect. Icy fear gripped him. He tried Ira whom he could see standing next to the car.

The call answered on the first ring. "Here, boss. Where are you?"

"This will sound crazy, but can you reach the dam? My radio isn't working. It conked out mid conversation with Frank, and I can't reach Lou's phone either."

"We lost contact with everyone on the dam the instant the fog rolled in. Where are you?"

"About one hundred feet above the dam and car park in the forest. If you turn to your left, you'll see me in that clearing."

Ira turned.

Evan waved. "See me?"

"How did you get up there?"

"That's a long story we don't have time for, so I'll give you the short version. The tunnel beneath the dam is filled with fog. I could hear voices and footsteps. I followed them, found a door and a staircase that incidentally aren't on the blueprints I've seen, and here I am." He paused. "In some ways it's worse than the west wing."

Ira laughed. "Yup, you're crazy all right."

Evan shook his head. "I don't pay you to agree with me. Anyway, I'm going back down there. I know you won't agree with me on that score either, but I have to find the others. Give me twenty minutes. Speak soon."

He hung up before Ira could argue against what, on reflection, was a stupid thing to do. However, it was the only, logical thing to do under the circumstances. There were members of his team down there, including Lou, and he had to go and get her back to the sunlight.

Evan climbed back down the stairs, taking care to fasten the hatch to the forest behind him. He wasn't sure why this wasn't on the blueprints he owned, but it made sense to give the dam workers an escape route to higher ground. He'd often wondered why there wasn't one.

As soon as he reached the second twist of the stairs, the temperature dropped like a stone. Evan zipped up his jacket and pulled up the collar. Fog swirled around his ankles. As he descended, the yellow, dank miasma rose until it swallowed him whole.

The flashlight made no difference this time, not even permeating the murk an inch. Evan used the tunnel walls as a guide to make his way forwards, shuffling his feet as he went. He stopped, once again hearing the voices ahead of him. He stood like a statue, straining to hear, to make out the words, the direction they were coming from. He took another step and his fingers met a gap in the wall.

An infinitesimal crack that could be a door; at least he hoped it was a door and not an actual crack. If the cracks had reached this deep they were in serious trouble. He pushed it a little and the voices became clearer.

"It's too big a risk," the first voice said.

"There's nothing left of the village now. And once the water is gone, we can get a team in properly to check."

"And if he did leave records as he threatened in the journal, and she finds them?"

311

the first voice argued.

"Her word against ours," the second said firmly. "Her reputation is as good as ruined anyway. Once we've made sure there are no records, we'll clear up. Kill her and anyone else who knows."

Evan moved away as quickly as the damp, blinding fog would let him. His pulse throbbed in his neck, his heart in his throat. There was no doubt in his mind that Lou was the 'she' they had referred to. That put her in immediate danger, and he had to warn her and get her to a safe place.

Whoever the men were, they wanted her dead. He recognized the voices, but not enough to put a name to them. However, it was a safe assumption they worked for Varian.

It seemed to take forever before he reached the stairs at the far end of the tunnel. He climbed as quickly as he could to the surface of the dam, this time exiting into thick fog. Completely turned around for a moment, he wasn't sure which way to go. He inched back to the doorway and closed his eyes for an instant, seeing it in his mind. He veered left and slowly made his way to the car park.

Suddenly he was back in bright sunlight. He glanced over his shoulder. Thick fog stood like a wall behind him.

Lou sprinted over to him and hugged him. "You made it out. I was so worried. It's weird, isn't it? The fog came down out of nowhere and hung there. It's like it's hiding something."

He returned the hug. "Yeah. Maybe it is. You shouldn't be here."

"Why?" Hurt glistened in her eyes. "I thought you wanted me here . . ."

His fingers covered her lips, cutting her off. "Go back to the house. Go over what notes you have from the other day."

"Evan?"

He shook his head and leaned down, kissing her gently. "I don't want to say much out loud," he whispered. "Just trust me." He leaned back and signalled Jack and Zach. "General, I'd like you and Zach to accompany Dr. Fitzgerald back to the manor. Don't let her out of your sight. Zach, I want you to make sure the manor is secure."

He kissed Lou's hand, taking note of the confusion mingling with the hurt in her face. "I know you don't understand, but I'll explain later. I promise."

"You better."

"I'll be home before dark." Evan opened the car door.

"You better." She slid into the seat, swinging her legs inside the vehicle. "Yes, I did say the same thing twice."

He grinned and tweaked her nose. "Just go home and stay safe. I'll text you the safe combination." He shut the door.

Jack studied him. "What gives?"

"I overheard a conversation down there," Evan whispered. "Someone wants her dead. Discrediting her isn't enough anymore. I don't want her alone or unsupervised for now. I need to stay here and work out how much time this dam has left before it falls. Otherwise, I'd come with you. Please, promise me you won't leave Lou alone."

Jack studied him for a split second. "She won't be out of my sight at all."

"Thank you. I'll be as quick as I can."

36

Lou photographed the notebook, making sure she had both digital and film images of each page. She'd resisted the urge to read, instead choosing to wait for Evan to come home first. This concerned him just as much, if not more so. She squinted over at Jack. He'd taken Evan's order extremely seriously and hadn't let her out of his sight since they'd left the dam. He'd even followed her to the kitchen and watched her make a banana sandwich.

Her bodyguard hovered safely outside the study. She'd been pleased she hadn't had to ask him to do that. Jack had insisted on wanting father-daughter time, uninterrupted father-daughter time were his exact words. The compromise was the door had to be ajar. She could see Zach through the crack, just standing there watching her. The security bloke gave her the creeps.

The door opened wide. Zach peered

inside. "Can I get you some coffee?"

She nodded. "I'd prefer tea, but a drink would be lovely, thank you. Dad will want coffee."

Sirens began to wail, permeating the building. The hairs on the back of her neck rose. "What's that?"

"The dam." Zach strode to the radio on the sideboard and clicked it on. He tuned it rapidly to the local station.

"— mandatory evacuation of Dark Lake and the surrounding twenty mile area. I repeat. There is now a red warning in place for the Aberfinay Dam. This means the village of Dark Lake and everything within a twenty-mile radius is under a mandatory evacuation order."

"Do we have to leave?" Lou asked.

"Sounds like it," Jack replied. "Though I imagine Evan would tell us himself."

"Assuming he can."

The phone rang, and Zach picked it up. "Hello. Yes, we heard on the radio. Oh . . ." He covered the phone. "Boss says the alert didn't come from him. The last one he issued was an amber alert, and that was yesterday morning." He spoke on the phone again then held it out to Lou. "He wants to talk to you."

Lou seized the handset and wandered over

316

to the window. "Evan? If you didn't issue the red, then who did?"

"I don't have long, so I need you to listen." He was talking fast, the words tumbling from him. "I don't want you leaving the manor or opening the door for anyone."

"What's going on?"

"I don't know. All I do know is that evacuation order didn't come from me or my team. Someone wants the village emptied. They want the manor empty as well."

"You reckon they're after the box?"

"I'm afraid so. I'll get Zach to patrol constantly. Your father can keep an eye on you. I know you don't like the idea, but stick to him like glue for me. Just sit tight and don't leave the main part of the house. No matter what happens. I'll be there as soon as I can, though it may be later than I'd hoped."

"It'll be dark in a couple of hours."

"I know. I also know that means the fog will spread. That's another reason for you to sit tight. The dam is in bad shape, yes, but it's not likely to fall down overnight. Lou?"

"Yeah?"

"I lo—" He broke off. "Give the phone back to Zach."

Lou held the phone out, sitting on the window sill. She shivered, cold and numb. What had he almost said? It sounded like "I love you," but what could have stopped him mid-sentence?

Zach thumped down the phone. "I have to secure this place. Please don't leave this room until I get back."

"Can't guarantee that." Lou tried to sound brighter than she felt. "But I'll either be in the bathroom or my bedroom if I'm not here. Dad won't leave my side; Evan said to stick to him like glue, so I will." She crossed back to the table and resumed photographing the book.

Half an hour later, Zach still hadn't returned. "How long does it take to lock up a house?" she asked rhetorically. "The manor isn't that big."

"Maybe he got lost or side-tracked." Jack winked at her. "Like someone else I know. Want me to go look for him?"

She poked her tongue at him as she packed the camera carefully into its case. "He's a big boy. I reckon he can take care of himself. However if he's not back before I die of thirst, then we'll mount a search party."

She repacked the box, taking care to lock

318

it again. This time she slid the key into her bra.

Jack raised an eyebrow.

"Least I know it's safe there, Dad," she quipped. "You'd kill any man who tried to retrieve it."

"Too right I would," Jack growled. "That includes Evan, by the way."

Lou picked up the box. "This is going in my room again tonight. I can lock the door from the inside and bolt it. No one will get in." She grinned. "You can leave the connecting door between our rooms open if you want."

He scrunched his nose at her. "Don't tempt me." He paused. "Maybe I'll bring my quilt and pillow in and sleep on your floor."

She laughed. "It wouldn't be the first time. Can you give me a hand with these, please?"

Lou headed up to her room and shoved the box and bags under her bed. "I still want that tea, but first I need the loo."

"You're not going alone," Jack said.

"If you believe you're coming in with me, you have another think coming." Lou shook her head. "Just because you want to go where no man has gone before, that doesn't mean the ladies' loo."

Jack rolled his eyes. "I'll wait outside."

She groaned. "You blokes take this protection thing way too seriously."

"Someone wants you dead, kiddo. They'll find a way to do it. Evan and I want to make it as hard for them as possible."

"Fine, but you sit outside the door." She shut the bedroom door behind her and headed down the hallway to the bathroom. "Maybe we should go and search for Zach after all. He might have got lost."

"He'll be fine." Jack leaned against the wall opposite the bathroom. "We'll go find him when you're done."

Lou went into the bathroom and shut the door, shooting the bolt across with a loud click. "You want me to sing? 'Sing a song of sixpence, a pocket full of rye . . .' "

Jack laughed. "Nah, I'm good."

"Maybe you should sing. I mean, I know I'm OK, but I can't see you to make sure you're all right."

"You really want me to sing? 'Four and twenty blackbirds baked in a pie . . .' " Jack launched into a very off key version.

Lou laughed. "No, please, don't sing. I'll be two minutes." She washed her hands, and pushed them through her hair. Turning her head this way and that, she did a quick restyle and then dried her hands.

She unbolted the door and opened it. The hallway was empty. "So much for waiting outside the door." She glanced up and down the corridor. "Dad? Where'd you go?"

No answer came.

"Dad!" Lou sighed. "Oh, come on. This isn't funny. First you tell me not to wander off and then you do the self-same thing." She stuck her hands on her hips. "If you want me to act like a grownup over being protected, this is not the way to do it."

Laughter echoed from the other end of the hallway. "OK. If you want to play hide and seek, which, under the circumstances, is very infantile, then fine. One, two, miss a few, ninety-nine, a hundred, ready or not here I come."

Lou slammed the bathroom door and stomped down the corridor, making sure her feet missed the carpet and hit the wooden floorboard edging instead. She flung open the door to the room in which she'd heard the laughter. "I said enough!"

The room was empty. A door disguised as a bookcase stood ajar. Running footsteps slapped against stone from behind it.

"OK. So this is how you want to play it." She raised her voice. "I'm not amused, Dad. I have work to do. I'm bringing the rest of the stuff up from the study."

She ran back down the main stairs and packed away her film camera. Noises came from the hallway. She huffed. For the time being she'd put this in the study safe. At least everything else was in her room. She checked her phone for Evan's text containing the safe combination, and opened the safe. She laid the camera on top of a pile of notebooks. Did they also contain the history of Dark Lake? She made a mental note to ask Evan when she saw him.

She locked the safe then swivelled as the study door swung open. Shaking her head she strode to the door. Laughter and running footsteps came from the end of the hallway. That really was enough. Lou strode down the hallway, following the sound until she found herself at the door to the west wing.

Evan's warning to stay out of there echoed in her mind, but no one else was around to investigate. A scream shattered her indecision. She had to go. She pushed open the door. "Hello?"

Mist or dry ice wafted over her feet. She shook her head. There was nothing there; just a product of an over active imagination. The screams came again.

"Where are you?" Lou called, making her way down the hallway. A glow came from the door at the end. The screams became louder, more insistent.

Lou pushed open the door. Flames engulfed the room. Carpet, walls, bedding, everything blazed. Smoke billowed. She raised a hand against the heat. A figure stood in the centre of the conflagration.

There wasn't time for thought. Taking a deep breath, Lou moved one step towards the blazing room. "I'm coming."

Someone grabbed her arm and pulled her back. The door slammed shut.

Hands swung her around.

A furious Evan faced her. "I told you to stay away from the west wing." His voice shook in anger, his eyes blazed.

She shook herself free. "Evan, there's a fire in there. Someone's trapped. We can't leave them." She took a deep breath, and then frowned. She could no longer smell smoke. Glancing behind her, the space around the door was no longer glowing. "I don't understand."

"There's no fire, Lou." Evan's tone was gentle now. "The door at the far end of the hallway is shut and locked for a reason."

"It wasn't locked." She stared at her surroundings, not believing what she was seeing. "Wait a second. This hallway didn't look like this a moment ago. There was wooden panelling, red carpet on the floor." The stone walls were blackened and the floor charred. In several places there were holes, and she could see through to the level below. "Oh . . ."

"Be careful where you stand." He caught hold of her hand. "One false move and you'll go straight through the floor."

"But . . ." Lou stared up at the door Evan had closed. It was burned and warped.

Evan held her tightly. "See." He opened the door.

Lou gasped. Nothingness filled the gap in front of her. Just a burned shell outlining what once had been a tall, imposing structure. The fading light of sunset poured in from above.

"You would have fallen three stories into the basement if you'd taken one more step."

She shook her head, desperately trying to understand what she was seeing. "Evan, I saw paintings on the wall, carpets on the floor. There was a room with a four poster bed, curtains hanging around it. Everything was on fire. I could hear the flames, even smell the smoke."

Evan closed the door before leading her back down the hallway. He closed that door as well. He locked the door, pocketing the key. "Come on. I'll show you from outside."

37

"The fire started up there." Evan pointed to a door that opened to nothing on the third floor. "That's what you were about to step through when I stopped you. The fire began on the first anniversary of the flooding of the villages."

"What used to be here?" Lou moved a step closer to him.

"The kitchen was on the ground floor — about right where we're currently standing. Above that was the library, the dining room, and a few guest rooms. The entire top floor was the nursery, so the nanny had her quarters there. As did the nursery maids."

"Who died?"

Evan sucked in a deep breath. He glanced around the ruins they stood amongst and shuddered. "The housekeeper was checking the house after the fog rolled in. The baby was in the nursery along with the nanny and Mabel, my great grandmother."

"Was the baby your grandfather?"

Evan nodded. "Yeah. Anyway, the housekeeper headed to the west wing. She got to the outer doorway, the one I keep locked. She could smell smoke. She opened the door. She said the smoke floated along the floor of the hallway like mist at first, swirling around her feet."

Lou wrapped her arms around herself.

"She could see a glow around the edge of the far door and could hear screams. She opened the door to find an inferno. A figure stood in the centre of the room, flames all around her. My great grandfather, alerted by the gardener, stopped her from going in. Instead he ran inside to save his wife and the baby. He got the baby out, handed him to the housekeeper and told her to run outside, to get the baby to safety. He went back in for his wife."

Evan led her to another part of the ruin. "The floor collapsed under him. He was found here, his wife in his arms. They were both badly burned. She died later that night; he died a year or so later."

"That's so sad." Lou rubbed her sleeve over her eyes. "Do they know how the fire started?"

"No. It could have been a candle left alight in the library. Or it could have been a careless maid in the nursery. I guess we'll never know. Anyway, apparently my great grandfather never forgave himself."

"Why were the caves so important to your grandfather if he never went there with his parents?"

"I don't know. I want to go and find out, but . . ." He paused, gazing up at the sky. "We should go inside. It's getting dark, and the fog will come down with it."

Lou followed him inside. "This doesn't make sense."

"What are you thinking?"

"I saw it. I was there. I —"

"It happens. That's why it's locked; aside from the fact it's dangerous. I keep meaning to have the ruins demolished and rebuilt, but what with one thing and another . . ."

Lou stopped. "What's up there?"

Heart pounding, Evan turned to study her. "Where?"

Lou pointed. "There. Tell me I'm not seeing things again."

Evan followed her finger and swallowed. He hadn't wanted to explain this at all. Not now, not ever. Light blazed from the only remaining part of the west wing. "No, you're not seeing things."

"Is there someone there?"

"Yeah. Lilly."

"Let me guess." Her gaze went from worried to angry. "You're married. She's your wife, but she's quite insane, so you keep her locked up in the tower."

"You read way too many romance novels," Evan retorted. "No. I'm not and never have been married."

"Well, what's up there then?"

He sighed, his heart heavy. "OK, I'll show you." He walked slowly into the house, Lou beside him.

Jack met them in the kitchen. "Where did you get to?" he demanded.

"Me?" Lou retorted. "You said you'd stay right outside the room. I was talking to you the whole time. Then when I came out, you'd vanished."

"I vanished?" Jack scowled. "You went quiet and when I broke the door down, you weren't there. The only person I found was Zach. He's still searching the grounds looking for you."

"Can't we do this later?" Lou tapped her foot. "Evan is introducing me to the other woman in his life."

Jack turned on Evan in disbelief. "What?"

Evan sighed. "Let me let Zach know we've found Lou, and then I'll show you." He sent a quick text, then put his phone away. "This way." He led them up the familiar back staircase to enter the remaining part of the west wing. "This is the only safe way up here now. Lilly's in here." He tapped on the door. "It's Evan."

The door opened. Dr. Carter stood there, Ira by her side. "I was about to send Mr. Miles to find you."

His heart sank further and his whole body went cold and numb.

The village vet smiled at him. "No, it's nothing like that. Come and see for yourself."

Evan took a step into the room then paused. "Lou, this is Maggie Carter. She's the village vet — multitalented as she does large and small animals. Maggie, this is Dr. Fitzgerald. I'm sure you've heard all about her by now from the news. Ignore it, none of it is true."

"I wouldn't go that far," Lou muttered.

"OK, well most of it isn't true. And this is her father." Evan's gaze flicked past Maggie. "Lilly?"

Three short barks came from the other side of the room. A golden and white collie pushed herself up to stand, tail wagging. No longer wearing a bandage, she stood tentatively on four legs, as if testing her own weight.

He strode over. "Hey, Lilly. How are you

329

doing, girl?"

Lilly sniffed and licked his fingers, barking loudly.

Emotion welled up within him. He wasn't sure how he felt. "You look so much better. Yes, you do." He glanced up at Lou. "I thought I'd lost her. She got her leg caught in a nasty trap in the woods — a poacher's trap that had been there for almost half a century . . ." He broke off, amazed as Lou turned and ran from the room, tears running down her face. "What did I say?"

Jack's face contorted. "Excuse me." He followed Lou from the room.

Evan refused to let his concerns cloud his joy at Lilly's recovery. He buried his face in the dog's fur, making a fuss over her. "Well, I'm pleased to see you. Yes, I am. Does this mean you're up for a w-a-l-k in the morning, huh? Only a short one, maybe around the top garden?" He glanced up at the vet. "You're a miracle worker. How can I ever thank you?"

Maggie Carter chuckled. "Pay the bill — that's all the thanks I need." She packed up her things. "Lilly should be back to normal in a couple of days, but she's to take it easy. She can go outside tomorrow." She paused. "But, yes, she can leave the room now and have free reign in the house. But no more running off unsupervised."

Evan beamed. "You hear that? Lilly is a free dog again. Shall we go? Shall we?"

Ira laughed from the doorway. "If only your colleagues could hear you now. They'd tease you for being childish."

Evan poked his tongue out. "That's me being childish. Otherwise, I'm talking dog. Can you see Maggie out, please?" He pushed upright and tapped his thigh. "Come on then, girl. Let's go find the others."

The corridor was empty, so Evan headed down to the lounge, hoping to find Lou there. What had upset her so? Was it him? Had he done or said something while explaining about the west wing? Surely, she wasn't jealous of a dog?

Jack stood by the window, coffee cup in his hand, watching the swirling fog from between a gap in the curtains.

"Where's Lou?"

"She's gone to bed. She's tired. She took the notebook with her rather than leave it in your safe down here."

Evan could hardly bear to ask, but he had to know. "Did I upset her?"

"When she was a teenager, she had a dog very much like yours. He died saving her life. It took her a long time to get over it."

"Oh." His stomach dropped as if it contained rocks.

"She'll be fine. She needed time on her own. I'm calling it a night as well. I ought to check in with the wife and find out how the ballet recital went." He paused. "Just so you know, I'm sleeping with the connecting door between my room and Lou's open tonight."

He balked. "Don't you trust me?"

"I'm keeping an eye on her, like you asked. Besides, it's that or her bedroom floor."

Evan grunted. "Makes sense, I suppose. To be honest, if you weren't here, I'd probably do the same thing. I need to ring the dam and get an update. See you in the morning. 'Night."

" 'Night."

He gazed at Lilly as Jack headed out. "Just you and me then."

Lilly barked and flopped in her bed under his desk. She rested her nose on her paws, sighed contentedly, and closed her eyes.

"Then there was one." Evan picked up the phone and called the dam but only heard the engaged tone. He set the receiver down. He had to go and find Lou, make sure she was all right. It didn't matter that Jack would be in the adjoining room with the door open. He wouldn't be able to rest without seeing her; he needed to explain, needed to make sure she really was all right. He padded upstairs and paused outside Lou's bedroom door. He glanced at Zach who stood in the hallway. "Call it a night. We'll make sure she's fine from here."

Zach nodded. "Good night, sir."

Evan leaned towards the bedroom door. Sobs came from the other side.

He knocked. "Lou?"

"One minute." Even if he hadn't heard the sobs, her emotion-laden voice told him something was very wrong.

After a brief pause, she opened the door. Her eyes were red and brimming with unshed tears, her cheeks wet, and shoulders shaking.

"Come here." He folded his arms around her distraught figure.

Lou clung to him as she struggled to regain her composure.

He didn't let go, but murmured quietly to her. He glanced up at Jack standing in the doorway between the two rooms and mouthed, "I've got this."

Jack nodded and pulled the door, leaving it open a tad.

Evan could hear him talking on the phone again.

Finally Lou pulled back. She accepted the clean hanky he offered. "Sorry."

"Don't be sorry, love. Jack told me you had a dog like Lilly once. Do you want some cocoa? We could go sit in the kitchen. Eat all the biscuits Mrs Jefferson made yesterday." He tilted his head.

He was rewarded with a faint smile.

"OK." He paused. "And, yes, I'll make it myself."

38

Lou ran her finger around the rim of the cup as she sat at the kitchen table. Steam wafted upwards and she inhaled deeply. "Smells good."

Evan sat beside her and pulled across the box of biscuits. He removed the lid. "Here you go." He waited until she'd taken one before he helped himself. He immediately dunked his into his cocoa.

"You know, Dad does this as well. He thinks he can get me to talk if he plies me with hot chocolate."

"We don't have to talk if you don't want."

"It's fine." She raised her cup and sipped. The smooth liquid slid down her throat. "You're right. It's much better made with melted chocolate, rather than the tinned chocolate powder."

He grinned. "Can I say I told you so?"

"No."

Lou wrapped both hands around the cup.

"His name was Deefer." Simply mentioning his name brought back the sharp stab of grief she'd felt when he'd died so many years ago. "He was a sheltie. Same colouring as Lilly."

He tilted his head. "Deefer?"

"Very bad joke. *D* for dog."

"Clever. So I suppose if you had a cat you'd call it Ceefer."

"Maybe. On reflection, I should have called him Shadow, because he followed me everywhere when he was a puppy. Mum said he'd sit in the hall when I went to school and pine for me every minute until I came home. He didn't even mind being on the boat for several months when we went to search for Jim and Staci's parents."

"Months? Sounds like a long trek."

Lou studied him, knowing he already knew but not saying as much. Instead, she swigged a long sip and then began to tell him about how they ended up shipwrecked on Agrihan on the other side of the world. "Anyway, in January, we set off for the abandoned American Air Force base. Deefer tried to stop me from wandering off the path and trod in one of those infernal, rusty traps. He died a day or so before we were rescued by Dad and his team." Tears ran unheeded down her cheeks. "We buried

Deefer on the cliff overlooking the beach."

Evan laid a gentle hand on hers. "Your stepfather rescued you?"

She wiped her tears on the hanky, which was now almost too wet to use. "Yeah. He was tasked with the rescue mission Jim's Morse code message triggered. Anyway, the surgeons couldn't save my leg, but Dad encouraged me to do the physio, learn to walk again and so on. I'd never have been in the world championships or been to uni if it hadn't been for him."

He squeezed her hand. "You never did explain that to me."

Lou sucked in a deep breath. "Jim and I took the dingy out to go fishing. I splashed the water to annoy him and attracted a shark. It knocked over the dingy. Jim made it back to our boat. I didn't." She swallowed. "I was out of it for a while. Jim did his best, but my leg got infected in the weeks between the shark and when we got rescued. They had to remove it to save my life."

She changed the subject. "I had another dog after Deefer, but it wasn't the same. When he died, I didn't bother having another. Besides, being as transient as I am, it's probably best. I'm hardly ever at home. I live in hotel rooms and out of a suitcase."

Evan set down his empty cup. "Lilly usually comes to London with me, but she's been in plaster, and I felt it best she stayed here. Plus, it was touch and go for a few days." He carried both cups to the sink. "Did you read any of the journal?"

"No. I was waiting for —" She broke off as the doorbell rang.

"Ira will get it. Go on."

"I figured we could read it together in the morning. That's if you wanted." She glanced at the door as loud voices came from the hallway.

"One moment." Evan headed into the hall, leaving the door open. "Can I help you?"

Lou got up and moved to the door, peeping through the gap.

A tall man in a green camouflage uniform stood in the hallway, helmet on his head and clipboard in hand. "Corporal Brown. I've been tasked with overseeing the evacuation of Dark Lake. You have to leave tonight, sir. Transport is being provided."

"That's not happening." Evan shook his head. "I own Xenon. I'm in charge of the dam. My team is currently working there in an effort to stabilize it."

"Is anyone else here?"

"My staff. Can I ask where the evacuation

order came from, because I didn't issue it, and I'm the only one with the authority to do so."

"It came from a Mr. Monty Sparrow from the Sparrow Foundation."

"Figures. By all means, evacuate the village, but it's nothing to do with me or my team. I'm not leaving nor are they." He lowered his voice so it no longer carried.

Lou went back to the sink and washed up the cups.

Rain pounded against the windows, thunder rumbled in the distance.

Evan strode back in, his brows furrowed and his lips set. "He's gone."

"So, tell me. If that dam goes, how long have we got?"

"I already told you, it's not likely to go tonight. Otherwise I'd have issued a red warning myself. The water level is now such that it wouldn't destroy as much as a full lake would." He paused. "Am I worried? Yes, I am. It's my job to worry. I have a bad feeling about all this, and it's nothing to do with the dam. Maybe, on reflection, you and your dad should take the jet and fly back to London where you'll be safe."

"That's a little extreme. Surely the flood won't go that far." She rolled her eyes.

Evan clicked his tongue. "You know what

I mean. Varian won't think of looking for you there."

"And you?"

"I have to stay here. The dam is my problem."

"No way." She shook her head. "I'm not leaving without you."

"I'm not arguing." He grabbed her shoulders. The firm touch sent shockwaves of pleasure through her. His intense blue gaze captured her. "I want you safe. I want you far, far away from the dam and Varian. I want . . ."

Lou raised her hands to grab his arms. "I want you," she whispered, not caring if that was forward of her. "Just shut up arguing and kiss me."

"Shut up? I'm talking about your safety and you want me to shut up?"

She reached up on tiptoe and kissed his lips lightly. "Yes."

Without further comment, his lips were on hers. His arms surrounded her, lifting her off her feet and setting her on the worktop, before pulling her against him firmly. Lightning flashed and the thunder echoed almost immediately, rolling off the hills. Each kiss sent her higher, his touch setting nerve ends afire.

She knew without a doubt that she loved

him, and she prayed this meant he felt the
same way.

39

A loud cough jolted them apart. Jack stood glaring at them from the kitchen doorway.

Evan's cheeks burned as he wished the floor would open up and swallow him whole.

"Dad . . ." Lou's rosy cheeks and wide eyes probably matched his own.

"Jack, I can explain."

Jack held up a hand. "I hope you can. Don't hurt her. Oh, and if you intend to sleep with her, you have to marry her first."

"Dad!" Horror and embarrassment covered Lou's face as she jumped down off the work top. "It was one kiss."

Jack raised an eyebrow. "Really? One very heated, passionate kiss from where I was standing."

Evan swallowed hard past the lump in his throat. He hadn't thought of marriage as the eventual outcome, but the general was right. Kissing like that usually led to something else. He needed to pull back, treat Lou with the respect she deserved, and lead them to the proper conclusion to this tentative relationship they were starting out on.

Lou still appeared indignant. "And if you must know I kissed him first, so don't you go blaming this on Evan."

Evan's gaze hit the floor. "Your dad's right. I should know better. I'm sorry."

Lou rounded on him. "You're sorry? For what? Kissing me?"

"No." He paused. "For not thinking before I acted."

Jack shook his head. "I'm too old for this conversation. Suffice it to say, sex is a wedding gift for your husband or wife. It's not something to be given away lightly."

"I couldn't agree more. I won't put either of us in this position again." He glanced at Lou and pressed his lips to her forehead. "At least not where he can find us," he whispered.

Lou giggled.

"Behave, kiddo." Jack frowned. "I do not want to have to tell your mother."

"You wouldn't?"

"Tell her I caught you kissing a tall, dark stranger? No. You can tell her when the time is right. I'm going to bed now. Can I trust you two to behave?"

Lou nodded. "I'm going to bed anyway. Evan, what time do you need to be at the dam tomorrow?"

"First light to see what damage this storm has done. Why?"

"I want to go over the notebook with you."

He glanced at his watch. "OK, so how about half six? Should give us an hour before I need to leave. Oh, I'm setting the burglar alarm tonight and the motion detectors. So if you need to come downstairs for whatever reason before I'm up, do it very carefully and keep to the walls. Stay out of the study and the library."

"Sounds good. 'Night."

" 'Night."

Evan waited for Jack to follow her, but he didn't. Silence fell, broken only by the rain and thunder. Evan's stomach clenched, expecting a lecture or at least a stiff talking to.

With a mercifully short glare, Jack pivoted and left.

Evan sank into a chair. He had to be more careful around Lou. He was too involved. Before he met her he'd thought he'd stop at nothing to keep her quiet. This started out as purely business, but now?

Now he'd let the little archaeologist into a tiny crack in his heart, and she was splitting him open as surely as that tiny crack had split the Aberfinay Dam wide open. And as surely as one would fall, he knew the other would also come tumbling down.

The question was which would fall first? Although a small voice inside him told him it was too late. Part of his heart was Lou's and always would be.

Either way he had to date her, to keep her in his life at all costs. He rose and ran into the hallway. "Jack?"

Jack paused halfway up the stairs and peered down at him.

"Can I have a word?"

"Sure."

Evan made his way up the stairs and leaned against the wall. "I'd like permission to court your daughter."

Jack raised an eyebrow, his expression quizzical. "Court her? As in . . . ?"

He pressed his heels firmly into the carpet. Nervous didn't even begin to cover the state his insides were in and the fear of rejection overflowed from every pore. "She thinks I'm quaint and old-fashioned. Courting seems to be the right way to go about this, as does asking your permission first. So, yeah, court, as in the old-fashioned way of dating."

The older man held his gaze for a long moment. Then a smile crossed his face.

"The ultimate answer will come from her, but I don't have any objections. Just keep in mind what I said back there."

"I will." His heart leapt as he headed back into the study to get an update on the dam. The phone rang before he reached it. "Close."

"Boss, it's me." Ralph's voice vibrated and ended on a high note. "Did you ask for extra water to be diverted to the dam? Because we're getting an influx from somewhere and it's compounding the problem."

Evan hit his forehead with the palm of his hand. "I'd forgotten about that. I did that last week, when the dam levels fell. Cancel it. The numbers are in the blue folder I left with you. Call them now."

"Sure thing. I'm increasing the overflow to compensate."

"Thanks." He slumped at the desk and rubbed the back of his neck. "Keep me informed. Oh, and I'm ignoring the evac orders and staying put in the manor."

"I hate to disagree with you, but this Sparrow bloke may have a point."

"And as I explained to the military blokes that came, he has a good reason to want the area empty as well. No one is getting into the manor to get their hands on the documents here."

"No offence, boss, but we need you alive. Take the documents and get out of there."

Evan shook his head. "No can do. Can't explain over the phone, but I have a good reason for staying."

Lou lay awake most of the night, tossing and turning. Lights flickered and rotated in the corner of her left eye, but the sleep that would avert the coming migraine eluded her. Around three she rose, showered, and dressed. She downed headache meds and then settled on the bed to read over all her notes.

When her alarm went off at five, she grabbed the notebook from the box, along with her camera and headed carefully downstairs to the kitchen to make some tea.

Evan glanced up as she came in. "Morning. You're up early." He moved over to her and kissed her gently. "I've just made a pot of coffee if you want some."

She shook her head. "I prefer tea. I only drink coffee to be sociable; despite living in the States for several years, I don't really like the stuff."

"One pot of tea coming up." He moved to the side and switched on the kettle. "About last night . . ."

She leaned next to him. "Don't worry

about it. Dad takes his role very seriously."
She giggled. "He's even worse with Emily.
She brought a boy over once, and Dad gave
him the third degree over the tea table."

"How old was this kid?"

"Nine or ten I think. I would love to be a
fly on the wall when her prom date comes
to pick her up in a few years." She threw
her head back and laughed. "Dad'll probably stand there, gun in his hand, and
demand Emily be home before ten."

"I wouldn't go that far." Evan made the
tea. "But I'd like to think I'd be protective
of any daughters I may have in the future."
He flicked her nose and then tucked her
hair behind her ears. "You look dreadful.
Did you sleep any?"

"No, my mind is too active. I also have a
headache, which doesn't help any."

He grazed his knuckles against her cheek
and kissed her forehead. "I'm sorry."

Lou leaned into his touch, allowing the
comfort and pleasure to mix. "It isn't your
fault. It happens some nights, especially this
time of year. September 30 was the day I
lost my leg. It's also the date of Mum's and
Dad's wedding anniversary, which is why
he has to be home by then."

Evan laid the tray with cups and pastries
and picked it up. "Let's take this into the

den. I've lit a fire in there."

She followed him, passing Zach in the hallway.

"September 30 is also the day the village flooded. And the date of the fire in the west wing." He set the tray down and paused. "It's almost as if everything is conjoining and centring around the same date."

She smirked. "This isn't a disaster movie, you know. The world won't end on September 30."

"It might." He plated the pastries and handed one to her.

"Thank you, and I hope not. But it is a little weird how all the dates are the same."

"Tell you something else that happens on September 30: my birthday."

"Fancy that. And how old will you be this year?"

He grinned. "The same age as my tongue and a little older than my teeth." He caressed her cheek with his thumb. "A lady should never ask."

She struggled to keep a straight face. "I'm no lady. I'm an archaeologist, and strangely attracted to old things."

Evan's eyes widened in shock. "Old?"

She waved a hand, clicking her fingers. "Yes, I went there. You walked straight into that one, mister."

Evan wrapped his arms around her and laughed, the tension between them falling away. "I'll have you know, miss, I'm not that old. I'll be thirty-four."

"Still older than me." She leaned against him, one hand holding her side. "I have a stitch from laughing too much."

"That will teach you to pick on older men." He kissed her forehead. "Does that make me a cradle snatcher?" he whispered.

Lou raised her face to his. "Not that much younger than you." She kissed him gently. "Are those pastries to be eaten or for looking at?"

He chuckled. "We can eat them." He let her go and moved to the tray. He poured the tea. "Did you bring the notebook?"

She nodded. "I figured we could read it aloud and record it. I have photos of each page, but it'd be good to have an audio recording as well."

"Sounds good but we should eat first."

Lou curled up on the couch and took the mug from him. "Thanks."

Evan said grace and began eating.

"Dad rubbed off on you." Her lips curved into a wry smile.

He shrugged. "An old habit I'd gotten out of. I was thinking maybe I should pick it up again."

"It's a good one to have. I've been thinking the same thing. Maybe once all this is over . . ." She wiped a crumb from her lips and licked her fingers. "Are we still checking out those caves you mentioned?"

"They're probably still sealed," he said in between bites.

"They might not be. Chances are the rocks moved during the land movement caused by the explosions. Or there may be a way in despite the rock fall."

He swigged his coffee quickly and topped up the cup. "I'll need to check in at the dam first so probably won't be until the afternoon." He paused. "I'll tell Zach to stay in the hallway, even though we've shut the door. I don't want any of this overheard."

They finished the meal in silence. Evan piled up the plates on the tray and refilled their cups. He rose and spoke quietly to Zach, before shutting the door. Then he settled on the couch next to her. "OK. Are you ready to do this?"

"Yup." Lou picked up the book. "There's a note at the start of the book, which states this is a private journal. I'm guessing the other one we found was the public one kept in the house. I'm also hoping this one will fill in the gaps caused by missing pages and faded ink in that other one. This one is in two sets of handwriting which, from what I've gathered, are his and hers. Fancy a bit of role play?"

His hand ran over her arm, before entwining in her fingers. "Why not? I'll be my great-grandfather and you can be my great-grandmother."

40

June 16

My name is Mabel Close. I used to be scullery maid at the manor 'til I fell in love with the third son, David. Our dalliance was forbidden by class status, society, and every other rule known to man. We hid our love for a time, playing with fire. We'd meet on my half day, several towns over, where he'd help me with my spelling and letters. Sweet, stolen moments in the orchard, the attics, or the caves.

We were seen by Michael, one of the servants. He's a sly man, always sneaking about trying to get people in trouble. He's valet to Mr. Close, David's father, and must have told him. Mr. Close forbade us to see each other. He threatened to give me notice without reference, said I'd never work around here again.

David stood up to him. He told him we were getting married. That only made things worse. His father threatened to disinherit him if we married. He sent David away to medical school, hoping the five-year separation would cure him of his infatuation with a servant.

It didn't. He wrote to me and spent time with me when he came home for holidays. Our love grew greater. He graduated and had plans to work in a big hospital in London.

We were going to leave together, marry, and set up home miles away from here. But both older brothers died leaving only his sisters, who could not inherit, David had no choice but to return home.

David kept seeing me. Things went too far, and when I found myself expecting, we had no choice but to marry. His father was furious and threw him out. Said he'd inherit over his dead body, and he never wanted to see him again. Then he sacked me.

We eloped, married over the anvil in Gretna Green. I'm not sure why, but we ended up back here in Abernay. David rented a small cottage opposite the church. He doctors from the back room. It's not ideal, but it will do for now.

June 17

Mabel makes my father sound like an ogre. He is just not as forward thinking as some of us. He still does not agree with women having the vote. He insists the classes shouldn't integrate, but I disagree. Mabel is all I want in a wife and always will be.

The villagers are beginning to attend my clinics and surgeries. I fear that half of them come through simple curiosity and to find out if the rumours are true.

This journal is running concurrent to the one in the main part of the house, with extra details where necessary. I don't want this one found. Neither do I agree with the decision to flood the villages. I may have come out publicly to agree, but having met privately with Tully Belton, my eyes have been opened to what is really happening here.

No one wants to leave. And why should they? They are being forced to sell their homes, having been told they will lose their employment if they do not. As most of the villagers are employed either by my father or by CS or at the mill owned by James Chapman, there can be no doubt in my mind who is behind this, as those three men will gain most from the dam and new power station being built there.

Lou picked up her cup. "This journal starts before the one you had in the safe. There must be another one somewhere."

"That one is pretty old and in a much worse condition than this one. The pages might have been lost or damaged over the

355

years. Or removed for one reason or another," Evan glanced down. "The next bit is yours."

June 24
There is a protest meeting tonight. David is insisting he attends. I don't want him to go. What if things get violent and he gets hurt? What will become of me then? His parents are still not speaking to us, and it's been four months now. Despite the fact David is the village doctor, we are essentially outcasts.

The position in London is looking like a good option. He has telephoned the hospital there and they are going to get back to him once the board has convened next week.

The babe within me is uneasy tonight. I don't want to stay here. There have been too many accidents on the construction site. It won't be long before someone is killed up there. The work progresses in the dark and the fog, as well as during the day.

The fog. A strange, unearthly mist that covers the dam each night. Never seen fog in June before.

June 25
Last night's meeting went well. Frank Philips chaired the meeting with Tully Belton as his second. Despite Mabel's misgivings, we

remained more or less as gentlemen, although tempers were high and voices raised.

A picket has been planned for the dam each day with placards. A petition will be raised to my father, though I have advised I cannot sign it. At least not yet.

June 30
Another meeting and, again, David insisted on attending. This time, I can hear the shouts from the hall across the street. The situation is becoming untenable here.

Mrs Teague, a widow of some sixty years, has sold her home and moved to be with her daughter in Dorset. She received only a fraction of what the house is worth. Those in the tithe cottages have no choice but to leave.

July 3
David was been called to the dam despite the late hour and the fog. Another accident. This time a young lad of nineteen, John Perkins, crush injuries they said. David was almost in tears when he came back. He could do nothing to save him.

July 8
I am attending the rally in London. Mabel is refusing to come. I am unhappy at the prospect of leaving her here alone, but this is

something I have to do.

July 9

David is away in London. The fog is thick tonight, so unlike July. The sounds are muffled, yet up at the dam, work continues. I have signed the petition against the dam and flooding on behalf of us both. One day all this land will belong to David. It is only right that history knows he wanted nothing to do with it; they should know his stance was firm against.

He wants no part of this dam or the flooding. No part of the destruction and loss that will accompany it. People will lose their homes, their livelihoods. We lose everything so a few men can profit.

July 10

The Prime Minister said he can do nothing. He didn't even come to the door, only sent an assistant to take the box containing the petition from us. We are betrayed by those meant to protect us.

Frank Philips is dead. Murdered. Again the police will do nothing. They are paid by my father to do what he wants.

That would change under my tenure, but once the village is gone, so will the position of squire. I will not inherit the title, for which my father is probably pleased. The land will belong to us but nothing more.

Tully Belton, Forest Phillips (Frank's son), Jonathan Keene, and I will meet in the church just before midnight. We will not let the village fall without a fight. We must come up with a plan and soon.

July 23

Our child, a daughter, came too early, barely six months. She did not survive. Mabel is doing as well as can be expected. I am . . . also. We named the baby Elizabeth, after Mabel's mother. She was born on July 12. We buried her in the church yard under the cover of the fog. Under the law, she would not receive a funeral as she was not deemed to be alive. There was another funeral the following day; we merely used the same grave. I am sure that God will not mind.

41

Lou wiped her sleeve over her eyes, trying not to sob aloud. "That's awful. Not even being allowed to bury your own child."

Evan pressed a tissue into her hand. "I had no idea. I guess back then the subject was as taboo as it is now."

Lou wiped her eyes. "It shouldn't be, but I guess just like we wouldn't know what to say, the parents wouldn't either." She stared back at the book, shivering. She glanced over her shoulder at the door. It was ajar and she could see Zach in the hallway. Snuggling against Evan again, she turned back to the book. "Me, again."

August 10
There is sickness in the village. David tells me its influenza, and we should boil water before drinking it and avoid contact with other people as much as possible. I cannot do that. I need to be out doing normal things. Other-

wise, my mind goes back to Elizabeth, and I grieve all over again. I've cried enough. David needs a strong woman at his side, especially now.

While he is at work, I run errands and take food to those who are sick. As his wife, they are my people, too, even though I am still one of them.

But it is strange. The symptoms, though not unlike influenza, do not make sense to me, but then I am not a doctor like David. It begins with a headache, fever, nausea, and weakness of the limbs. It then turns into what appears to be pneumonia. My brother died of that when he was twelve, so I know that well.

But then chest pains and a cough begin. The sick cough up blood. I have seen it myself and looking through David's textbooks, that does not happen with influenza.

August 12

Mabel is right. I fear plague has come to Abernay. Finlay is similarly affected. Soldiers surrounded the villages late last night, erecting barricades. The cottage hospital is full. If more cases develop, as I suspect they will, I will either need a larger building or have to confine them to their homes. I will be remaining with the sick in order to prevent me giving this to Mabel. It is only those who protested in

London and their families who are sick.

Though that may well change in the coming days. It seems too much of a coincidence, and I will be running tests to determine what manner of plague this is.

I am leaving out of the journal kept in the main house certain details of the plague and will do so for as long as I can. I do not wish to start a panic.

August 13

I have barely seen David. He came home long enough to pack a bag saying it would be best if he stayed away to keep me free of the disease. He wouldn't even kiss me before he left. The first time ever he has refused me his touch, and I cannot help but think it is a bad omen.

August 15

I have to go to the barrier each day to collect food. Armed soldiers shoot anyone who attempts to leave. I saw young Daniel Masters shot. All he did was kick his ball over the barricade and try to get it back. What kind of sickness is this, that the outside world fears a small boy running after a ball?

August 18

I continue to help where I can. Mrs Jones is

sick, as is her husband. I am caring for their six children. The baby is poorly.

There is still no news about this sickness on the wireless. No outside help apart from the soldiers who deliver the food and guard what is now our border. Jimmy and Peter Thornton from Finlay tried crossing the barricade this morning. They were shot and killed.

August 21

David is sick. I am helping nurse him and the others now. Some of the servants from the manor are also sick. It is spreading. We lost another ten people today. Nurse Mount thinks the death toll will rise swiftly. It is a horrid way to die. She says so far none of the infected have lived.

I cannot lose David as well as Elizabeth. I pray every day that he will recover.

September 1

No time to write the past few days. David was near death several times, but praise God, he is now recovered, although very weak.

I am tired, but so far untouched by the sickness.

September 10

My parents are both dead. The lack of entries here show how little time there is to write, never mind grieve.

Each night we burn the bodies of the dead and place the ashes in a lead-lined casket. So far over a hundred of our friends, acquaintances, and families are gone.

It can't be a natural occurrence. I am carrying out what tests I can to discover the cause.

September 15

It is, indeed, not a natural occurrence. From what I have discovered it is deliberate. The first case was Johann Wilkes, a migrant worker at my father's farm. He attended the clinic in Finlay the day before we went to London. His wife said he received a routine vaccination, which caused his arm to swell and the injection point to rupture within a few hours. He became sick a week later.

Whether or not my father was involved I do not know. And as he is amongst the dead, I cannot ask him. All I know for sure is that we are being slaughtered like cattle for our land and our homes.

The dead vastly outnumber the living. They have begun constructing a concrete vault under the dam in which to inter the burned ashes of the dead. They are afraid even the ashes could spread the sickness.

Evan glanced up. "I don't remember seeing a vault under the dam on any of the blueprints I have." He pulled over the tablet computer and pulled them up. "Nothing here. Why alter the blueprints?"

Lou shrugged. "It does explain that tunnel you found that also wasn't on the blueprints. Maybe after this, they covered it all up completely. Buried the dead and the original plans and drew up new ones." She tapped her fingers on the arm of the couch. "Maybe that's what's hidden in the caves?"

He nodded. "It's possible, yes. And I want to get to the bottom of the cave part of this mystery. But first, let's finish reading and find out what happens next."

Lou chuckled. "This isn't a Saturday morning movie cliff-hanger."

He grinned. "It's better. I'm beginning to see the appeal of archaeology. Uncovering the past can be quite exciting."

September 21

It's over. The remaining bodies have been burned and interred. The vault under the dam is sealed. CS and Chapman have drawn up new plans of the dam. Ones that don't show the vault and tunnel leading to it. This is one secret they want hidden forever.

Mabel was one of eighteen people in the villages who didn't get sick at all. Only one other, aside from myself, recovered and survived. Twenty out of two hundred in Abernay still live. No one in Finlay survived.

The twenty of us have decided to stay. We will not move. The dam has cost us too much. The authorities want to cleanse the village, so we are all living in the manor house for now.

Father's papers prove CS and Chapman are behind the forced land sales and the deliberate infection of the village. I have placed them, along with the original blueprints of the dam, into a locked box and will take it to the caves in the morning. It is essential they do not fall into the hands of either CS or Chapman.

As of this point, I am cutting all family ties with CS. He may have been my mother's cousin, but he has proved himself unworthy of the name.

September 22

Today, David and I hiked into the caves and hid his father's papers. The key we are leaving in an envelope in the safe, with a note for it to be handed down through our children until either the box is found or this journal is discovered.

David blames himself for not being able to save anyone. But what chance does anyone have against what he termed biological warfare? No one can fight that.

He wants to seal this record as well. I agree as should this fall into the wrong hands then who knows what will become of us.

September 27
Fire! I heard several explosions, at least five, in various parts of the village, one after the other. *Boom, boom, boom, boom, boom.* The fire is spreading rapidly, leaping from building to building. With so few of us left, and no outside help, we can do nothing except watch it burn. We have no fire brigade, and the soldiers are standing on the other side of the barricade, refusing to help.

Some have fled — around twelve. I fear they will be shot on sight, like the others.

Mabel fears we will burn alive for our stubbornness and our refusal to leave what is now our only home.

September 30
It's over. The waters come today. The village will be flooded despite our best efforts. David will remain here in the manor. CS wants him to oversee the dam. He has threatened to go to the medical council and have him deregistered if he does not. As the dead are buried beneath it, David feels obligated to remain here. He fears some remnant of the plague may remain in the ashes and thus still

be a problem in the years to come.

David wants to place this notebook in the crypt before the church is flooded. This is the last entry. Our new life will begin with the death of the village. I can hear the sirens and the church bell. I must go. The water is coming.

Lou pulled out a piece of paper. "That's it."

Evan removed the book from her hands. "Wait." He peeled back the corner of the back cover where it had come loose and pulled out a piece of paper. He unfolded it.

September
The vault was drilled deep into the concrete foundations of the dam. This caused a huge crack, some fifteen inches wide in places to form, running the height of the dam. I fear the entire dam may give way at some point, especially if the ground becomes unstable or there is an earthquake similar in size to the one at Dogger Bank in 1931.

Fresh concrete was poured into the crack and the dam sealed. It's been given approval by the board, but it's possible they were paid to say that. The dam looks whole on the outside, but it's rotten to the core. It is a house of cards waiting to fall.

Lou closed the book and raised her head. Her throat constricted. "If that was plague and has a long half-life . . ." She broke off. "How deep does that crack go? Evan, we may have a major disaster on our hands."

42

Evan met her gaze, his heart pounding and stomach clenching. "I don't know."

"Do you have the number for the CDC?" Lou reached for her phone.

He frowned. "The what?"

"Centre for Disease Control or whatever it's called here. I can't remember off the top of my head."

"Ah. We don't have one. You've been in the US for too long. I'll ring the HPA — Health Protection Agency — but they'll probably send in the military from Porton Down."

"That's the other end of the country." She sounded as worried as he felt.

"What choice do we have?" He pushed his hands through his hair. "First we find those documents and discover exactly what we're dealing with and what the half-life is. Maybe the ashes are no longer contagious."

"And maybe they are."

Evan made a grab for the phone. "Either way, I'm calling the dam and issuing an immediate evacuation order. I also want a two-mile exclusion zone set up and enforced. We then go to the dam and check those blueprints and find this cave."

"You need more coffee." Lou ran a hand over his arm. "You're not making any sense."

"Forgive me for being a little freaked out about this."

She rubbed her temples. "You're not the only one, but we can freak out later." She raised her phone. "Right now we have both calls to make and a dam to evacuate. We'll need hazmat suits. Can you get some?"

He nodded. "Yes."

"Good. Four: you, me, and two spare suits. You call and organize those. Let me handle Porton Down. I have a friend who works there. I can cut through all the red tape in getting an alert raised. If it's a false alarm, it won't matter."

"Seriously? Where don't you have contacts?"

"I have them everywhere." She pulled a face at him and dialled her phone. "We met at uni and went out for six months before we realised I wasn't his type. We stayed mates though.

"Hey, Peter, it's Lou Fitzgerald. Yeah, I'm good, thanks. You? That's great, congrats. Listen, I have a massive favour to ask as I'm in a bit of a bind right now."

Evan tuned her out and called the dam. "Ralph, it's me."

"Nothing new here, boss. Water level is still dropping and we stopped the new stuff coming."

"Good. I'm on my way as soon as I can. I have to do a few things first. Right now I need you to listen and listen good. You have to do exactly what I say. Evacuate the dam immediately and get a perimeter set up. Nothing in or out for a two-mile radius. I also need the hazmat suits left in the car park for us. Make sure that every blueprint and plan there is of the dam is left in the office. And that's everything, dating right back to the original ones from when it was built."

"Evac? Hazmat? What's going on?"

"I don't have time to explain. You need to get everyone out and stay out. Keep an eye on it from somewhere safe, and let me know the instant something changes."

"Hang on, boss. The military just showed up in force."

"Good. Let me speak to the officer in charge." He gazed at Lou, but she'd turned her back to him and stood by the window, talking rapidly.

The phone in his hand crackled. "This is Colonel Davies."

"I'm Evan Close, head of Xenon, owner of the land and dam and in charge up there. We have a situation, Colonel. I'm in touch with Porton Down, and I need an immediate evacuation of the dam with a two-mile perimeter for now. Set up a command point immediately, half a mile from the dam. No one is to go on or near it with the exception of myself and Dr. Fitzgerald."

He waited for the officer to object. When he didn't, Evan carried on speaking. "I've explained to Ralph that I need hazmat gear. It's vitally important, and I can't stress this enough, that no one from the Sparrow Foundation gains access to the dam at all."

"Boss, it's me again." Ralph sounded breathless. "The sensors flipped out big time. There's movement along the entire base of the dam."

"Then we can't delay. Open the gates completely. Drain it as quickly as possible. I need you with the guards they'll post on the road. I can't risk having anyone other than Lou or myself up there. A team from Porton Down may arrive, but unless they're cleared via me, even they can't get near the dam."

"What's going on?"

"Trouble." He paused as Lou touched his arm. "One minute."

She shook her head. "Is that the dam?" As he nodded, she held her hand out for the phone. "Can I have a word with whoever is in charge up there?"

"Ralph, put Colonel Davies back on."

Lou snatched the phone. "Yes, this is Dr. Lou Fitzgerald. I've just got off the phone with Peter Dorchester from Porton Down." She paused. "Yes, that Porton Down. He'll be bringing a team up by military helicopter within the next couple of hours or so. It's possible we're dealing with a version of the pneumonic plague. There is no cure for this if he's right. Antibiotics won't work. Therefore, we have to evacuate the dam now and keep it clear. Mr. Close and I will be over there as soon as possible. We'll need full hazmat gear."

Evan watched in amazement as she transformed while she gave orders. At the same time shock rolled through him, making the hair on the back of his neck stand on end. Could that plague still be active down there?

Lou scrunched her face. "I understand that, Colonel, really I do. However, no one knows the dam like Mr. Close, and he needs to get up there to determine how long we have before it fails and whether the vault below it possibly containing plague samples is at risk. I'm the only person who knows what we're searching for once we find the vault."

She paused and raised her eyes heavenward. "Thank you."

She handed him the phone.

"Actually Colonel, we'll be there in twenty minutes." Evan hung up. "We need to leave."

She rubbed her temples again. "I thought we were doing the caves first? I know Peter needs those samples ASAP, and it'll be quicker if we do it. We can go down there, retrieve the samples, and leave them for him. We can give him the paperwork at the same time if we do the caves first. Because he won't be here for —"

Evan cut her off. "Ralph said the seismometers at the dam show movement."

"Then you're right, we don't have time to waste. We'll assume the worst, and if your records prove us wrong, so be it. Peter is concerned enough by my description of the symptoms to drop everything and come up here. He agrees with your great-grandfather's notes that the plague wasn't a natural occurrence. He said there had been genetic work done on that strain of plague that predates World War II."

Evan's blood ran cold. "They used the villagers as guinea pigs."

"It's looking that way." She stood and hung onto the edge of the couch to steady herself.

Evan grabbed her arm. "Are you sure you're all right?"

She rubbed her head. "I've got a headache. It's turning into a migraine. I'll repeat the meds in an hour or so. I'll be fine."

Lou's stomach roiled as Evan sped to the dam. "Killing us on the way won't help," she complained as he rounded a blind bend on the wrong side of the road.

"Do you want to drive?"

"Love to." She swallowed hard and cranked open the window.

"No." He rounded another corner. A horn blared, and he pulled into the hedge just in time to avoid a head-on collision.

"Evan!" Her voice came out more like a squeak than the scream she'd imagined in her mind.

Both of them thudded back into their seats, breathing heavily.

Lou's fingers gripped the door handle and

dashboard tightly. "Well, that escalated quickly," she gasped.

"Sorry." Evan's knuckles were white, and he levered them off the steering wheel. "Are you OK?"

She rubbed the back of her neck. "Yeah." Actually, she felt lousy, but at least the headache wasn't yet impinging on her vision. "So, am I driving or are you slowing down a bit?"

"You drive." He paused. "Have you driven an automatic before?"

She nodded. "Heaps of times as the car I drive in America is automatic. However, I did learn to drive the same way all Brits do — on a manual car. That way I have a choice what I can drive here, rather than being limited to just automatics."

They changed places, and Lou settled into the driver's seat. She took a minute to move all the mirrors and position the seat. "OK." She set off sticking to the speed limit, which was slower than Evan had been going. "Nice wheels."

"Thanks. Ira prefers automatic. I don't. But then I haven't driven much the last six years or so."

"That accounts for a lot, but then I guess you don't need to. You know, if you'd woken Ira or Zach . . ."

"They are evacuating the manor — removing some of the paintings and so on. Just in case."

She raised an eyebrow. "Paintings?"

"Some of them are worth a fortune. Along with some of the vases. I've been meaning to clear out stuff and donate it to a museum anyway. This gives me reason to do it."

Lou slowed to a halt at the barricade and opened her window. "Hi, I'm Dr. Fitzgerald and this is Evan Close. Colonel Davies is expecting us."

"I need to see photo ID from both of you."

"Of course you do." Lou pulled out her driving license and handed it over.

Evan reached past her with his. "Look, we really don't have time for this . . ."

Lou glanced at him. "Hey, the exclusion zone was your idea."

The soldier handed back the cards. "Colonel Davies is at the dam."

She frowned. "Doesn't he know what a total exclusion zone means? Tell him I'm on my way." She closed the window. "Thought you said to make the command point half a mile away? Not at the dam itself."

Evan scowled. "I did. Now put your foot down."

Lou did so, and it wasn't long before she swung into the car park. She stopped the car and gazed in horror at the dam. Water was beginning to seep through the gap in the middle. "That will not last."

"Then we need to be quick."

43

A team of people in hazmat suits sprinted over to them holding out gear.

Lou shivered as she climbed into hers. She'd always hated these things. Her eyes blurred, and she leaned back against the car, closing her eyes tightly. She pinched the bridge of her nose, wishing the headache would go away. Maybe driving wasn't such a great idea.

Evan's hand landed on her shoulder. "Are you sure you're all right?"

She picked up the empty sample case. "Yeah, tired from not sleeping and sick from the drive, never mind the headache. I'll be fine. Come on. Let's do this."

Evan checked that her suit was secure before he walked with her to the office. His hand gripped hers tightly until he pushed open the door.

Ralph and another man, both suited up, stood by the table.

"I thought I said evacuate out of here."
Evan's tone was icy, his eyes piercing.

"Boss, this is Colonel Davies," Ralph said.
"Jasper was just leaving. He brought all the
plans he could find in the library."

Evan nodded. "You leave, too, Ralph. This
dam will collapse, and I don't want anyone
near it when it does. Colonel, I'm Evan
Close, this is Dr. Fitzgerald. We spoke on
the phone."

Colonel Davies tilted his head. "I wish I
could say it was a pleasure. Peter Dorchester
called a few minutes ago. His team will be
here within the hour."

"Good," Lou said. "Don't let anyone up
here unless it's him. No one named Sparrow
is to come anywhere near this place."

Colonel Davies blanched. "I wasn't aware
of that. Monty Sparrow went below five
minutes ago. He had all the correct Xenon
papers. I assumed he was part of your team
and sent him down."

Evan would normally have sworn, but he
managed not to. "Where were you, Ralph?"

"Organizing something else," Ralph muttered. "Else he wouldn't be within ten miles
of this place, never mind two."

Evan gritted his teeth. "Well, it's done
now. Where is he?"

"In the control room," the Colonel said,

"with what he claims are original blue-prints."

"He stole them. Monty Sparrow is not part of Xenon, nor will he ever be. He's part of the whole reason this dam is about to collapse. Call him back up here now." Evan trembled with fury. "I gave explicit instructions . . ."

Lou tuned him out. There really wasn't time for this. "I'll head down there."

None of the three men were listening to her. Gripping the case in one hand and the stair rail in the other, she trotted down the stairs as fast as the dizziness would allow her.

Monty glanced up as she entered the control room. "I was wondering when you'd get here. You had to stick your nose in, didn't you?"

"Your father sent me up here," she retorted.

"I know. According to him he couldn't simply fire you or discredit you because you're the best in your field. No one would believe his side of things. This way you investigate, he fires you, whatever you say looks like a vendetta against you." He pointed to the blueprints. "What you're searching for is here."

"Where?" Vibrations ran through the dam,

causing her to lose her footing. She gripped the table.

Monty pointed. "The problem is, even if we reached the vault, when this thing goes it'll take the vault with it."

"What?" Evan spoke sharply from the doorway.

Monty grabbed Lou and pulled her towards him. "Don't come any closer."

"For Pete's sake, Monty," Lou hissed. "Are you really doing this now? We have a bigger problem here than you, me, and your father."

"You think I like what he does? Letting me tidy up after you? Take what should have been your glory, your papers, and put my name on them first? He treats me like a child. I made one mistake, and he's making me pay for that the rest of my life."

"You're acting like a child now." Evan moved slowly across. "Why don't you show us what you found? You could share the discovery."

Lou raised a hand and gripped Monty's arm. "Evan's right. We should do this together. I no longer work for your father. I quit and have no intentions of going back. He doesn't deserve my loyalty any longer."

"You did? I thought he was winding me up with another promise he wasn't keeping.

I never wanted your job. I still don't."

"I quit all right, and if I were you, I'd do the same before this all comes crashing down on him. What did you want to be growing up?"

"A fireman." Monty let go of her.

"Then do it," Lou told him. "Do what your heart tells you and not what Daddy wants for once in your life."

Evan stepped to her side. "I'd phrase it differently, but I agree with her."

Lou nodded. "Let the docs check you over first. It's the same for everyone who's been around the dam and the lake. I need you to bring me up to speed first, and tell me what you know."

Monty frowned. "I always thought the stories of the sickness were to keep me away from here when I was a kid."

"What?" Evan exploded. "He knew all along before he did the blasting down there?"

Monty nodded. "He's always known from his Grandad's journals."

Lou shook her head, instantly regretting it. She closed her eyes, head reeling.

"Lou, are you sure you're all right?"

She forced open her burning eyes. "Yes, Evan, I'm fine. Stop fussing." She focused on the blueprints on the table. "I love the overlay of the two. Did you do this, Monty?"

"Yes."

"It's a great job. So we're here." Her finger ran along the tunnel. "The crack runs down to there and . . . there's the sealed vault. How come no one knew about this?"

"I haven't seen these before. May I?" Evan pored over them. "These are original plans from when it was first built, and these show the vault and access tunnel. These were supposedly lost in the fire at the manor." He glanced at Monty. "Where did you get them?"

"Dad had them in his office. There's other stuff there that belonged to your family, too. Didn't you know that his grandad set the fire at the manor?"

Evan's eyes glowed hot. "He. What?"

Lou put a hand on his arm. "We can discuss that later. Monty, why don't you go and get checked over and find those other papers for us? You can take them to Evan's offices in London. They'll be safe there."

"OK." He headed over to the door.

Evan studied the blueprints. "So, if I'm right, there should be an access tunnel right behind that panel."

The ground moved beneath their feet. Lou's gaze flicked up, locking with his. The same terror shone in his gaze that she knew was in hers. "Tremors are getting worse. Whatever you're gonna find, do it quickly."

44

Evan grunted as he crawled through the access tunnel to what the plans said was a ladder. He wasn't large, but the people who built this must have been midgets. The vibrations were worse here, and he could hear the dam creaking. He knew the dam was collapsing; the only uncertainty was when.

He reached up to the radio attached to his suit. "Ralph, it's Evan."

"Hey, boss. How's it going?"

"We don't have long. Get everyone to a safe distance and higher ground."

"No can do. At least not until you and Dr. Fitzgerald are out of there."

"Don't argue. I want that two-mile exclusion zone adhered to. The dam is collapsing." He reached the top of the ladder.

"You're the boss. Tell Dr. Fitzgerald the team from Porton Down just arrived."

"I heard that. Tell them we'll be as fast as

we can." She sneezed.

"Bless you." Evan's concern for her grew. "Have you got a cold?"

"Allergies pick the wrong times to show up. Remind me to take my migraine meds when we get up top."

"Have you still got that headache?" The plague symptoms ran through his mind.

"Yes, and my vision is beginning to get impaired. The meds will sort it."

Praying she was right, Evan shone his torch down the hole. "OK, we've reached a long ladder." He began climbing. "Forgive me for not letting ladies go first."

She snorted. "Age before beauty every single time, mate."

"It must be a couple of hundred feet." He glanced down, still not able to see the bottom.

"The plan said one hundred and fifty." She paused. "The vibrations are almost constant now. Hurry."

Finally, Evan reached the base of the ladder. A small steel room, no more than five-feet square was lit by a single bulb. A steel door and locking ring set to the far wall. He twisted the ring slowly and the door swung open.

"I'll go down," Lou said.

He shook his head. "It's my job."

Lou held his gaze. "No, it's mine. I want you to stay up here and keep watch." She squeezed his hand. "I won't be long." She climbed over the door and vanished into the blackness.

Evan stepped to the door. "Lou?"

"Still here." Her breathless, tense voice crackled over the mic.

He shone his thermal camera over the walls, checking the structural integrity. "Hurry. We don't have long." The blue cold spots highlighted on the screen in front of him grew. "You have one minute. Then I'm going to toss you over my shoulder and carry you out of there."

"I'm coming." She appeared a few seconds later, tears running down her face, her suit covered in what appeared like dust. She gripped the sample case tightly.

"Are you OK?" He went over to her, but she moved backwards. "Lou?"

"Don't touch me," she whispered. "Just in case your suit has a hole."

His stomach dropped as he realised it wasn't dust she was covered with. "You go first. I need to do a thermal check of the vault itself."

She nodded and began climbing up the ladder.

Evan moved to the doorway and aimed

the camera around the walls. Watching the readouts, relief filled him. The vault was intact. So far. He shut the door, making sure the wheel was tightly locked.

"Evan?"

"I'm coming." He began climbing the ladder. "Good news is the vault doesn't show signs of the breach."

Lou sneezed.

"Bless you. Are you topside yet?"

"No."

It didn't take him long to catch up. The climb was long and arduous. The dam shook constantly. Worry for Lou increased with every rung as her upward momentum slowed. "Maybe you should go see the doc when we get up there."

"I'm fine. I get migraines all the time. I don't usually climb ladders with them. I have the meds in my bag in your car."

"Boss!" Ralph's panicked scream came over the radio. "It's going. The dam is going. Get out of there."

"We're in the control room. Give us two minutes."

"You don't have two minutes."

Evan caught hold of Lou's arm, his other hand grabbing the blueprints off the desk. "Run." He half-pulled, half-propelled her along the corridor leading to the surface.

Brilliant sunshine blinded him as they emerged on top of the dam. Overhead a helicopter hovered, dust blowing around them as it landed on the shaking dam.

Two men in hazmat gear leapt out and seized them. "We need to get you clear. Now."

The dam swayed under their feet as they were helped into the chopper. "Go, get out of here," one of them yelled at the pilot.

Before the door was even closed, the chopper lifted into the air.

Evan stared in horror, his heart in his mouth, as the dam gave way with a roar and a crash, the resulting cacophony a sound he could never put a name to. Rocks, concrete, and water erupted outwards and downwards, turning the river into a swirling mass of destruction.

He glanced at the officer, not wanting to think how close a call he and Lou had had. "Is everyone out?"

The officer nodded. "Two miles away. We'll land you there."

Evan's gaze returned to the destruction beneath them. Frozen, he watched his car float away on the tide.

"My meds . . ." Lou whispered. She closed her eyes. "Need to go back to the manor to get the others."

"We'll get you some more. How bad is it?" He reached out for her.

She pulled away from his touch. "Don't."

He held up his hands. "Already covered, see?"

Lou leaned against him, and he wrapped an arm around her. "Pretty bad," she whispered.

Evan glanced at her. "Ralph, you still there?"

"Yes, boss."

"Ring Ira. Get him to bring Lou's meds to wherever you are. They'll be in her room at the house. He'll need to use her car. Mine just got swept away. We'll also need a change of clothes each. Warm ones, preferably."

After another few minutes, the helicopter landed in a clearing. Evan helped Lou out. "Let's sit you down."

She shook her head. "Where's Peter?"

"Here." A tall man came over to them. "Did you get it?"

Lou handed over the case. "The vault is about two-hundred feet below the dam. It should hold." She closed her eyes and wobbled.

Evan grabbed her, holding her securely. "I got you."

"Are you all right?" the man with the case queried.

"People need to stop asking me that. It's only a migraine. It'll go once I take the meds."

"OK. I'll get this analysed."

Lou leaned heavily against Evan. "Sorry."

"Let's get you decontaminated and then your meds will be here. Ira's bringing them in your car."

"OK."

He led her over to where men with hoses and a curtained area stood.

"You might have to support me," she whispered. "Just don't tell Dad . . ."

"It's fine." He wrapped his arms around her, keeping her balanced as the water sprayed the suits. He didn't let go as they removed suits and clothes, standing there shivering in their underwear as the water drenched them.

Once finished, Evan tenderly wrapped her in a towel and carried her over to where Jack and Ira stood waiting. "Did you bring the meds?"

"Yes." Ira held out the box.

"Lou?" Jack touched her dripping hair. "You OK, hon?"

She opened her eyes. "Hi, Dad. This doesn't look good, does it?"

Jack's eyes twinkled. "I thought we'd had this discussion, to be honest."

Evan sighed, knowing the man was teasing, but playing along. "In my defence, we're surrounded by a million or so people." He set Lou down in the front seat of her car. "Let's get you dried and into warm clothes."

"I'll do that." Jack nodded. "You see to yourself."

"OK." Evan stepped back, not wanting to leave her.

"I'll be fine, Evan. Don't want you catching a cold on my behalf."

"Honey, here's the meds," Jack said. "How many?"

"Two."

Evan turned away to find Ira holding out a towel. "Thanks." He changed quickly, pulling the jumper on as well. "How bad is the flooding?"

"It could have been worse, had you not ordered the run off increased." Ira held out his jacket. "Zach asked for a couple hours personal time. I didn't see a problem as you, the general and I would be with Dr. Fitzgerald."

"He gives me the creeps anyway. You know he was listening earlier right when we read that journal? Just like he listened in on me and Dad last night." Lou slid her small hand into Evan's. "You're cold."

He studied her carefully. Her white face, along with sunken, red eyes set a million alarm bells ringing in his mind. "And you look sick. You need to go see a doctor. Jack, tell her."

"I have, and she's not listening to me."

She pinched the bridge of her nose and sneezed. "I'm fine. Let's go find these caves of yours. How far away are they?"

"Twenty minutes by car."

"Then let's go. Ira or Dad can drive us. I can doze on the way, and I'll be better when we arrive." She glanced over at the raging river.

"It could have been a lot worse," Evan said. He held her gently. "I'll rebuild the dam. Clear the bottom of the lake properly first. Maybe use the rubble to build a monument to all those villagers who died."

"All of them?"

He nodded. "Yeah, all two hundred of them from Abernay and however many it was in Finlay." He glanced at Jack. "I'd like you to come as well. Ira, you can drive."

45

Evan shook Lou gently as Ira stopped the car. "Lou, we're here. You can stay in the car if you want."

Her eyes fluttered open, and she raised her face to stare at him. It was all he could do not to recoil. She looked awful, almost gaunt. She shivered in his arms and sneezed again. A faint smile creased her lips. "I'll come with you."

Evan had never had a migraine, but his mother had occasionally. She'd go to bed in a dark room and just stay there. "Maybe we should get you to bed. We can do the caves later."

She shook her head, wincing, and was that a moan?

Jack turned around and studied first her, and then Evan. "Honey, I really think you should do what Evan says."

"Not married. Therefore, I don't have to obey him," she quipped. "I can sleep later.

We're here now."

Evan put a hand on her forehead. "You're burning up."

A half smile greeted him. "Are you trying to tell me I'm hot, mister?"

"Well, yeah." He kissed her forehead.

She chuckled, her cheeks rosy. Too rosy. "Should you say things like that with my dad in the car? Besides, I'm not that hot." She shivered again and sucked in a deep breath. "Come on. Sooner we're done, the sooner I can go sleep off the darn headache."

Evan kept hold of her hand as they walked slowly along the narrow path leading to the cave. Jack walked on the other side of her, Ira right behind them.

Evan stopped as they came to the cave entrance. He pointed. "Lou, look. Those stones have moved. They covered the entrance the last time I was here."

She scrunched her nose and rubbed a hand over her eyes. "Maybe they did it themselves. Fell in a landslide or something."

"Even you don't really believe that." He shook his head. "No. They'd be everywhere if they had. Those are in a neat pile."

"Then maybe use your phone and call Ira and get him and his gun to go first," she said. "In case they need shooting or something."

Evan looked askance at Jack and Ira, and then twisted her to face him. "Lou?"

"Though if Dad were here, he'd say man up and just go in there." Her eyes shuttered.

"Yup, that's exactly what I'd say, kiddo." Jack clutched her hand. "Maybe we should stay here and let Ira and Evan go in."

"Dad? Good, you got out." Her eyes closed again, and she wobbled. "Stop the world. I want to get off."

Evan caught her. "This isn't a good idea. Let's get you back to the car."

"I'm fine," she objected.

Jack glanced at Evan. Concern etched into the lines on his face. "I don't like this."

"Me either."

"Will you stop talking about me as if I'm not here?" Lou's voice was stronger and clarity shone in her gaze. "Are we doing this or not?" She pulled away and straightened her shoulders before heading into the cave.

"For crying out loud," Jack muttered.

"Lou, wait!" Evan called.

She stopped. "Waiting . . ." She glanced over her shoulder. "Christmas is ninety-six days away and will likely get here before you do."

Evan pushed aside the fact she was counting the days until Christmas.

Ira pulled out his gun and nodded. "Ready."

Evan strode over to Lou. He held her hand. "You could get lost in here easily. So just stay with me."

Lou started singing "Stay with Me" under her breath.

"Thanks. That will be stuck in my head for the rest of the day," Evan muttered.

"You're welcome."

Evan flicked on his torch and led them through the network he knew so well. Up ahead, there was a light and at least two voices. He turned off the torch and pulled Lou against the wall, motioning to the others to keep still and quiet.

"It has to be here somewhere," Varian's voice carried. "There's nowhere else those papers would be. You're sure Evan said the documents were in the caves?"

"Yes. I heard them myself."

"That's your security man, isn't it?" Shock filled Lou's tiny voice.

Glad he couldn't see anyone's reaction, Evan scowled. "Yeah, Zach. Hence his sneaking around, listening at doors, and demanding personal time as the dam fails."

Ira whispered in his ear. "Let me handle this." The sound of a gun slide echoed.

Evan put a hand on Ira's arm. "Not yet."

"And they proved my grandfather's role in all this?" Varian raised his voice. "We have to find and destroy it. I can't have any of this coming back on me. Not after all I've done to keep it hidden."

Lou pulled away from Evan. If she were being honest, she felt like death warmed up. The migraines hadn't been this bad for a long time. She wanted to sleep. Forcing one foot in front of the other, she moved into the light, throwing up a hand to protect her eyes. Pain seared her sockets, piercing her brain and making her gag. "You hiding evidence again, Varian?" she managed. "Rewriting history so you come out intact? Making yourself and your family the victor rather than the perpetrator?"

Varian spun around. "Lou."

"Yeah, it's me." She leaned a hand on the wall, desperate to stay on her feet long enough to resolve this. "And this is your fault. If you hadn't sent me up here and then followed me to destroy the evidence, none of this would have come to light. The burned bone would have been explained by the scorch marks on the church walls. The records and history mention the huge fire that destroyed the villages. Because you sent

400

me, we found the journal that proves the villagers were murdered."

"You're sick. You don't know what you're saying."

She ignored him. "I have a headache, not memory loss. You planted those bombs that destroyed the ruins and destabilized the dam. That's why it failed. You killed AJ. What your grandfather did wasn't your fault. What happened today and this last week is."

She pinched the bridge of her nose. Her head was beyond painful now. Rotating triangles captured ninety per cent of her vision, and her eyes blurred. "You could just have let me resign. I was leaving anyway after Llaremont was finished. I'm tired of you giving all my notes to Monty. Well, not this time." She shivered and coughed. "It's too late. It's published."

Varian scowled and moved a step towards her. "What?"

She groaned, leaning against the wall. "It's published. AJ brought all my notes up himself. I didn't ask him to. I could have, but I didn't. I have some honour."

Evan stepped into the confined space and wrapped his arm around her waist. "I told you to wait."

"I'm fine."

Zach pulled out his gun. Ira lifted his.

Lou sighed. "Seriously? You two have seen way too many movies where the bad guys threaten the good guys so the bad guys stand a chance of winning. Ain't gonna happen. Good guys always win. Put the guns away, and let's talk like grownups. Varian, you win." She glanced up at Evan. "We're leaving."

"We can't," Evan said. "Not without those files."

"Yes, we can. The scientists from Porton Down have the samples from the vault. Truth always wins. Varian can keep the files that are here. We don't need them." She closed her eyes, swallowing hard, her head pounding, fit to burst. "I'm going to be sick."

Evan held her as she threw up.

She straightened, coughing hard. Her hand came away covered with blood. "Evan? Dad?"

Evan swung her into his arms. "We need to get you out of here. Ira, run ahead and call an ambulance or a helicopter or something." He glanced over his shoulder at Varian. "I suggest you also get yourself to a doctor."

"Why? What's she got?"

"I have no idea. She says it's a migraine,

but it could just as easily be your grand-father's plague." He paused. "And, Zach, you're fired."

46

Evan raised his head as Jack slumped into the plastic chair beside him. "How is she?"

"Not good." Jack's eyes were red, and he appeared to be as tired as Evan felt. "I've sent for her mom. She's flying over. How are you?"

"They've started antibiotics, and it's a seven day course, so too early to tell. How about you?"

"The same."

Evan rubbed the back of his neck. "They won't let me see her. They say it's family only."

"I'll tell them you're her boyfriend." Jack shot him a smile. "It's the truth; you are courting her."

He sighed. "I never had a chance to ask her. Things got rather fraught this morning and stuff happened really quickly."

Jack agreed. "Is anyone else sick?"

"Ira, Varian, and Zach. A couple of the

underwater search and rescue divers are running a fever. Charlie Brampton and Jasper Steele were found dead in their home this morning. They house share and have both been up at the dam a lot. My team is on antibiotics the same as everyone else."

"Mr. Close?"

Evan glanced up. "Yes?"

The tall man sat beside him. "Peter Dorchester from Porton Down. I thought you'd like to know before the press gets hold of it. It is pneumonic plague, but not a genetically modified version. It's still highly contagious but treatable. As yet, we don't know the source of the outbreak, but we'll keep searching. Could you let Dr. Fitzgerald know?"

"She's in intensive care. She's really sick, but yeah, I'll tell her."

Jack's phone rang. "Fitzgerald. Hey, honey." He stood and walked to the window, talking quietly.

Evan gazed out of the window, and then pushed upright. He headed down the hallway to the chapel. Inside, it was dark and quiet. A stained glass window lit the area behind the altar, a huge cross set on a table at the front.

Evan sank into one of the chairs and buried his head in his hands. He wasn't sure how long he lingered before he became aware of someone beside him. "I never told her how I felt." Guilt tied his insides in knots. "I mean, she knows, because I've kissed her often enough, but I never said it out loud. I even asked her father for permission to court her, but I never told her. And now, it's too late. Well, probably too late."

"It's never too late. While there's life and breath, there is always hope. It's a cliché, but it's true."

Evan glanced sideways. The man beside him wore a suit and dog collar. "You reckon?"

The green eyes twinkled. "I know so. Things always seem darker just before dawn."

"Dawn's a long way off, Padre. It may never come." His nails dug into the palms of his hands.

"All the more reason to tell her. She'll hear you. Would it help to pray or light a candle?"

"No, but thank you." He paused. "Not really a praying kind of a bloke, haven't been for a while. But being here, it's peaceful. Comforting."

The man nodded. "You may have forgotten God, but He hasn't forgotten you. I'll add your friend to my prayer list. What's her name?"

"Lou, and thank you. She'd like that." He stood. "I'd better get back to ICU."

Evan picked up two coffees from the vending machine on his way and held one out to Jack, who sat in the waiting area. "Here."

"Thanks." Jack sipped the hot liquid. "I told the nursing staff you're family. You can see her when you want."

Evan set his cup on the table. "Thank you. I might go see her now. There's something I need to tell her." He headed over to the ward and rang the bell.

The nurse opened the door.

"Evan Close. I'm here to see Lou Fitzgerald."

The nurse smiled. "You're her boyfriend, right? Pop on the mask and suit. Then wash your hands before you put the gloves on. She's in the side room with two beds. There are specific instructions on the door you'll need to follow as she's in quarantine."

Evan did as requested and then crossed over to the occupied bed. Shock flooded him, almost knocking him backwards. She lay there, wired up to monitors and on a ventilator.

The nurse at the end of her bed, also wearing a suit, mask, and gloves, smiled.

"It's not as bad as it looks. You must be Evan."

"Her boyfriend, yeah. I hadn't realised she'd be . . . no one said." He sat beside the bed. "Can I hold her hand?"

"Sure."

He gripped her hand tightly, blinking hard, unprepared for the onslaught of emotions that charged through him. "What are all these machines for?"

"Right now she's in a medical coma, to give her body a chance to rest and fight the infection. This machine here records her heartrate, blood pressure, and oxygen levels. This one is breathing for her."

Evan raised Lou's hand and kissed her fingers through his mask. "How sick is she? I know they've sent for her mum from the States, so it's not good."

"She's critical. Probably won't know anything for at least the next seventy-two hours. If she makes it that far, then she might have a chance."

Evan's eyes burned, and he was grateful the mask hid his trembling lips. He squeezed her hand tightly. "Don't you die on me. You hear me? There is so much I want to tell you about how I feel, but I'd rather you were awake to listen. I . . . I love you. There I said it."

He took a deep breath. "Your headache is contagious." His vision blurred, and he dropped her hand.

The nurse tilted her head. "Are you all right?"

"Headache. I think I might go home. Sleep it off." He stood, and his legs gave way. He slid to the floor, gripping onto the bed as he fell.

An alarm rang somewhere, echoing. A door slammed open.

"I need some help in here." Gloved hands caught him. "Let's get you onto a bed."

"I'm fine," he protested. Someone lifted him onto a bed. He assumed the empty one beside Lou. The cool pillow under his head felt good.

"Doctor, this is Evan Close. He's Lou Fitzgerald's boyfriend."

"Evan, I'm Dr. Halstead. I'll just check you over."

Evan shook his head, instantly regretting it as the world spun. "I need to rest for a few. Then I'll go home. Probably allergic to those antibiotics someone gave me."

"Humour me, OK? I need a full set of bloods run. FBCs, U and E's, LFTs . . ."

Evan groaned. "Sounds like I'm in an episode of *Casualty.*" He closed his eyes. "Lou, honey, if you've given me the dreaded lurgy, I shall have to marry you and make you regret it forever."

47

Lou opened her eyes. This wasn't her bed.
A nurse in a mask and gown sat at the end
of the bed. That meant it was a hospital.
OK, that was a little excessive, even for a
migraine as bad as this one had been.

Three people, also wearing gowns and
masks, hovered around her bed, but not one
of them the one she longed to see. "Where's
Evan?"

"Charming," Jim complained. "We fly
thousands of miles to be here, an emergency
flight, I hasten to add, to sit by your deathbed, and your first words are 'where's
Evan?' It's nice to see you too, Lou."

"Hi, Jim. Well, as I recall, you only visit
me for the chips, so fair's fair." She turned
her head slowly and reached for her mother.
She sat beside Jack, and as usual they were
holding hands. "Mum."

Mum clutched her hand. "He's teasing.
How are you feeling?"

"Better. What happened? And what's all this about my deathbed? It was a migraine."

"What's the last thing you remember, kiddo?" Jack asked.

Lou thought for a moment. "The dam fell. Evan and I went to the caves with you and Ira. I had a massive headache, and you and he wanted me to go home to bed."

"That was ten days ago," Mum said.

"Ten days?" Lou frowned, trying to get her head around the idea. "Really?"

"We've been here almost eight now." Mum glanced at Jack. "Not the best way to spend an anniversary."

"Is that today?"

Jack pushed the hair from her face. "Yeah."

The nurse stood beside her. "I need to run a few tests now you're awake." She shoved the thermometer into Lou's mouth.

Jack raised an eyebrow. "Don't even think about it."

She scrunched up her nose. Did that man remember every single thing she'd ever done? "You didn't answer my question."

"And don't talk with your mouth full."

Lou rolled her eyes. Some things never changed. Being visited in hospital for one thing, and Jack moaning at her about thermometers, for another. As soon as the thermometer was removed, she asked again.

"Where's Evan?"

"He's in the next bed. He's been sick, too, but not as bad as you. He's sleeping right now."

"Sick?" She pushed upright, to have the nurse lie her back down. "Someone tell me what's going on?"

Jim pulled a face. "You got the plague, and you don't even remember?"

Plague? That made no sense, but now wasn't the time to ask. She tilted her head. "That explains the very sexy masks everyone is wearing."

Jim snorted. "Did you just call your mother and stepfather sexy?"

She struggled to keep a straight face. "I might have."

Jack groaned. "She's feeling better. I think it's time for lunch while you have those tests done. We'll be back later."

Lou arranged the blanket as they all stood. "Nothing changes, look, it's like old times. Leaving me alone in a hospital bed with a nurse brandishing needles."

Jim laughed and cleared his throat. "You know you love it, really. We'll be back. Fret not."

"All these years, and you still do a rubbish impression of that actor." She glanced sideways at the nurse. "Let's do this."

Fifteen minutes later, the nurse pulled back the curtains between her bed and the one next to her. "The doctor will be in shortly."

Lou glanced to her right. "Evan . . ."

A huge grin split his face. "You're awake." He threw the covers back and got out of bed. He sat beside her, leaned in, and hugged her tightly. "I was so worried about you."

She hugged him back. "Happy birthday."

"You remembered."

"Of course I did." She paused, leaning against him as he settled onto the bed next to her. "How sick was I? I mean they got Mum over here, and Jim said something about death beds and the plague."

Evan kissed her forehead, his arm settling around her. "Yeah, plague. They wanted to give you the last rites at one point, but Jack said no. He prayed a lot."

"It does work. Perhaps you should try it."

"Tell you the truth, I have been." His hands moved slowly through her hair. "There is so much I should have told you. How I feel about you for one thing . . ."

"Evan," she began. She twisted to look up at him.

"Let me finish. I love you. I don't want to lose you. And I don't want you taking a job

414

at the other end of the country or moving back to your family home in the States."

"You work in London. I've been offered that job up here in the university. Not that I've accepted it yet."

Evan's face fell. "I see."

"You seriously think I'd pick a job over you?" She cupped his face in the palm of her hand. "I love you. I could never put work over you."

"You do?"

She tapped his ear. "Maybe you should turn your hearing aid up or have one fitted."

"Did you say something?" He grinned at her, shaking his head.

Lou giggled. She mouthed, "I love you."

"Speak up. I can't hear you." He leaned forward and kissed her.

She closed her eyes, kissing him back.

Footsteps stopped by the bed, and Jack coughed.

Lou beamed at Evan, and then glanced up, her cheeks burning. "Nasty cough, Dad."

"I thought we'd had this conversation," Jack teased. "You know, the one about kissing my daughter in compromising places." He pointed to the bed. "They don't come much more compromising than a bed. Do we need to have it again?"

Evan laughed. "And once again I'm kissing her in front of an audience."

"Dad . . ." Lou began.

"It's OK, kiddo. I've already given him my permission."

"Permission for what?" she asked, confused. "What did I miss?"

Evan held her face towards his. "The night before you got sick, I asked your dad for permission to court you."

"Court?"

"Yeah, an old-fashioned way of dating. As an archaeologist you should know that."

"I do, but . . ."

Jim groaned. "It's a bit early for the 'I do's', isn't it?"

Evan kissed her. "It's never too early. We'll figure out the jobs and the living arrangements further down the line."

Lou leaned into him. "Sounds good to me. We have plenty of time to do that. Just promise me it won't be in Dark Lake."

"OK."

"What happened to Varian? Did you find the rest of your great-grandfather's papers?"

"Varian got sick, but he's recovering. The police have charged him with various things, including AJ's murder and attempting to kill you."

"What about Monty?"

"He left a letter with my office in London. He's handed over all the papers Varian had pertaining to Dark Lake, and he's left the company. He said he's doing what you told him to do and following his dreams."

She snuggled into him. "Sounds like a plan."

Evan snorted. "You told him to be a fireman."

"Did I?"

He nodded. "Yes, you did. Doing the same?"

She shook her head, gazing up into the eyes of the man holding her. The man she'd do anything for and follow to the ends of the earth. "I'm doing what my heart tells me."

"And what's that?" Evan asked.

She reached up and kissed him. "Follow the man who loves me and love him back." She pulled away. "Hang on. Do I still work for you?"

"For as long as you want," he whispered.

"Isn't there a company law against marrying the boss?"

His hand curved around her face, fingers moving gently. "My company, I make the rules. If you'll marry me."

"Yes, I'll marry you . . ."

ABOUT THE AUTHOR

Clare Revell is a British author. She lives in a small town just outside Reading, England with her husband, whom she married in 1992, their three children, and unfriendly mini-panther, aka Tilly the black cat. Clare is half English and half Welsh, which makes watching rugby interesting at times as it doesn't matter who wins.

Writing from an early childhood encouraged by her teachers, she graduated from rewriting fairy stories through fan fiction to using her own original characters and enjoys writing an electronic mix of romance, crime fiction and children's stories. When she's not writing, she can be found reading, crocheting or doing the many piles of laundry the occupants of her house manage to make.

Her books are based in the UK, with a couple of exceptions, thus, although the spelling may be American, the books contain British language and terminology.

The first draft of every novel is hand written.

She has been a Christian for more than half her life. She goes to Carey Baptist where she is one of four registrars.

The employees of Thorndike Press hope you have enjoyed this Large Print book. All our Thorndike, Wheeler, and Kennebec Large Print titles are designed for easy reading, and all our books are made to last. Other Thorndike Press Large Print books are available at your library, through selected bookstores, or directly from us.

For information about titles, please call:
  (800) 223-1244

or visit our website at:
  gale.com/thorndike

To share your comments, please write:
  Publisher
  Thorndike Press
  10 Water St., Suite 310
  Waterville, ME 04901

421